Burtrum Lee

To Nick + Ashley,
What a pleasure to know
you! I hope you enjoy!
Keep on bookin'!

Mary M Maurice

Also by Mary Maurice

Fruit Loops the Serial Killer
Burtrum Lee

Burtrum Lee

By

Mary Maurice

HOLLISTON, MASSACHUSETTS

BURTRUM LEE
Copyright © 2017 by Mary Maurice

Cover Art by Joel Nakamura.

First printing November 2017
10 9 8 7 6 5 4 3 2 1

ISBN # 1-60975-197-3
ISBN-13 # 978-1-60975-197-5
LCCN # 2017950964

Silver Leaf Books, LLC
P.O. Box 6460
Holliston, MA 01746
+1-888-823-6450

Visit our web site at www.SilverLeafBooks.com

To Aunt Pat, Thank you!

Burtrum Lee

1

Santa Fe, NM, 1960

"Burtrum, I'm not going to tell you again, slow down! You're going to lose control in this weather," Katie Lee pleads, as the wheels of the black sedan catch a patch of ice. Katie feels the Buick fishtail, clipping a nearby snow bank.

"Shut up, Katie! You know how important this child is to us. We might never have the chance again, and I'm not going to let anything happen to him."

"You're going to kill us all, and then where will we be? Please, Burtrum, I beg you, just ease up a little."

Katie Lee cannot believe this tragic turn of events. She knew it was a bad idea when Burtrum insisted she come to New Mexico with him, she in her ninth month. Now her instincts are proving true. The contractions began an hour ago, and here they are, out in the middle of nowhere, lost in a snowstorm, miles away from any hospital.

Doubts began to surface early on in the pregnancy; messing with nature and all. Even though Burtrum, a world-renowned fertility scientist, guaranteed his new experiment, artificial insemination, was fail-safe, she still had her misgivings. But what else could she do? Refusing was out of the question.

As the months progressed, and her terms eased along, Katie began to relax and trust her husband's genius, joyfully planning the future of their baby son.

Now, though, as she sits in water soaked panties, those happy feelings are replaced with fear, as she prays her husband will pull over for a minute and let the gale force winds pass them by. Katie sees a smile in the black window as she wonders what her son will be like.

The wheels skid on the icy road a second time, and Katie clings tightly to the armrest, her knuckles turning whiter than the snow outside.

"Damn-it, Burtrum! Now, please, let's stop for a minute!" Her cursed words echo in the silent cab. Her pleas are futile. She can see the crazed intensity in his blackened eyes, as he speeds down unfamiliar snow packed roads, oblivious to the ghostly dangers lurking.

"I'm fine, I know what I'm doing, there's no need to get belligerent. Just relax and hold the baby in until we get to the hospital. Is that too much to ask?" His words are firm and direct.

Leaning her head against the frosted window, Katie sees an ashen reflection mocking her terror. Large blue eyes sparkle as she recalls first meeting Burtrum Lee. How gruff he acted with her at the beginning, kind of like now, but then after a while softened up to her. For Katie, it was love at first sight.

Even though Burtrum is twice her age, they married almost immediately. Their union, up until now, has been a good one, and Katie speculates things will change between them with the child.

Vicious winds whip the heavy car back and forth, making it impossible for Katie to see out. She glances over at Burtrum, hunched and leaning closer to the icing windshield.

"Honey, please!" Katie softens. "We can wait until the winds ease up and you can see better. I'm fine. The contractions are still pretty far apart, so we have plenty of time."

Katie hates to lie. The pains are closer than ever and she knows the baby is coming. Clenching her fist to her mouth, she holds back her moans as a jolt rips through her gut. Burtrum's determination overrides any trace of common sense as he continues to plow through the unforgiving swirling gales. Katie leans her head against the window again and closes her eyes. The coolness on her forehead helps to soothe the increasingly intense labor pains.

2

Santa Fe, NM, 2004

Lee Conner flicks her hand toward the sound of Lucy's meowing.

"Shut up, will you? I'm trying to sleep," she snaps, pushing the feline off the mattress and rolling over.

The cat's begging continues to grate on her nerves.

Whipping her legs over the side of the bed while she wrestles with the comforter, Lee tosses a pillow at Lucy as she dashes away, disappearing down the hall. "All right all ready, I'm up. Are you happy now?"

Unfolding the Venetian blinds, Lee gazes out her window at a sky full of gray clouds, and wonders if the much needed rain will arrive today. Turning, she catches her image in the full length mirror on the opposite wall. Her knobby knees redden in embarrassment as she studies herself.

Spotting the clock on the bookshelf, Lee realizes she

needs to hurry or she'll be late for work. Slipping on a pair of shorts and a t-shirt, she contemplates her employment at the Casa de Magdalena B&B. It certainly isn't her dream job, and she knows it's just a short term gig until she finds her niche, whatever a *niche* is. Chuckling, Lee jumps when the phone rings, and reaches for the receiver.

"Hello!" Sleep clinging to her voice.

"Birdy, I'm sorry, did I wake you? I thought you'd be out of bed by now and ready for work." Clair Conner knows her granddaughter isn't the most motivated person on earth, and has a tendency to oversleep.

"Grandma, I'm just leaving, and I wish you'd call me Lee."

"You know I prefer to call you Birdy. Just thank your stars I don't use your birth name."

"You know I hate it, and will always question their decision to name me after Great, Great, Grandpa Conner. But listen, I don't have time to get into this," said Lee, becoming slightly agitated. "Why are you up so early?"

"I wanted to catch you before you left for the B&B."

"What can't wait until later?"

"Nothing important, I just wanted to call you at home."

"But Grandma, you know you can reach me at work anytime."

"Yes, but I don't like to bother you there."

"It's no problem. Now, what's up?"

"I'm wondering if you'd like to come over for dinner tonight. There's this nice man who works down at the nursery, you know, where I get all of my plants and trees." Her granddaughter's multiple job history and Lee's association with men hold a similar track record. She either gets bored with them, or finds something wrong, ending the romance. No man is ever good enough!

Rolling her eyes, Lee snips. "Yes, Grandma, I know the place."

All of her life, both her parents or grandmother have tried to set her up with men, but with no success. She feels guilty for not falling in love with at least one of her suitors, but none of them are ever what she wants. Lee has never felt that rush of excitement her friends describe when they meet the loves of their lives.

"What a load of crap," Lee said, accidentally whispering out loud.

"What did you say, sweetie?"

"Oh, nothing, Grandma. Listen, I'd love to come over for dinner, but I don't want to meet anyone, okay. I'm not in the mood."

"All right, honey, that's fine, I just wanted to bounce it off you before I invited him," disappointment echoed in Clair's words.

"Thanks, Grandma." Silence wiggles across the line. "Hey, I really appreciate everything you do for me, trying to help me find the right guy and all, but don't you think maybe we should just let it rest, and if it happens, then it happens?"

"Whatever you say dear, I just don't want to see you lonely."

"I'm not, don't worry. Now, what time is dinner, and what are you making?"

"How about around six, and I'm not sure what's on the

menu yet. I'm thinking maybe green-chile-chicken enchiladas."

"Yummy, you know how I love those."

"Great then, I'll see you this evening."

"Can I bring anything?"

"Just your beautiful self."

"I'll do that. I've gotta run though, I'll see you later. Hope you have a nice day."

"You too, sweetheart. I love you, bye."

"Love you, too. See ya."

Lee listens to the phone click and then hangs up.

Rubbing her hand through her auburn hair, she reaches for a jacket dangling on a hook behind the door. Strolling to the kitchen she sees Lucy waiting patiently to be fed. Squatting down, she pets her feline friend.

"I'm sorry, honey. I forgot all about you." Darting over to the cupboard and opening it, she grabs a handful of dry food and tosses the morsels into Lucy's bowl. "There, how's that?" The calico sprints to the food, making Lee grin.

Buttoning up her coat, she opens the door and is blasted with a brisk whirlwind. Dirt and leaves spin in the air, whipping around the dry dustbowl Lee calls a front yard, reminding her more of October than March.

Covering her mouth, she lumbers down the driveway, and out into the street. Luckily for Lee, the B&B is a ten-minute jaunt from her home. Reaching the plaza, she crosses the square and heads down Palace Avenue, smiling to herself as she studies the brown adobe structures lining the streets. Everything here in the City Different is soft and earthy; one of the things she loves about Santa Fe.

Lee has lived here all of her life, and considers herself blessed to have been raised in such a beautiful place. The surrounding mountains are always breathtaking, inspiring people from all over the world to come and find their true artistic selves.

And that is exactly what happened back in the eighties when the city boomed. Everyone came, driving the economy into a chaotic state. But then, as with all booms, it ended, leaving the natives with a high cost of living and low hourly wages. Lee's parents and grandmother made their money back then, selling off the land they owned on the mountain to developers, who later lined the hills with houses, half of which stand empty now.

Passing a dark window, Lee glimpses her misplaced features. She certainly doesn't resemble any of her family members, who all possess the classic Hispanic traits of dark hair and eyes, with a soft brown skin tone. But she, with her auburn hair, green eyes, and a pale complexion, resembles none of them. As a young girl she would ask why she looks so different, and all they'd say is that she'd inherited her Great, Great, Grandfather Conner's characteristics. So, not only did she acquire his awful name, but also his British traits.

From the story told, he'd been an English officer sent to explore the Southwest territories, and falling in love with the land, stayed after his commission ended.

As Lee turns down Faithway Street, the white gingerbread house with blue trim comes into view. Strolling up the walk, she bends over and picks up the *New Mexican*, knowing the thin paper offers little news.

Unlocking the front door, she quietly enters and eases the portal closed. Everything is silent. A stillness hangs in the air, as Lee suddenly remembers the house is empty. The only guests are those staying out back in the casitas.

Hoping for an easy day of mindless cleaning and housekeeping, she switches on the coffee machines, listening as they gurgle to life. Deciding to whip up some pancakes and sausages for breakfast, Lee pulls the instant mix out of the cupboard and searches for the maple syrup hidden behind the honey.

While preparing breakfast, her thoughts wander to Clair and how persistent she's been over the past few months, always trying to set her up. Lee knows her grandmother only has her best interest at heart, but still, it's starting to annoy her.

It's not as though she spends every night on her couch. She goes out and meets men, but none of them hold her attention. There's never a spark, never any desire to devote her time to someone. Maybe she's just a loner. Nothing wrong with that.

Pulling the white tab off the concentrated juice can, Lee pours the orange sludge into the pitcher and then holding it under the faucet, dilutes the semi-frozen mixture. PMS sings ballads in the back of her mind, and she wonders if that's the reason she's been feeling so spacey today, not hearing the back door open.

"Morning, Lee."

Yelping, Lee whips around and sees Kim, the reservation secretary, standing there giggling.

"That's not funny," Lee scolds, unable to control the

slight smirk creasing her lips. "You should make more noise. You almost gave me a coronary."

"A little edgy today?" Kim jokes, unlocking the office.

"No, I was just deep in thought."

"Don't drown."

"If I do, I'm taking everyone down with me." Both women laugh, as Lee asks, "Would you like a cup of coffee?"

"Yes, please, that'd be nice," Kim said as she tossed her backpack on the desk. Grabbing two mugs off the hooks, she turns to the still dripping pot.

"I tell you," Kim yells from the small closet they call *control central*. "Today already feels weird. Don't you think?"

"Yeah, but I figure it's because I'm about to start my period."

"I think it's the chem-trails. They're already lining the sky and it's not even eight yet."

Gesturing with her hand in the air, Lee spits, "No, no, let's not get into that right now.

It's way too early and my brain can't take it."

She is well versed in Kim's conspiracy theories, and knows the young rebel always searches for an opportunity to try and discuss what she believes to be just and real. Strangely enough, none of her predictions have ever come true.

"You're right, get me started and neither one of us will get any work done."

She hands Kim her coffee, who takes a sip, eyeing Lee over the rim.

"How is it?" Lee asks.

"It's fine, just how I like it, nice and strong."

Sliding the griddle off the shelf, she glances back at Kim. "You hungry?"

"Extremely," Kim exclaims. "What are you making?"

"Pancakes and sausages."

"What kind of cakes?"

"I'm thinking of ginger-banana," Lee replies, meticulously placing the sausage patties into the frying pan.

"Sounds good. Let me know when they're ready."

As the clock strikes three, Lee whispers a silent thank-you, and grabs her things.

Saying good-bye to Kim, she glides out the door and skips down the sidewalk, glad the weekend has finally arrived.

Kim is getting restless. Her replacement, Chris, who promised to come in early, has yet to arrive, and is on the verge of being late for his own scheduled time.

"To hell with this," Kim hisses.

Standing to leave, she hears the back door open, then close. Sighing in relief, she mouths, 'finally,' and reaches for her backpack on the floor. Quickly turning, she almost runs into a man standing in the office doorway. Taken a little off guard, Kim backs up, snapping at the stranger. "May I help you, sir?" She notices his breathing is heavy and tiny pebbles of sweat cling to his forehead, even though it's a cool spring day.

"I'm looking for Burtrum Lee Conner," his voice is raspy as he coughs.

"Who?" Kim thinks for a minute. "Oh, Lee, she just left, can I help you?" She asks feeling a little sorry for the guy. She can tell he's not from Santa Fe.

"When do you expect her back?" His body tightens.

"Not until Monday. So, if you want to leave her a message, I'll make sure she gets it." Feeling trapped, she tries to edge around the pudgy, balding, middle-aged man. Aren't they all starting to look the same, she thinks to herself.

"I really need to talk to her." His brow furrows.

"I'm sorry, but there's nothing I can do."

Digging in his pocket, the odd man pulls out a crinkled twenty. "Here, I'll give you this if you tell me where she is." He takes a step closer.

Stuffing her hands in her pockets, Kim backs away. "I'm not going to take your money, and I think you better leave now, or I'll call the police," her voice squeals.

His face begins to shade crimson as footsteps approach from the living room.

Bobbing his head like a prairie dog from its hole, the goon wipes his brow with a plump hand, and stumbles out the door.

Seeing Dionna, the night manager, Kim spits frantically. "Did you see that guy who just left? What a weirdo. He demanded I tell him where Lee was, and when I wouldn't, he cornered me in the office. Heaven only knows what he might have done if you hadn't shown up!"

"I didn't see anyone. Is he a guest?" Dionna voice twangs in disbelief. She knows how Kim likes to dramatize.

"I don't think so. I haven't seen him around. Maybe I should call Lee, she might know something about it."

Retreating back to the office, Kim dials Lee's number but only gets the answering machine. After leaving a brief message, she hangs up, stretching for her pack.

"Listen Dionna, I'm going to cruise, even though Chris isn't here yet. If Lee calls, tell her I went home, okay?"

"I'm sure it's nothing, Kim."

"Yeah, you're probably right. He just acted so desperate and out of place."

"There are a lot of those here in Santa Fe. What if he comes back?"

"Explain to him that we don't give out employee information. And if he wants to talk to Lee, she'll be in on Monday. And then call me."

"Yeah, okay."

Striding out into the pre-spring air and taking a deep breath, Kim day dreams about the big fat joint she has waiting, and smiles.

❈   ❈   ❈

Strolling home, Lee whistles in anticipation of a relaxing couple of days. And there's no better way to start it, than to have dinner with her grandmother. She loves Clair Conner, and at times feels like she is more of a parent to her than her own.

Over the past few years, Lee has begun to notice that Jed

and Jane Conner pay less and less attention to her. This is hard in itself, but it's compounded by the fact that Lee feels like she needs more support than ever, but doesn't know why.

Clair stepped in though, and picked up the slack. Lee figures her parents are too involved with their hoity-toity social scenes to concern themselves with their only daughter.

Smiling as she approaches her hovel, Lee reaches out to slip the key in the lock, but instead pushes the door open. Shaken and scared, she steps back, unsure of what to do. Lee knows she bolted it this morning, and can't think of any reason why it should be open. Carefully easing in, she's taken off guard by the state of her living room. At first the mess doesn't compute, but then Lee realizes her home has been burglarized.

"Oh, my gosh," she exhales, suddenly remembering her cat. "Lucy, Lucy. Come here kitty, where are you?"

Lee's heart skips a beat when she doesn't hear a response, but then, out of nowhere, the calico curls around a corner, meowing and seeming a little skittish.

Quickly stepping forward, Lee bends over and lifts the twelve-pound cat to her chest. "Oh, Lucy, I'm so glad you're all right." She kisses her friend on the head. "What happened? Did you see anything? Or were you a smart girl, and hid?"

Setting the feline on the floor, Lee is amazed at the damage lying before her. "Man, oh man, can you believe this?" Surveying the room, she senses something unusual about the intrusion, but can't pinpoint it. Sweeping to the back of the house, Lee notices the kitchen has barely been touched. A few drawers and cabinets are open, but it's nowhere near the destruction in the living room.

Entering her bedroom, she's greeted by the same scene she found in the front of the house. Lee's first instinct is to call the police, but a nagging sensation prevents her. Glancing at the phone she sees a red light flashing on the answering machine. Pushing the play button, she listens as the tiny tape reels backwards.

"Lee, hey Lee. You there? This is Kim, pick up. Listen, some weirdo guy came looking for you. He wanted to know where you were. I didn't tell him anything, and then he split when Dionna showed up. Thought maybe you might know something about it. I don't think he's a guest. Call me."

Lee stands still, baffled. What is going on? What is Kim talking about?

Deciding the safest thing to do is grab Lucy and head to Clair's house, she calls out, but again receives no response. Dropping food in her bowl to ease the cat out of hiding, Lee knows the poor creature is genuinely spooked, and hates to take her away from familiar territory.

Just then it dawns on Lee what's so strange about the break-in: nothing's missing. The TV, VCR, stereo and all of her CDs are untouched. Even her golf clubs, sitting in the corner neglected, have been overlooked.

Is this person after something specific?

What does she, Lee Conner, have that would inspire someone to ransack her home?

Questions reel in her mind as she hoists Lucy in her arms and heads out the door. Tucking the cat into the back seat of her VW Jetta, Lee jumps behind the wheel and tries to start the car. It sputters at first, not having been driven in a few days, but then the sparks catch, and the engine revs.

Racing down Bishops Lodge Road to her grandma's adobe home snuggled in the foothills of the Sangre de Cristo Mountains, Lee feels tense. When Clair Conner first built her home, it stood alone. Now hundreds of brown structures dot the countryside, with more and more construction sounds ringing throughout the valley each year.

Parking behind the house, Lee snags the angry cat and holds her tight. Trudging up the long stone path to the back porch, she stops to catch her breath, catching a glimpse of the Manzano Mountains off in the distance.

Sighing, she lets the beauty of her native home relax her. Juniper burns in her nostrils, spicy and sweet, as deep blue skies, and burnt orange horizons sooth her eyes.

Turning the doorknob, Lee is surprised to find it locked. Trying hard to embrace the struggling kitty as she rings the bell, Lucy finally wriggles out of her grip just as Clair opens the door. Immediately, the cat plunges out of Lee's arms, racing into the house and disappearing.

"We won't be seeing her for a while," Lee says, hugging Clair and slipping past her. "Birdy, are you all right? You're rather early." Closing the door behind her, Clair follows her granddaughter into the kitchen.

"Oh!" Lee sits down at the table. The warmth of the fireplace fills her with comfort.

"Why did you bring Lucy?" Clair pours her granddaughter a glass of cabernet.

"Oh, my word, Grandma, you won't believe it," Lee said, her hands shaking as she tries to steady the glass.

"I get home to find my front door open, and the whole place in shambles. There's nothing stolen, so I think they're searching for something special."

"What are you talking about? You're not making sense." Clair eases down into a chair.

"Then there's a message on my machine from Kim at work. She says some man shows up after I left, asking about me."

"Who?"

"I don't know. But I think he has something to do with the condition of my house."

"Did you call the police?" Genuine concern laces Clair's voice.

"No, I thought I'd wait to see what you had to say."

Clair is silent for a long time. She finally speaks, although, hesitantly. "I think the best thing to do is to keep this between us. Maybe this man just saw your picture on the B&B's website and wants to talk to you personally because he knows you're the manager. You know how Kim sometimes likes to blow things out of proportion," Clair sighed, then continues. "As for your house, it could be some random break-in, and since nothing was stolen, maybe we should wait until tomorrow and decide if it's necessary to involve the authorities."

"I guess you're right," she said, rubbing her forehead. "I feel a headache coming on."

"Why don't we go to your house in the morning. I'm sure things won't seem as bad then." Clair hopes Lee doesn't detect the tension in her voice. She has a strong sense of who's behind this.

"You're right. I'll be able to think more clearly once I get some rest." Standing, Lee continues, "I need some fresh air. I'm going out back for a little while."

"You go right ahead dear. Just take it easy and I'll call you when dinner's ready."

Lee kisses Clair on the cheek. "Thank you Grandma. I knew you could calm me down. Let me know if you need me for anything."

"I will, I promise." Clair studies her granddaughter, her eyes etched in worry.

Jane Conner glances in both directions as she pushes the number three button on her cell phone and raises it to her ear. Spotting a police car approaching from the other side of the street, she lowers the device, cursing as she does. It'd be just her luck for a cop to bust her for talking on a cell while driving. Jane thinks it's a ridiculous law, and one that infringes on her liberties. Still, she doesn't want to get caught and have to pay the standard sixty-five-dollar fine.

"Hello?" She hears a muffled voice against her thigh. "Hello! Is anyone there?"

"No, no, Clair don't hang up," Jane shouts down into the phone.

"Jane? What are you doing?"

"I'm in my car, and a cop just drove by." Lifting the receiver back to her ear, Jane's voice becomes clearer.

"Oh, I see," Clair said, agreeing with the cell phone law. There are too many people out there driving around gabbing and not paying attention to the road. "Do you need something?" Clair's tone is cool. She too has noticed how, over the past few months, Jane and Jed have been treating their daughter.

"Yes, I'm looking for Lee. She isn't at home, so I figure the only other place she can be is at your house. I don't know why in the world that girl won't get a cellular so I can contact her when I need to."

"Maybe that's one of the reasons, Jane," Clair snips, once again becoming annoyed with her daughter-in-law.

"Well, anyway," Jane said, sounding slightly put off. "Is she or isn't she there?"

"No, she's not."

"Clair Conner, I know you're lying."

"Come check for yourself."

"Maybe I'll do just that."

Having overheard the conversation, Lee saunters inside. Shaking her head, she taps her grandmother's shoulder, and indicates to Clair to give her the phone. Handing the receiver over without a fuss, Lee laces her palm across the mouthpiece, and says, "I don't know why you two can't just get along."

Holding the phone to her ear. "Hello, Mother."

"Lee, is that you?"

"Who else would it be, Jane?"

"You know how I feel when you call me by my name, plus, why is your grandmother being so difficult?"

"Don't start, Mom. What's up?"

"I just want to know how you are. We haven't talked in the past couple of days, and I'm wondering if you're all right."

"Yes, everything's fine. What's the real reason for your call?"

"Well, your father and I are throwing a little dinner party tonight and we thought you might like to join us."

"Don't you think it's a little late for an invitation?"

"No, not really. We figured you might not have anything to do this evening, and we don't want you sitting home alone on a Friday night."

Rolling her eyes. "Trust me, Mother, I enjoy sitting home alone. It's awfully nice of you to think of me though, and I appreciate the invite, but I'll have to pass," Lee's tone rings sarcasm.

"You can't tell me you have other plans."

"Well, as a matter of fact, I do. Grandma is making dinner. She invited me over this morning."

"I swear, you're always at that woman's house, and you never spend time with your parents anymore."

"Mother, I'm not going to get into this now. Dinner's almost ready and Clair needs my help. I'll call you in the morning, okay? Give Dad my love. Bye."

"Fine, good-bye then," Jane's voice is razor sharp.

Lee lingers in silence for a moment after hanging up. For the past few months she and her mother have been at each other's throats constantly. They have always gotten along in the past, but now it seems like nothing Lee does can satisfy Jane Conner.

"Birdy, you okay?"

Hearing her grandmother's voice stream in from the living room, Lee clears her throat. "Yeah, you know Jane,"

Sadness shimmy's her words.

Appearing in the doorway, Clair shuffles over to her granddaughter and pats her on the shoulder. "Oh, boy, let me tell you, I'm not sure what's going on with her. I mean, it could be menopause, but Jane should be pretty much over that by now. Who knows? To be honest, I'm getting a little tired of trying to figure her out."

"Hey, let's talk about something else, okay? I'm already upset as it is."

"Your mom and I go way back, you know," Clair said, clearly not ready to let the subject rest. "I knew her as a child. She and Jed used to play together all the time. I saw from the start that they'd marry each other. So did everyone else. She was a sweet thing then. I think life has made her a little bitter. But enough is enough. Are you hungry?"

"Yes!"

"How about I fix us those enchiladas?"

"Are you sure it's not too much trouble, Grandma?"

"Don't be ridiculous. You just sit there and keep me company." Clair smiles at her granddaughter, and touches her chin.

Feeling weary Lee says, "I'm going to go find Lucy, and make sure she's all right."

"Yes, that's a good idea."

Lee exits the kitchen, and Clair slyly slips into the pantry. Reaching to the top shelf, she pulls down an old coffee can and removes the plastic lid. Making sure Lee is out of sight before removing the contents, Clair examines the yellowed newspaper articles in the dimming light.

3

Santa Fe, NM 1960

Jane Conner is crazed, the bedroom walls are closing in on her as she thrashes back and forth on the blood soaked sheets. "No, Jed, don't say that. You're lying. Why are you doing this to me? Just give me my baby!"

Jed Conner plops down next to his hysterical wife and reaches for her hand. His heart is heavy with sorrow as he lays her cool fingers inside his. She's lost a lot of blood, but fortunately he's been able to stop the flow before she bled to death. He glances away from the pale face of his distraught wife, wiping away an escaped tear slipping down his cheek.

"I'm sorry, Jane. There was nothing I could do. He wasn't breathing."

"I want to see him," she howls. "Give me my son." She bolts upright, flinging her arms at Jed. He reels back, barely being missed by the flailing fists. Trying to calm her down, Jed attempts to restrain his manic wife.

"Jane, honey, Please, just lay back down. We don't want the bleeding to start again."

"What difference does it make, Jed? What is there to live for now?"

Jane begins to sob, leaving her gasping for air. Rising, Jed steps over to the dresser for a tissue. Jane, weak and wobbly, stumbles out of bed and rushes past him, knocking Jed to the floor. He watches in awe as his wife snatches up their dead son lying in the cradle, and runs out the front door in her sheer nightgown, heedless to the dangerous blizzard conditions.

Jed's stunned; he can't move, get up, go after her. Nothing makes sense. Returning to the now, he jumps up, and scurries out the door. The howling winds slap his chapped cheeks, blinding him with pebbled snow.

"Jane, Jane!" He bellows, his words vanishing in front of his eyes.

She won't last out there for very long, he cries to himself.

Wrestling his coat over his shoulders, Jed grabs a blanket from the couch, and stands outside his house in the white night, searching for a sound, a clue towards the direction in which he should turn.

4

Massaging his temples with his plump, white hands, Calvin Kramer keeps questioning his purpose for being here in Santa Fe; trying to locate some unknown woman. He knows he should be back in San Francisco, attempting to mend matters with his wife, Carla. It's bad timing on Lyman's part to send him to New Mexico as Calvin's marriage is about to explode.

Furthermore, he's a man of science and not a sleuth. He doesn't understand why Lyman Stone didn't just hire a private detective, or send someone from lab security. Anyone would have been better than him.

Attending to an itch directly above his right ankle, Calvin looks around, hating what he sees; everything is so small and brown. Easing his finger out of his sock, he examines the tip. Blood underlines his nail. The bite continues to sting, screaming out for more attention.

His stomach grumbles in neglect as Calvin remembers he hasn't eaten since the Egg McMuffin earlier at the airport. He's been in such a hurry to find Burtrum Conner, he's forgotten to eat, which is unusual in itself for Calvin.

Breathing in deeply and exhaling, Calvin feels his nostrils burn from the dry air. He inspects the road outside of Lee's house, but sees no sign of her. He'd returned to her house, hoping to catch her getting home from work, but to no avail.

The small adobe structure is pitch dark, as Calvin decides to call it quits. The chill air has also begun to take its toll on him, and if there is one thing he doesn't like, it's being cold.

Starting the engine, he reflects on how crazy this whole situation has become. He wonders what's so special about Conner? Lyman just tells him bits and pieces, and this disturbs him, but figures the less he knows the better.

Pulling away from the curb, Calvin recalls seeing a restaurant close to his motel. He'll get some food to go, return to his room and try calling Carla again., maybe she's calmed down enough to answer this time.

Calvin Kramer hates it here in Santa Fe.

I am walking in unfamiliar woods with Lucy pouncing along beside me. She is chasing birds and butterflies around in the beautiful surroundings. She sees a fly, and in her pursuit of the insect, jumps into a pond. I'm terrified as she sinks beneath the water. As I kneel on the muddy edge, panicked, I watch her resurface. I immediately pull her from the water and hold her close, thinking how terrible I'll feel if something happens to her. As it suddenly begins to

snow, I notice she has a brown wallet clinging to her paws. I reach out to grab it, but it falls into the pool and disappears beneath the swampy, green water.

Lee jerks awake, and, in doing so, erases the dream from her memory. Laying back down, shaken, she tries to get her bearings.

Moaning, she lays her arm across her forehead. She knows she shouldn't have drunk so much wine this evening. Regret can't help her now as her tongue, thick and purple, aches for moisture.

Stumbling into the kitchen, Lee prays there is a cold Coke in the refrigerator, as she yanks open the icebox. Spotting a red can, she grabs it, pops the top, and gulps down a large swallow, feeling the acid fizzle against the back of her throat.

Behind her, Lee hears Clair trudging down the staircase.

"Birdy, honey, are you okay?"

Shielding her eyes as Clair flicks on the light, Lee whispers groggily. "Grandma, do we really need those?"

Clair swats the switch back off. "Sorry, honey. I can't see anything." The room darkens, except for the sliver of light coming from the gaping fridge.

"Sweetheart, you're going to burn the bulb out." Clair shuffles over and turns on a nightlight under the cabinets. Shutting the Maytag, she glides Lee to the table and helps her sit down.

Shadows skip across the walls, as moonlit winds rustle the dried leaves left on the trees from last summer. Lee feels like crying. She turns her head so her grandmother can't see her eyes.

It doesn't matter. Clair senses something is wrong as she reaches out to touch Lee's shoulder.

"Honey, what's the matter?

Turning to Clair, Lee wipes a tear off her chin. "I don't know, Grandma. It's as though suddenly I feel like my whole world is displaced. Do you know what I mean? Like the person I am, isn't really me. I don't know. Maybe I'm just going through a midlife crisis, or something."

Clair pats Lee's hand. "Sweetheart, don't worry. We all go through this at one time or another. It's natural."

"Is it though?" Lee still feels drunk from the wine, and a sharp pain has begun to crease her brow. Rising, she announces. "I think I'll just go upstairs to bed. I'm sure my mood has to do with the wine I drank. You know how that stuff affects me." Leaning over, she kisses Clair on the cheek. "I'm going to get up early and go over to my house, maybe start straightening things out."

"Do you want some help?"

"It might be better if I go alone. I'll get more done if I'm by myself." Lee turns toward the staircase, "Night."

"Good-night dear," Clair replies, anxiety finding its way into her brain. She needs to do something, and quickly before all hell breaks loose. Grabbing the rail, Clair ascends the stairs.

San Francisco, CA

Dr. Lyman Stone paces back and forth on the worn beige rug. His office décor is dull and drab, as he fumes over his own misjudgment. He should have made the trip to Santa Fe himself, and not send that baboon, Calvin Kramer. What was he thinking? Such a delicate subject, at last discovering the whereabouts of his daughter.

Lyman is well aware that Katie never had a son, he himself made sure of that when the experiment began. Dr. Stone wanted a girl. Then when the crash happened and a male child was found with Katie Lee, Lyman Stone knew something was very, very wrong, he just didn't know what took place at the scene of the accident. But now, after all of these years, he's finally going to get to the bottom of it, no matter what it takes.

5

The sound of the coffee grinder awakens Lee as she opens her led filled eyelids. Scanning the clock on the dresser, she hisses. "Damn-it!" Unraveling her legs from beneath the blankets, she hurries to get dressed. Scampering downstairs, she snake-eyes Clair as she reaches the foyer.

Smiling, her grandmother turns her attention back to the frying pan on the stove, and asks. "You hungry?"

Knowing it's pointless to be angry, Lee replies. "Yeah, sure, why not, it's already getting late."

"What are you talking about? It's barely nine o'clock."

"I know, but I wanted to get up two hours ago."

"Well, I guess your body needed more sleep."

"What does it know?" Lee picks up a juice glass and takes a sip of the orange liquid, sweet and tangy, with just enough pulp.

"There's more in the fridge if you want. It seems like you

could use a couple of doses of vitamin C." Clair wheels around toward Lee. "The coffee will be done in a minute." She turns away and then back. "You don't look so good. Are you feeling okay?"

"Not really. I'm just worn out, plus, drinking all that wine didn't help. I'm sure a good night's sleep will cure everything." Wiping her nose with her sleeve.

"For Pete's sake, use a Kleenex." Clair slides the box across the table, hitting Lee in the elbow.

"Ouch! Quit being so mean to me," Lee jokes.

"Keep it up young lady and you'll be flipping these eggs for yourself."

"Eggs?" Lee's gut wrenches.

"Yes, why?"

"I don't know, I'm not sure if my stomach can handle huevos."

"Then what would you like?" Clair turns the flame out from beneath the cast-iron skillet.

"I don't know. Maybe a little oatmeal and toast, something, soothing."

"Okay, no problem." Filling Lee's cup with coffee, she nonchalantly feels her cheeks and forehead for a fever. Her skin is cool and clammy beneath Clair's touch.

Lee glances around. "Hey, have you seen Lucy?"

"Yeah, she was up early with me. I fed her and now I think she's sleeping on the afghan at the bottom of my bed. I think she likes it here."

Studying her grandmother standing by the stove, stirring the porridge, Lee wonders for the millionth time if she'll end up spending the rest of her life in Santa Fe, doing nothing, and going nowhere.

"Breakfast is ready," Clair announces, as she scoops steaming cereal into a bowl.

After only a few bites, Lee feels full and pushes the food away. "That's all you're going to eat, young lady?" Clair inquires.

"Grandma, my gut's a little queasy."

"You barely touched it. You need your strength." Sliding the dish closer. "Just a tiny bit more."

Red rage blisters her brain as Lee hurls back her seat and stands up abruptly knocking the chair over. She's tired of her grandma treating her like a little girl. Shocked by her uncharacteristic actions, Lee scrambles toward the door, grabbing her coat, and without a word, races out.

Watching in astonishment as her granddaughter speeds down the driveway, Clair can't believe what just happened. Lee has never acted this way before, and she fears this might be the beginning of the end for the Conner clan as they know it.

Tremors ripple through Clair as she hurries into the living room. Opening her desk drawer, she pulls out a worn address book. Flipping to the L's, she thumbs through the aged pages until she finds the unused number. Punching the digits into the touch-tone phone, Clair prays this is still the right connection. After all, it's been almost four decades since she has last dialed the 415 area code.

❋   ❋   ❋

Santa Fe, NM 1960

"Hello!" Katie Lee's voice is coated rust as she speaks into the telephone.

"Is this Katie Lee?"

"Yes, who is this?"

"It doesn't matter. I just want you to know that your daughter is alive and safe, and if you tell me where you are, we can bring her to you."

"My daughter? I never had a daughter. I had a son," Katie chokes out. "And he died in the accident." Katie's anger flares. "What kind of cruel joke is this? Who are you, why are you saying these things?" She screams.

The woman gasps, as the phone goes silent.

❀ ❀ ❀

Santa Fe, NM 2004

Seething, Lee isn't sure what made her so angry. Her grandmother talks to her that way all the time, and she's never reacted like this before.

Pulling into her driveway and turning off the Jetta, Lee sits for a moment, evaluating her house. She's owned the adobe abode for over twelve years now, and recalls how exciting it was the day she moved in. Now that it's almost paid for, with a lot of help from her parents, she wonders how much longer she's going to live here.

Lugging herself up the walkway and onto the front porch, Lee unlocks the door and is greeted by a silent welcome. Chills vibrate her nerves as she maneuvers through the living room picking up a lamp and setting it upright. A sense of foreboding enters her thoughts, as she suddenly feels uncomfortable. It's as though she's been personally invaded. A stranger, touching her belongings.

Having second thoughts about being here alone, Lee stares at the phone, wanting to call the police. But her grandmother convinced her to wait, which now, is starting to seem a little strange.

Retreating to her bedroom, she grabs a few cloths and a tote bag. Cramming everything into the canvas case, Lee scampers out the door, resolving to return later with her dad, but wondering if she'll ever feel cozy at home again.

Calvin Kramer impatiently taps his fingers on the dash as the traffic on Guadalupe Street comes to a complete halt. He didn't even think there were enough people in Santa Fe to cause a tie up. Closing his eyes, he listens to the sound of the spring birds chirping. Examining the computer image Lyman gave him, Calvin's not sure he'll even recognize Lee Conner if he saw her, the photo is so bad.

Cars creep forward giving Calvin a line of sight to the front. An accident, that's what's causing the hold up. Shaking his head in frustration, his thoughts wander back to Carla, as worry crosses his brow. She's been acting very strange lately. Becoming unresponsive and distant. When he asks her about her mood changes, she tells him he's just being silly and to think nothing of it. It's all part of menopause, she insists. He knows better, though.

A honk brings him back to reality, and as his foot touches

the gas pedal, the car jerks and stalls. Embarrassed, he jams the gear into neutral and restarts the engine, this time inching slowly as he coasts forward.

Turning down Paseo de Peralta, and onto Santa Fe Avenue he doesn't notice the Jetta passing him, or the auburn haired woman behind the wheel.

Stopping in front of Lee's house, Calvin spies to see if there are any indications that she's home.

Pulling over to the side of the street, he slides the address book he stole from the house out of his pocket. It's the only significant thing he's found, and it certainly will not prove this is the woman Lyman seeks.

Flipping through the pages, he notices very few entries, and wonders if she has any friends. Coming to a name under C, *Clair Conner, 4143 Bishops Lodge Road*, Calvin assumes it to be a relative because of the same last name.

Locating the street from his tourist map, he realizes how close he is, and decides to drive there. Maybe he'll get lucky today and find her. Then he can get back home where he belongs.

San Francisco

Katie Lee hangs up the phone, and breathing deeply, listens to the gurgling sound coming from her oxygen line. Reaching out for the green plastic tube, she runs her blue-veined finger along it, checking for clogs. Finding none, she leans her head back against her pillow, and tries to relax. Excitement makes it hard for her to breath.

BURTRUM LEE • 43

How can she keep calm, though? Dr. Stone found out about her daughter, the baby she's tried to hide all of these years. She has no idea how Lyman made the discovery. All Katie knows is that her child is in danger, and she needs to act, and act fast.

Katie relives that mysterious call right after the accident, telling her the infant she thought was dead, is alive. Why didn't she believe the caller? At first she thought it was some sick joke, but then there was that feeling she just couldn't shake, and hoped that whomever had her child, would try to contact her again. But they didn't. Not for four decades.

When Clair Conner called her private phone, one that even Wanda doesn't know about, Katie couldn't explain the sensations she felt. Desperation, exaltation! She knows she has to get to Santa Fe before Lyman finds Lee. Katie's aware that Dr. Stone tampered with the experiment, and it wasn't for the betterment of the research, but for his own personal agenda.

Pressing the call buzzer on the arm of her wheelchair, Katie Lee gazes out the bay window and into the deep darkness of the Pacific. Another storm is rolling in over the vast ocean, as she tightens her shawl around her shoulders.

Carla turns her phone off and tosses the device into her overnight bag. A trip alone with her lover, maybe tonight he'll insist she leave Calvin and run away with him, why else does he want her to pack her bags.

Her marriage is over, Carla knows that. Her suspicions

were verified that Calvin is having an affair, when he suddenly up and left her on this so-called-business-trip for the lab. Why would he get sent to Santa Fe, or Los Alamos? Who cares? All she knows is that a bright, fun and loving future is in store for her, as she slips a strand of Trojans into her purse.

❋ ❋ ❋

Santa Fe, NM

Clair Conner's mood lightens as she diligently works in her garden preparing the soil for spring planting. She knows with the lack of snow this past winter the summer will be dry and hot. If she wants a healthy garden this season she has to start saving gray water, now.

Twisting her head back toward the house, Clair thinks she hears footsteps, and assumes Lee has returned. Standing to greet her granddaughter, she bends over to slap the dirt off the knee of her slacks.

Straightening up, Clair is caught off guard by a stranger appearing in front of her, and sways on her feet. She immediately feels ill-at-ease. "May I help you?" Her voice, shaky.

"Are you Clair Conner?" The man takes a step closer and extends his hand. "It doesn't matter who I am, you're on private property and I'd appreciate it if you would leave." Clair's not usually this rude, but she has a bad sense about this guy, and believes he might be the man hunting down Lee.

"Excuse me ma'am, I don't want to cause any problems, I just want to know where I can find Lee Conner."

"What do you want with her? Who are you?"

"It's of a personal matter."

"There's nothing too personal when it comes to Lee."

"I just have a couple of questions for her. So please, the sooner I speak to her, the faster I can leave you nice folks alone."

"I know why you're here and I think it's best that you leave." Clair sees frustration begin to build in his face, like a red powder keg. "So, please, I'd like to get back to my gardening." Turning to the flower beds. "You can let yourself out."

Uncharacteristically, Calvin grabs her arm. "Listen lady, I don't want any trouble. I just want to get this over with, and then go home. Got it? So, just cooperate, okay."

Hearing Jane's voice float out from the house, he releases Clair's wrist.

"Clair, you out there?"

Cursing, Calvin turns and runs away.

Feeling dizzy, Clair sits down on the bench.

Stomping out the door, Jane sees Clair and rushes over to her. "Clair, oh my gosh, are you all right?" Squatting down in front of her mother-in-law.

"Yes, yes, I'm fine."

"What happened?"

"That man was here?"

Jane twists her head from side to side. "What man?"

Clair remembers that Jane doesn't know about Lee's pursuer.

"Yesterday, when Lee got home, she found her house ransacked. Then at work, some guy shows up asking about her, and just now he was here demanding me to tell him where she is."

Jane stands and helps Clair up. "Who is he?"

Glaring at Jane, Clair's response is chilling. "I think you know."

"What would they want with her after all these years?"

"I believe the wrong person discovered she's alive, and now he's coming for her."

Jane glances up at the sky for a moment. "You mean that crazy genetic scientist, Dr. Stone? The one accused of performing illegal experiments back in the sixties, but was never convicted."

"Yes, him."

"What would he want with Lee?" Jane's brow crinkles.

"I can't get into it, we'll talk later. Right now, what we need to do is guard Birdy." Clair begins to head toward the house.

Jane stops mid-track. "Clair Conner, you come clean with me, and come clean, now."

"I told you, later." Clair's voice strains. "Now, where's Jed?"

"He's on a business trip."

"What do you mean? I talked to him yesterday and he didn't mention anything."

"It was sudden; he had to fly to Los Angeles for a meeting."

Clair senses her lying, and wonders if there's more to what she's being told.

"We'll call him later on his cell phone. If he just left, he's still in flight."

"I'm a little worried," Jane sighs.

"Me, too," Clair whispers.

Calvin Kramer bends over the trunk of his car, trying to catch his breath. He wipes his sweat-soaked forehead with the sleeve of his powder-blue oxford shirt.

"Darn it," he yells, kicking the tire, and igniting pain in his foot. "That's it! No more, I'm done!"

Calvin hears Carla's voice ranting inside his head.

"See, I told you not to go. Now you're going to end up in jail because you don't have a spine, and are too afraid to tell Lyman, *no.*"

Shaking his head, he views the Sandia Mountains rising in the background. The morning mist has burned off, leaving a slight layer of haze over the watermelon-colored peaks.

Taking a deep breath, Calvin feels like he's barely inhaling any air at all. This high altitude does not agree with him, making Calvin wonder if maybe the lack of oxygen to his brain is the source of his erratic behavior.

Climbing back into his rented Ford Taurus, Calvin tells himself he can't blame everything on the atmosphere in Santa Fe.

Deciding to go back to his motel, Calvin figures he'll call Lyman and tell him this assignment is a failure and he wants to come home.

Dr. Stone knew from the beginning that the chances of finding Lee Conner were slight. Calvin still doesn't understand what is so important about this woman, and Lyman is still being tight lipped.

"Bastard!" Calvin curses.

He'd witnessed Stone receiving the telegram that started this crazy business. After that, everything changed. Lyman became unusually excited, and the next day Calvin found himself on a plane feeling confused and angry. Definitely a case of being in the wrong place at the wrong time.

He ponders the idea of searching for another job when he gets home. There are always research labs looking for qualified physicists. But he's pretty comfortable at Lee Labs, plus, Carla has gotten used to a certain kind of lifestyle, and he'd hate to have to make any sacrifices because of a pay cut. He'll just have to buck up for another day or two, and see what happens.

Jane Conner sits in her S Series Mercedes parked in her mother in-law's driveway and opens the glove compartment. Concealing her silver cased flask, she twists off the cap, and tilting the decanter up to her lips, gulps down a shot of vodka. She can't believe the circumstances suddenly arising, and she's pissed that Clair isn't talking.

Slamming the car into gear, Jane races down Bishops Lodge Road. She has to find her daughter, and find her fast, maybe she knows something about what Clair's not telling.

6

Megan Masterson tosses the stained blue polo shirt in the hamper as she rummages through her drawers searching for a clean one. How could she forget about spilling soup on her uniform yesterday, and now she's going to be late for work.

Spotting herself in the mirror as she scrounges around, she thinks her face looks like death warmed over. Splotchy red cheeks to match her blood-shot eyes. She now regrets drinking all that Jack Daniel's last night.

Contemplating calling in sick, Megan knows if she does, Dennis will fire her. She's already skating on thin ice. And this isn't the first time she's feigned illness due to a hangover.

Rushing into the bathroom, Megan rinses her parched mouth. All she wants to do is crawl back into bed, but knows she has to be at the Bistro in forty-five minutes.

Her head, beginning to spin, tells Megan she needs to lay off the booze for a while. Her drinking has become a nightly pastime for a couple of months now, ever since Sarah, her ex, moved out.

At last discovering a wrinkled work shirt, Megan slips it on, figuring Dennis will be angrier at her for being late, than for coming into work looking sloppy.

Trotting out of her small apartment and into the sunshine filled day, Megan experiences a sudden heat-wave rush over her as she crosses the deserted rail yard. Quickly glancing around, she bends over and vomits. Heaves rush out of her as she grasps for air.

Wiping her mouth with her hand, she takes a deep breath and continues on her way, legs shaking with each step. The sun penetrates her alcohol saturated body, forming pools of sweat under her arms. Pulling her sweater off, she slings it over her shoulder, letting the coolness of the breeze coat her perspiring body.

Wheeling through the blue door of the restaurant, Megan smells burnt toast, and gags. Mariachi music blares from the radio and Megan feels her aching brain cringe with every blast of the trumpet.

Knowing food will help, she heads to the back storeroom and opens a bag of rye bread. Stuffing a piece in her mouth, she chews steadily, the seeded crust tasting like cardboard.

"Who's back there?"

Hearing Dennis's voice, Megan swallows, and hanging her sweater on the hook, grabs an apron, dusting crumbs off her chest before Dennis sees.

"It's just me, Dennis."

"You're late," he grumbles. "Again."

"I know, I'm sorry, my mom called me just as I was leaving the house."

"She seems to call you a lot."

"I guess she just loves me." Megan brushes past her boss, disgusted by his smell. Dennis has always been known for letting one loose every now and then, and shows no discrimination as to where or when he'll pass gas.

"Just get to work," he growls.

Feeling like she's aged ten years, as she watches the last customer leave, Megan sighs, and stuffing her tips into her pockets, lumbers out the door. She doesn't have to be back until Monday, and is anticipating some quiet time alone.

Reaching her apartment and feeling lonelier than ever, Megan contemplates the idea of getting a cat or some goldfish, something to keep her company when these blues arrive.

What she really needs, is to get out of this one horse town, after all, it was Sarah's idea to uproot their lives from Minneapolis and move here, not hers. Plus, this city hasn't given her anything but grief. Maybe it's true what the locals believe. Either Santa Fe welcomes you with open arms, or spits you out. Well, right now, Megan feels like a big goober.

Feeling overwhelmed, she goes upstairs to take a nap. Maybe later if she's hungry she'll order a pizza, but now all Megan wants to do is sleep. Crawling back into the unmade bed, she pulls the covers up over her shivering body and closes her eyes, drifting off quickly.

What's her mother doing at Clair's house? Lee asks herself as she watches the silver Mercedes race down the road, oblivious to any other traffic.

Pulling into her grandmother's driveway, Lee gets out of the car and hastens up the steps. "Grandma, where are you?"

Lost in her thoughts, Lee doesn't notice Clair laying on the floor until she almost steps on her.

"Grandma, Grandma, are you all right?" Bending down next to the unmoving woman, Lee turns Clair onto her back, and notices her lips are slightly blue. Thinking she's suffered a heart attack, terror rips through her.

"Birdy," a faint voice whispers.

Leaning in closer, she tries to hear what Clair is saying.

"Honey, you've got to get out of here."

"What are you talking about? I'm not going anywhere. Just relax while I get some help."

Placing her hand on Lee's arm, Clair warns. "No wait, you have to protect yourself. We've been hiding the truth from you all these years."

"Truth, what truth? You're not making sense. Now be quiet and save your strength."

"They switched you!"

"I don't understand what you're talking about."

"Jed and Jane, they…" Taking a deep breath Clair falls unconscious.

"Grandma!" Lee gently shakes the frail woman.

Reaching up, Lee grabs the phone from the end table and dials 911. Tears slowly roll down her cheeks as she listens for the operator.

Presuming the worst, Lee is startled when she hears a

crash come from upstairs. Recalling Clair's words, she kisses her cool, white forehead, and stands up, dropping the phone to the floor.

Fear rips through her as she hears floorboards creek.

"This is 911, how may I help you?" A shallow sounding voice speaks out of the telephone. "Hello! Is anyone there?"

"I love you Grandma," Burtrum Lee whispers as she dashes out the back door.

Slamming the receiver down in its cradle, Megan curses. "Damn telemarketers." Whipping the covers off her body, she scurries to the bathroom. Her head feeling like it's about to explode.

Opening the medicine cabinet, Megan yanks the Excedrin from the shelf, and twisting the cap off, shakes three aspirin into her palm. Dry mouthing the tablets, Megan swallows, feeling the pills lodge in her throat before slithering down.

Shuffling to the couch, she melts into the saggy cushions, and reaching for the grimy remote, flicks the TV on. The local news blares, as she quickly presses the mute button. Flipping through the channels in silence, she lands on an episode of the Simpson's. She feels like crap. There is no way she can continue this life style. Megan has never been so unhappy, and realizes that her stay in Santa Fe is coming to an end. After all, what is keeping her here? It's apparent by now that Sarah is never coming back, her affair *isn't* just a fling. So what's left?

Turning the volume up, Megan closes her eyes. Cottoncandied ghosts float behind her trembling lids, easing Megan into dream filled sleep.

❋ ❋ ❋

Pulling in front of her parent's house, Lee glimpses her mother's sedan parked around back. Frantic, she races into the foyer shouting, "Mother, where are you?" Running up the stairs, she steps into Jane and Jed's bedroom and sees her mom poised at the vanity.

Raising her hand in the air as she catches the reflection of her daughter coming closer, Jane says, "You don't need to shout."

"Clair's had a heart attack."

"What?" Jane turns away from primping in the mirror. "I was just there and she was fine."

"Well, when I arrived I found her laying on the floor."

"Why did you leave?" Jane stands up.

"Grandma told me to run. I think that man is in the house."

"You think? Is he or isn't he?"

"I guess. I heard something crash upstairs after I called 911, and figured the paramedics would arrive soon, so I left. Why don't you go over there, she shouldn't be alone.

"He must've come back."

"Come back? He'd been there earlier?"

"Yes, I was at Clair's this afternoon looking for you, and found her in the backyard, a little shaken up. She said it was nothing. I should have stayed, but she insisted she was fine."

Rubbing her forehead, Lee begins to pace back and forth.

"I can't believe this. The whole situation is getting out of control. I don't understand what's going on." Lee wants to ask her mother about what Clair said; how she's been switched, or something like that, but decides to save it for another date. First, she needs to talk to Clair again.

Placing her hands on her daughter's shoulders, Jane stares into her eyes. "What you need to do is relax. I'll go to Clair's house and make sure everything's all right. You stay here, and don't answer the door or telephone. Okay?"

Melting into a beige Queen Anne chair, Lee sighs. "I don't get it, Mom, what's going on?"

"Honey, we'll explain everything once your father gets back."

"So, you've heard from Dad? I'd really like to talk to him right now."

"No, he hasn't called yet. But once he does and I tell him about Clair, I'm sure he'll be on the first plane home."

"Oh, Mom. I'm so confused."

"I know you are dear." Jane bends over and kisses Lee on the cheek. "I'll call you later to let you know how Clair is. Right now I should get to her house."

"Okay. Tell Grandma I love her."

"I will. Try to get some rest, all right."

"Yeah, I will."

Watching as her mother leaves, Lee lies down on the bed. Staring up at the white ceiling, she wonders what Clair meant. Closing her eyes, Lee has a sinking feeling something bad is going to happen, but she has no idea, *what*!

7

Katie Lee's head jets forward as her eyes snap open. She glances at her husband, whose face has tightened in horror. His foot keeps pumping the brakes, but they weren't slowing down.

"Burtrum!" She tries to scream, but no voice comes out. All Katie can hear is the crunch of the tires as the Oldsmobile spins out of control and off the road, plunging into the shallow embankment, and colliding head-on into an unexpected Ponderosa.

As Katie floats out of her seat, a sensation of being in space surrounds her. Glancing over, she watches as her husband catapults through the windshield. She, following right behind into the white darkness.

The contractions subside as she breezes through the air, wondering if she'll ever land. Hearing a thump, dread suddenly attacks her thoughts, as she howls in agonizing pain.

Time slows down, as streaking moonlight glimmers on the diamond snowflakes tickling her nose. The drifts of snow sparkle like a summer lake as the still beaming headlights dazzle Katie's eyes.

"My son!" Her brain screams, instinctively baring down, as her heart palpitates and adrenalin surges. Fear is on the rampage as Katie cries out.

Every fiber in her soul rips apart. The lights begin to blink in and out, she needs to stay conscious, it'll be their doom if she passes out. Katie's mind reels as she tries to grasp her surroundings; quiet, dark, heavy.

At first the footsteps seem out of place, like an echo from a lost dream. Is it Burtrum? Has his vigorous will and drive kept him alive and uninjured?

Laughing to herself, Katie feels like she's disappointed him. Freezing drops roll from her eyes as silver stabs ripple through her body. She can't hold the blackness back anymore; her mind refuses the torture. Slowly, Katie Lee slips into unconsciousness, silently whispering, "Burtrum, I'm sorry."

8

Calvin's whole body trembles as he stands over Clair Conner. He can't tell if she's breathing or not, and he certainly doesn't possess the guts to bend down and take her pulse. Now what is he going to do?

He's blown his opportunity to confront Burtrum Lee, not realizing she was right downstairs as he rummaged around upstairs. It's like being on a treasure hunt with no clues. This whole game baffles Calvin and when he tries to get more out of Lyman, all his boss says is. "Damn-it Calvin, just find her."

"How absurd," Calvin whispers as the oncoming sirens make him realize he has to split. Giving the room a once over, Calvin makes sure nothing is out of place.

Slipping out the back door, he creeps through the darkness to his car still parked on the shoulder. A fire truck and ambulance rush past him, whipping dirt and rocks in their wake. Grimy dust clings to his sweaty face.

Liking his lips, he climbs into the Taurus. Digging into his pants pocket, Calvin pulls out his cell phone, and tapping number three, holds it up to his ear as it rings.

"Lee Research Laboratories. How may I help you?"

Recognizing his friend's voice, he feels a sense of warmth. "Penny, hey it's me, Calvin."

"Calvin, how are you? How's the great Southwest?"

"Not so great. Is Lyman around?"

"He's in a meeting."

"Isn't it kind of late?" Calvin glances at his watch, realizing it's only six o'clock on the west coast.

"It's an impromptu conference."

"How long do you expect him to be tied up," Calvin said, becoming agitated.

"It's hard to say, you know how these sessions go. Just lucky I don't have to stick around till the end, I could be here all night."

Calvin can hear the fog horns over the phone and feels a deep sense of home sickness. "Well, just tell him I called, okay?"

"Yeah, sure." Penny hesitates for a moment. "Hey Calvin, is everything all right?"

"I guess so. I just don't want to be here." His breathing quickens. "Hey, Penny, have you seen Carla around at all?"

"No, I haven't." Penny suspects there's something more to Calvin's phone call. "Listen, I've got to get going. I'll give Dr. Stone your message, and I'm sure he'll get back to you as soon as he can. Okay?"

"Thanks Penny. Have a nice night."

"You too."

Calvin sits in the Ford watching the silent sirens whirl around in the black night.

❋   ❋   ❋

Clair Conner's eyes shoot open, as the bright lights above make her squint. Something smells funny, she thinks. Mumbled voices float in the haze surrounding her.

She tries to talk, tries to move her hand to get someone's attention, but her body will not move, it's as though she's paralyzed, caught in this dream like state.

Closing her eyes, Clair drifts off, riveting images tumble around in her mind. Where is Birdy?

❋   ❋   ❋

Lee jolts up from her mother's bed and swiftly runs downstairs, grabbing her coat and sprinting out the door.

She's going to find out the truth, and that's that. Obviously, her mother isn't going to be of any help, and her father is MIA, which seems to be more common these days. Guilt rips at her as she tells herself maybe she should be with Clair, but her grandmother's words of warning ring out.

Driving to the B&B, Lee figures she can ditch her car in the parking lot without anyone knowing. Being on foot, she'll be less likely to be seen.

Reaching the plaza, Lee sits down for a moment to make sure she's not being followed. A few people stroll around in the cooling air, nothing out of the usual.

Standing, Lee turns toward Guadalupe Street, deciding to go to the Cowgirl Hall of Fame, assured that the trendy restaurant will be packed, so she can blend into the crowd.

❊   ❊   ❊

Megan can't sleep. She keeps tossing and turning, back and forth, from side to side, her mind racing like a hamster on a wheel.

Flailing the blankets from her legs, she rolls off the couch and stands on the cold tile floor. Shivering as she slips her feet into her tattered moccasins.

Hollow noises echo inside her stomach, as acid churns against empty walls. Groaning, she stumbles into the kitchen hoping to find some food to tantalize her hunger.

Opening the fridge, Megan realizes that the ice box has gotten a little sparse over this past binge, filling it with beer instead of food.

Slamming the door shut, Megan tries to think of what restaurants will still be open. There's only one place nearby serving this late, and even though she's not in the mood to deal with the Saturday night drunks at the Cowgirl, her options are minimal.

The night is cool as Megan strolls down Agua Fria Street. Breathing deeply, she coughs as the crisp air stings her lungs. She is only half way down the block and she can already hear a ruckus coming from the haunt. The Cowgirl always seems to be a hit on week-end nights.

❊   ❊   ❊

Lee's nerves become unsettled as the mob keeps brushing up against her even though she stands tucked close into a corner. She's hoping to run into someone she knows, maybe convince them to let her spend the night. She'll make up some story about how her house is being painted and the fumes are starting to make her ill.

She sees no one though.

Watching a woman stand up and push away from the bar, Lee slithers quickly over to the empty seat and sits down.

"What can I git ya?" The slang talking bartender stands in front of Lee, seemingly perturbed at something.

"A Sierra Nevada, please."

Eternity passes before the tiny woman places the amber beer in front of her.

"That'll be tree-fity."

Pulling money out of her pocket, she lays a five-dollar bill on the tin-topped bar. "The rest is for you, and may I please see a menu?"

Snatching up the cash, the bartender flips a menu on the bar and chugs away without so much as a thank you. Shaking her head, Lee decides the next tip won't be so generous. Leaning back in the wrought iron chair, she listens to the mediocre band playing some rendition of a Rolling Stone's song. A few people are dancing on the cramped makeshift dance floor encamped by tables, where surprisingly, undisturbed diners sit and eat.

❋ ❋ ❋

Calvin flips his Verizon cell phone off and stuffs the black device into his pocket, wishing Lyman had not returned his phone call so fast. The conversation did not go well. He was basically told to stay put until further notice.

Dr. Stone's sudden obsession with this woman flusters Calvin. The Nobel Peace Prize scientist can get any woman he wants, why go after this particular one?

Before he left for this bizarre voyage, Calvin heard rumors about how Burtrum Lee Conner is Lyman's illegitimate daughter. Which kind of makes sense by the way he's acting. Calvin has never seen his boss so anxious, and now he is really thinking crazy, ordering Calvin to kidnap this woman.

Feeling lost, Calvin thinks about calling Carla and telling her everything, but he's been warned to keep his mouth shut, and he knows all too well what will happen if he disobeys Stone. Plus, Carla hasn't returned any of his messages since he left, so she must be really mad at him.

Suddenly feeling small, Calvin grabs his suit jacket and rushes out into the chilly night air. He'll go for a walk, calm down, and then try to contact Lyman again. Explain to him that he's not the man for the job, and he needs to find someone else to do his dirty work, even if it does cost him his career.

Jane Conner taps her fingernails on the fake mahogany nightstand as anger begins creeping up her spine. Being in a hospital on a Saturday night is not her idea of a good time.

She doesn't know what is taking them so long. Clair's fine, she just had a mild arrhythmia, but they're going to keep her overnight anyway.

Much to Jane's delight, the nurse at last arrives with a sedative, and Jane, walking over to the bedside, watches Clair swallow the peach colored pill. Waiting for the RN to leave, Clair finally whispers. "You need to go find Birdy, and protect her."

"She's at my house, so don't worry." Jane glances at her watch. Patting Clair's hand, she continues. "Nothing's going to happen as long as she's with me. Got it?"

"Yes, I got it." A slight smile appears on Clair's lips. "Oh, I'm tired. I think I'm going to go to sleep now. Good-night, Jane."

"Night Clair. I'll be back tomorrow to pick you up." But Clair Conner doesn't hear her daughter in-law's words as the sleeping pill takes hold.

Tip-toeing out of the room, Jane stops outside the door for a moment and tries to compose herself. She needs to think clearly now, the safety of her daughter is at risk.

❀ ❀ ❀

It's no surprise to Megan how packed the tiny bar is, as she slips through the wall of bodies, smashing up against breasts, buttocks and backs. Finally pushing her way up to the bar, Megan is surprised to find an empty stool.

Jumping onto the metal seat before anyone else has a chance, she crosses her arms and waits for one of the bartenders to notice her.

"Hey, Megan, what can I get you?" Leslie asks hurriedly.

"A sea-breeze, and a menu, please?" Megan says, taking the plastic folder from the busy woman as she splashes vodka into a glass.

"You guys are slammed," Megan said, stating the obvious.

"Just another Saturday night in paradise," Leslie says, sloshing the drink in front of Megan. "What'll you have?"

"Just some catfish fingers."

"That it?"

"Yeah, thanks."

Leslie turns away and Megan takes a sip of her drink. It's strong, and the taste makes her feel a little nauseous. As she lifts the cocktail to take another swallow, her elbow is nudged and some of the pink liquor splatters onto her white t-shirt.

"Great!" She sneers, turning to her left to see who the duffus is that ruined her shirt.

"Oh, my gosh, I am so sorry."

Before she knows it, a hand filled with napkins is in front of her. Megan grabs them and starts dabbing the stain.

"That's all right. It's a pretty tight fit in here tonight, and I should know better than to wear white."

Twangy country music rings out of the speakers as the band announces they're going on break.

"Man, I'm glad that's over."

"They're not very good?" Megan looks up.

"They're not terrible. They do a lot of different songs, but not very well."

Megan laughs, and extends her hand. "You're a kinder

woman than I am. My name's Megan Masterson."

Lee introduces herself. "I'm Lee Conner, and I hope you'll let me buy you a drink?"

A sense of familiarity comes over Megan as she studies Lee. It's like she knows this woman but has never met her before tonight.

"Are you new in town? I don't recall seeing you around, but I feel like I know you."

"I'm a native Santa Fean."

"Wow, I haven't met many of you. What a nice place to grow up."

"It has its ups and downs. I tried to get out once, but ended up returning. Guess there's something about Santa Fe that keeps bringing people back." Lee drinks her beer. "And you? Where are you from?"

"Minneapolis."

"Wow! You're a long way from home. Visiting or living?"

"Kind of both. Moved here a year ago, but it still feels like I'm just passing through. I've never really unpacked." Megan has no idea why she's becoming so philosophical. "Metaphorically speaking."

"What brought you to the Land of Enchantment?"

"A relationship."

"And where is he tonight?"

"She."

"Oh!"

"And she's with her new girlfriend."

"Okay, how about another drink?" Lee says, feeling a little nervous all of a sudden, and not knowing why.

"Smooth change of subject. I don't want to hear about it either."

Leslie comes over and sets Megan's meal down in front of her, asking. "Anything else right now?"

"A couple more drinks please," Lee chimes in. "If you could put those on my tab, and then I'll settle up. Thanks."

"Great, coming right up."

The bartender seeming a little nicer once Megan sat down.

Megan pushes her plate closer to Lee. "Here, would you like some?"

"No, no thank you, I just had a burger and I'm stuffed."

"Are you sure?"

"Positive."

Leslie places their drinks on the white paper napkins, and the two ladies lifting them, clink the glasses together.

"Cheers," Megan toasts.

"Cheers," Lee responds.

Megan's tongue begins to ache as the steam from the deep fried fish tantalizes her taste buds. Blowing on a hunk of catfish dripping with tartar sauce, she eats ferociously, trying to fill the empty pit in her gut.

Wiping her mouth, she side-glances Lee. "Sorry if I'm eating like a pig, I'm famished."

Megan eats for a while longer, and then asks. "So, what do you do for a living?"

"I'm a manager at a B&B."

"Oh, yeah, which one, even though I wouldn't know it if you told me."

"Casa de Magdalena, up on Palace Avenue."

"Do you like it?"

"It's pretty easy. And quiet whenever the boss isn't there. You?"

"I'm a waitress at the Boys Town Bistro."

"Yeah, I've heard of that place. Sandwiches and soup?"

"Yup, that's it."

"Do you like working there?"

"Not lately."

The band begins to play again, screechy music blares from their out of tune instruments. Leaning over, Lee says, "I think I'm going to split." Opting to just spend the night at her mother's house.

"If you wait a minute, I'll walk out with you." Catching Leslie's attention, Megan signals for her bill, as she digs into her pocket for some money. Slapping more than enough down on the bar, she pushes away from her chair and follows Lee out the door.

The floor vibrating from the pounding noise.

Feeling his luck change as he moseys into the Cowgirl Hall of Fame and spots Burtrum Lee sitting at the bar, Calvin ducks behind a group of drinkers, peering out between their shoulders. He is certain it is she.

Suddenly, a pain creases his bladder, and he cringes. Cranking his head around, he sees a bathroom behind him, and dashes toward the john, hoping to get back before Conner leaves.

His clover wilts upon his return, when he discovers no

sign of the two women. The chairs they sat in, stand empty, awaiting another occupant. Calvin is stunned as he twists his head back and forth searching for her face. Frustration roars, as his low-blood-sugar body stumbles through the increasing crowd.

Pushing his way out to the middle of Guadalupe, he stretches his neck north, then south, down the dimly lit street. Wiping his face with his hands, Calvin sits down on a stack of piled up railroad ties, tears on the verge of dripping from his eyes.

❋ ❋ ❋

Clair Conner awakes not knowing where she is. Still groggy, she's having a hard time recalling what happened. A heart monitor beeps in the silent night as visions of Lee standing over her flicker in and out of her memory.

A tear drizzles down her dry skin, and she quickly wipes it away. She is not going to do this, fall victim to her aging body. Her granddaughter needs her, and Clair Conner will be damned if she'll ever let anything happen to Birdy.

Unable to keep her eyes open any longer, she closes them, the sedative from earlier still coursing through her system as she falls into a deep sleep.

❋ ❋ ❋

The night air is cold as Lee wraps her coat tighter around her body. "It's freezing out here," She groans, shivering. "I wonder if spring is ever going to arrive."

"Soon, I hope." Rubbing her hands together, Megan asks, "Where did you park?" Hoping to hitch a ride home.

"I'm on foot."

"So you live around here?"

"No, not really, but within walking distance. But now I wished I'd driven." Lee looks around cautiously.

"Is everything okay?" Sensing something peculiar, Megan reaches for Lee's arm to stop her.

"Yeah, everything's fine." Lee continues strolling down Guadalupe Street. "I'm just a little wary about walking at night, you know, with all the crazies roaming around. Santa Fe used to be so much safer."

"I think they call it progression."

"Well, progress or not, it still isn't what it used to be."

"Why don't you move then?"

"Because I love this place, plus, my family is here."

"Would you like to get a cup of coffee or something?"

Lee glances at her watch. "I don't know. It's getting kind of late."

"Then why don't you at least let me give you a ride home."

"You have your car around here?"

"No, not really, but it's just down Agua Fria, about a five -minute walk."

"I don't know. I'd hate to put you out."

"Oh, you won't be, I'm a little wound up now, so this will be good for me." Megan skips up next to her. "What do you say?"

Shaking her head and smiling, Lee agrees. "Okay, if you insist."

Waving her hand in the air, Megan gestures. "Come on then, this way."

Twirling around, she starts prancing in the other direction. Lee stops and turns, then follows her.

"Hey, wait up," she says, smiling.

Megan halts in her tracks to let Lee catch up.

Matching strides, Lee inquires. "What kind of car do you own?"

"A '63 Bug. It's painted all adobe with turquoise trim."

"You're kidding, right?"

"Nope, not at all. I bought it like that when I first moved here."

"You know, come to think of it, I have seen it around town. Yeah, that's a pretty cool car."

"I don't drive a whole lot, so I hope it starts. But if it doesn't I'll pay for a cab ride home for you."

"That's awfully nice, but you don't have to do that." Lee is beginning to feel comfortable with Megan. She seems genuinely nice.

"So, is life offering you everything you thought it would?" Megan asks out of the blue.

Pausing for a moment, Lee replies. "I suppose so, up until recently."

"Why what happened?"

Lee's not sure if she wants to talk about her sudden woes with a woman she just met, but replies. "Well, my grandmother is in the hospital. I think she had a heart attack."

"Oh, I'm so sorry to hear that. Is she going to be all right?"

"I don't know. I haven't spoken to *Mother* yet. I'm worried sick."

"That's understandable. If you'd like you can use my phone to call whomever you need to."

"Oh, thanks Megan. You're so kind. Are you always like this?"

"Yeah, I guess so." Feeling a little flushed, Megan points ahead, "My apartment is just right up the road."

"Great!" Lee's voice sounding far off.

Unlocking the door, Megan lets Lee through first.

"The phone is on the kitchen counter, make yourself at home while I take a little potty break."

"Thanks Megan." Lee waits until she disappears down a small dark hallway, and then moves over to the retro-phone. Picking up the receiver, Lee punches in her mother's cell phone number.

It rings several times before Lee hears a sleep thick voice gurgle. "Hello."

"Mother? Are you sleeping?"

"Yes!" Jane yelps. "Where are you? I thought I told you to stay put. You never listen to me." Anger and concern lace her words.

"I had to get out, I couldn't just sit around and do nothing."

"Where are you?"

"At a friend's."

"Well, I think you need to come back here. It's the safest place to be right now."

"See, I don't think so. It's the only place he hasn't been. Don't you think you're his next target? Maybe you should get out of there."

"I'm not going anywhere. The only reason he hasn't been here is because it's impossible to get in through the security gate."

"Every system has flaws." Lee's exasperated. She's not in the mood to argue with her mother.

"How's Grandma?"

"She's fine. It's nothing, they're letting her go tomorrow."

"Oh, good, at what time."

"I think around ten."

"Are you going to pick her up?"

"I thought we both would."

"Maybe the best thing for me to do is meet the two of you at Clair's house at around noon. He might be staking out the hospital."

"I don't know, Lee. You need to be a little more careful."

"Trust me, Mother, I'm being very cautious. He could never find me where I am, so don't worry, and just meet me at grandma's tomorrow. I got to go now. Bye."

Before Jane has a chance to say another word, Lee hangs up.

Hearing her house guest sigh heavily from the kitchen, Megan appears.

"Things okay?"

"Yeah, it's nothing, a slight flicker in her heart."

"Nothing's slight at that age. She still should take it easy for a day or two."

"You don't know my grandma!" Suddenly yawning, Lee sits down on the couch. "Guess I better get going."

"Listen Lee, I know we just met, and you seem like the

type I can trust, so why don't you just crash here. I'll sleep upstairs, and you can have the sofa. That way neither of us have to go out in the cold."

"The offer does sound good. I don't want to inconvenience you, though."

"Oh, you're not." Megan walks over to a closet, and opening the folding doors, produces a blanket and pillow. Tossing them over to Lee, she says. "Bathroom's down the hall, towels are on the linen shelf. Just make yourself at home. I'm going to bed."

Megan starts up the staircase.

"Hey, thanks a lot, you don't know what this means to me."

"Think nothing of it. Night."

Lee watches Megan vanish into the shadows.

"Night."

Megan quietly closes her door, and stands against it. Something's not quite right, she thinks, trembling, she hopes her instincts aren't off on this one.

San Francisco, CA

Katie Lee grows more and more restless. Why hasn't she heard from Lyman. It's been hours since he called to tell her they located Lee Conner, and that he'll get back with more information.

She can't believe the turn of events. What are the chances of her landing on that particular B&B's web site as she was browsing, searching for a getaway for a couple of days, when all of a sudden she came upon their home page, with the whole staff gathered in the living room, she knew the face immediately, it was her own, and the name, what was the likelihood that it'd be her dead husband's, Burtrum Lee Conner?

Katie knows she has to find this woman fast, uncover who she is, discover if there's a connection? Without thinking, she instructed Lyman to send someone down to Santa Fe right away, someone from security. But instead, he sends Calvin Kramer, a-mediocre physicists, with no experience. She doesn't understand his reasoning.

Katie's impatience grows thicker.

Where is he?

Lyman has a lot of explaining to do. The resemblance between her and that woman is uncanny. It has to be her daughter, but how?

The possibilities are alive. After all, she knew her little girl was out there.

Katie glares at the door as it's pushed open. Expecting Lyman to rush in, she's disappointed as Wanda scampers into the room, sleepy and slightly incoherent.

"Why are you still up?" Wanda scolds.

"How did you know? I'm being quiet?"

"I can hear your bones creak." Wanda shuffles over to Katie's bed and tucks her blankets tighter. "Now, I'm turning out the lights, and you're going to go to sleep."

"But what about the phone call? I need to know, is she my child?"

Wanda pats Katie's hand. "Come on, honey, don't get yourself worked up. You won't be any good to anyone if you don't get some sleep. Lyman will call in the morning and then we can find out who this woman is, okay?"

"How can I not be excited. You saw her, she looks just like me, and come on Wanda, what are the chances. And if that's not enough, what about her name?"

"So, she has the same name as your husband, there is such a thing as coincidence."

"Not in my book."

"Listen, Katie, I'm tired and want to go back to bed, but not until you promise me you'll try to sleep."

Katie Lee stares at Wanda. The woman has been with her since the accident. Never leaving her side, always there for her. They'd grown old together and Katie considers Wanda to be her best friend. "Okay, how can I say no to that face?"

"Excellent!" Wanda leans over and kisses Katie on the forehead. "Now you get a good night's rest, and tomorrow we'll see what progresses."

"Good night, Wanda. Thank you."

"You're welcome." Wanda flicks off the lights as she leaves the room, softly closing the door behind her.

There's no way Katie is going to sleep. Her mind races a million miles an hour, as she lies stiff in her bed.

❂   ❂   ❂

Santa Fe, NM

"Great!" Calvin yells down the deserted street. He's lost the women. Now what is he going to do? Lyman will kill him.

Heading back into the bar, Calvin notices that the crowd is leaving and they weren't letting anyone else in. Realizing he'd left his jacket behind, he walks up to the bouncer.

"Excuse me sir, I left my coat inside, may I go get it?"

"Sorry, no one gets back in. You can come by tomorrow and pick it up."

"But you don't understand, I'm leaving first thing in the morning, before you open."

"Well, leave a name and address, and we'll mail it to you."

Right, as if that's ever going to happen, Calvin thinks, clambering out into the street, thankful that he keeps all his belongings in his pants pockets.

Stumbling to his car, Calvin can't think of a time where he's hated a place more than he does right now. Ever since he arrived yesterday, he's experienced nothing but rude people and unpleasant weather.

All he wants to do is get the hell out of Santa Fe, and if Lyman has a problem with that, well then, he can go to hell, Calvin tells himself, crawling into the sedan.

9

Lee awakes in a panic, not knowing where she is at first, she bolts up knocking her knee on the coffee table. "Ouch!" She exclaims.

Glancing around ignites her memory as she recalls last night with Megan. The woman is nice enough, but, there's something a little off about her.

What she should do is leave before her hostess comes down. Make it easier for the both of them, plus, Lee isn't sure she really wants to involve a stranger with her problems.

First, she needs to get to the hospital to see her grandmother. The worry is eating away at her, and even though Jane has reassured her that Clair is going to be all right, she still has to see for herself.

"Well, good morning." Megan bounds down the stairs. "How did you sleep?"

Standing, and being more careful this time with the closely placed table, Lee responds. "Surprisingly well. And how about you?"

"Okay. I tossed and turned a little bit, but I think that's because there was someone else in my apartment."

"Yeah, I'm the same way. When I have a guest over, I just can't seem to feel at ease." Megan heads toward the kitchen. "I'm going to make some coffee, would you like a cup?"

"Yes," Lee replies. "Do you mind if I use your bathroom?"

"No, please, help yourself. I left a towel, washcloth and soap on the hamper for you."

"That's awfully nice."

"Ah, think nothing of it."

"I'll be right out."

"I'll be right here," Megan giggles, knowing she sounds corny.

"Great!" Lee spurts, half smiling as she closes the door behind her.

Pouring water into a teapot, and then spooning Folgers into a Meleta, Megan begins humming as she takes two mugs down from the shelf.

Tinkering around in the kitchen, Megan doesn't sense Lee tip-toeing up behind her, and jumps when she hears.

"All done!" Chuckling, Lee places a hand on Megan's shoulder. "I'm sorry, I didn't mean to startle you."

"That's all right, my heart needed stimulation anyway. You know, get a jolt first thing in the morning and your day will be fine from then on in. Or something like that."

Lee smiles. "The java smells good. Is it ready?"

"Almost." Megan turns back to the stove, and removing the boiling water, pours it through the ground filled filter, turning her face away from the burning steam. Handing a mug to Lee, Megan asks. "Cream, sugar?"

"No, no, thank-you. I like my brew black."

"Okay, then. I'll be right back."

Dashing away, Lee feels lighthearted as she glides back to the living room, sitting down on the couch.

Comfort fills the small apartment, like a fresh coat of yellow paint. Around her, planted in precise placement, are a multitude of broken toys, and pictures of the San Francisco skyline thumb-tacked to the walls.

"So what's with the toys and Frisco?" Lee inquires as Megan comes out of the bathroom.

"Well, I consider myself a toy guardian. If I see a figurine abandoned, or broken on the street, I bring it home, and take care of it."

"Interesting." Lee rubs her chin. "And the pictures?"

"I love San Francisco. It's a great city, and when I was younger I always wanted to live there. For some reason I feel a connection to the bay area. Who knows, maybe that's where I'm really from."

"What do you mean, 'where you're really from'?"

"Oh, nothing." Megan shuffles into the kitchen. "Anyway, I've always wanted to live there, maybe that's where I should move."

"It's an idea." Lee sips her coffee and oddly enough, feels a little sad over the prospect of Megan leaving Santa Fe. "Yeah, if you're not happy in the Southwest, what's keeping you?"

Shaking her head, Megan replies. "I don't know." Quieting. "Hey, this isn't what I anticipated as a topic of conversation. It's Sunday, and by the looks of it, the weather might be nice. So, what do you have planned, Burtrum Lee?"

"I need to go to the hospital and see my grandma. Then run a few errands." Glancing at the clock. "I really should be taking off pretty soon." Lee places her empty cup on the counter.

Megan isn't ready to let her go yet. "Wait, aren't you hungry? I think eating might be a good thing."

"I have to get to St. Vincent's. I can grab a bite in the cafeteria."

Megan looks up at the clock. "I don't think they allow visitors this early."

Lee also realizes how early it is. "Oh! Damn-it."

"Let's go get something to eat, my treat."

"No, if anything, I'm buying. You were nice enough to let me sleep here last night, it's the least I can do."

"Okay then, I won't argue. Any place particular?"

"Somewhere we can walk to. How about the Plaza Restaurant, I know they open early, and their breakfasts are good!"

"Sounds fine to me. Let me go slip into some warmer clothes and I'll be right down."

"Excellent!" Lee stands up and starts folding the blankets.

"Leave those, I'll take care of them later." Megan runs up the stairs, as Lee watches her, wondering if she's making a mistake hanging out with this unknown woman.

❊   ❊   ❊

Jane Conner is beside herself. She's still upset at how Lee left after Jane insisted she stay at her house, and out of sight.

But no, once again her increasingly defiant daughter slaps her in the face, metaphorically speaking.

Plus, Jed still hasn't called, and now Jane is beginning to get worried. Snatching her cell phone out of her purse, she checks for messages, but finds none.

Her pounding head makes her nauseous as she reaches for the Bloody Mary sweating on the nightstand. Having a drink first thing is becoming her latest habit. She misses her and Jed's intimate breakfasts. Now that he's gone most of the time, she has to find company in something, and right now, the closest thing is a cocktail.

Her mood becomes more bitter, as Jane assumes the worst about Jed. He's been acting rather strange over the past few months, taking more and more trips to LA. He assures her that it's only business, but Jane senses otherwise.

Downing her drink, Jane realizes if she doesn't hurry she'll be late getting to the hospital, and heaven forbid that.

Stepping into the steaming shower, Jane feels herself relax and lets the hot, penetrating jet streams pound her aching muscles. Maybe today will be a better day than the past few, Jane Conner hopes, wiping away the tears streaming down her face.

❋   ❋   ❋

Clair Conner rolls her head back and forth, disgusted with the slop they call food. Taking a sip of the waterdowned decaf, she spits the swill back into the cup, pushing the tray away.

Easing the bed back into a horizontal position, Clair gazes up at the ceiling. She's glad to be going home today, not making her stick around for more tests.

She feels fine, just a little tired and sore. What is she to expect, fainting and all. She'd been assured that it was only an arrhythmia, and with a few day's rest, she'll be as good as new.

That's what Clair Conner needs to hear. With Lee being in trouble, she has to get home and stop the avalanche from happening, otherwise, someone might get hurt.

In hindsight, Clair should've put her foot down all of those years ago, insisting they do the right thing. But when they found out who the baby really was, the situation had gotten so out of control, there was nothing to do but keep their mouths shut.

So, over the decades they tried to safe guard Lee, keeping her away from the truth, that she's not a Conner, but that she's one of the first artificially inseminated babies in the world and that they abducted her from her real mother.

Wishing to see Lee, Clair wants to tell her how sorry she is for not being forthright, after all, doesn't the woman deserve to know who she truly is?

Envisioning Lee's face as Clair tells her about the accident and how Jed and Jane rescued/stole her from certain death, makes her cringe. And then the article about Lee's parents, and who the little girl really is, scared Clair so deeply, she hid the write-up, never telling anyone the total truth, not even her son.

And now she's going to pay for her deceit by losing Lee.

Closing her eyes, Clair suddenly feels overly tired. Clouds dance in her thoughts, soft and white, like large cotton balls.

10

Santa Fe, NM 1960

Jane Conner runs blindly, cradling the dead baby's body tightly in her arms. Driving ice flakes whip across her almost naked body, freezing tears to her face. Her mind rambles out of control, like little mice running around in circles. Tiny carnival figures dance in front of her eyes, as the cold, frigid air taps at every red, raw nerve.

"Jane, where are you?"

She hears Jed's raspy voice and pauses for a moment, searching for a place to hide. If he finds her he'll take her son away, steal him right out from beneath her breasts.

Jane Conner kisses his head and rubs her cheek against the lifeless skin.

"It's okay, honey, Mommy's here, and I won't let anyone separate us. But we've got to be quiet. We don't want anyone finding us."

Jane slashes her head around, searching for signs of Jed.

Figuring he must've turned toward the swamp, she decides to head for the highway, hoping to hitch a ride to Santa Fe.

In her delirium, Jane doesn't see the covered branches lying in her path, and tripping over them, slips down a slope of virgin white powder. Frantically grasping the child, Jane tumbles onto the iced-coated road below. Feeling dizzy, she shakes her head, and attempting to balance herself, slowly rises, her bare feet tingling. The trees are illuminated by a crooked beam of light, so out of place in the crisp night.

11

"Brrrrrrr, it's freezing!" Megan squeals, as the two women step outside into the cold, frigid air.

"Hey, why don't we drive. I'm sure my car will start now, plus, then I can bring you to the hospital." Megan unable to bare the blistering winds.

Standing still, shivering, Lee contemplates Megan's idea. It's a pretty good one, after all, the man looking for her doesn't know what kind of car Megan drives, so the chances of her staying undetected are greater.

"Yeah, okay."

"Wonderful!" Megan exclaims, opening the door to the VW Bug. "Get in."

Lee runs around to the other side and jumps into the iced pod. "Man, I think it's colder in here."

"Well, don't plan on it getting any warmer. At least it'll protect us from the winds."

Gazing out the window, Lee watches Agua Fria putter by as Megan slowly drives down the empty street. A light snow has begun to fall from the gray clouds, and Lee thinks to herself what an awful spring they're having. All of the trees are starting to bud, and she knows one good cold snap will freeze the blossoms, then there'll be no fruit.

"Some weather we're having, aie?"

"Yeah, I was just thinking that. It seldom snow's this late in the season. The trees don't know what to do."

"Me either," Megan jokes.

Within no time the women are downtown, and have no problem finding a parking spot as the square usually stays quiet until around ten on Sundays. That's when all of the church goers get out of mass and bombard the tiny plaza. Bells ring from the steeple of St. Francis Cathedral, alerting the parishioners the service is about to begin.

"Did you wanna stop and say a quick prayer before we eat?" Megan teases.

"No, let's just go in." Opening the glass door, the women are wafted with scents of bacon and chile. Lee's mouth waters as the hostess leads them to a table by the window.

"We got lucky, we beat the crowd," Lee observes.

"Good, I'm starving, and I don't know if I can wait."

The waitress takes their order and the two women sit sipping hot coffee in silence.

"Do you want to give your mother a call?"

"Maybe I should, I can find out when Grandma is getting released. I'd hate to go there, only to find her gone. Do you have a cell phone?"

"Are you kidding. Those cancer causing devices. No

way. But I do have fifty cents."

"That's how much it cost now?"

"Yup."

"Well, okay. I owe you," Lee laughs.

Standing, Lee glances around and sees an oblong silver and blue box clinging to the wall in the rear of the restaurant. "I'll be right back." Extending her arm.

"Yeah, sure." Megan reaches her hand out and drops two quarters into Lee's pink palm. "There, that should work." She watches as Lee strolls to the back, feeling something twitch, inside of her.

Megan shakes her head, recognizing the sensations, but immediately dismissing them. Nope, there is no way she is ever going to allow herself to feel something again. Picking up her cup, she blows on the java, and takes a sip.

"You've reached the Conner casa. Leave a message and we'll get back to you." Lee listens to her parents' answering machine, but hangs up without leaving a message. Her mom must be gone already, she speculates, digging in her pocket for two more quarters. Opting to try her mother's cell phone, Lee is unable to find any coins, and as she's about to ask the cashier for change, she sees the waitress setting down the food, and decides to wait.

Returning to the table, Lee figures it is way too early for her grandma to be released, plus, she won't be any good to anyone if she doesn't get something in her stomach. Sliding into the booth, she licks her lips, drooling over her burrito. "Wow, this looks great, and I'm famished."

"Did you get hold of your mom?"

"No, I got the answering machine, I'll try her cell after I

eat. Oh, man, this smells good," Lee exclaims, shoveling a fork full into her watering mouth.

"I don't know how you can eat that stuff?" Megan says, shaking her head.

"What, chile?" Lee looks at Megan's plate of plain eggs, hash browns and bacon. "You don't like chile?"

"No way. The first time I tasted the red and green, I almost choked. It's just not for me."

"Maybe you need to try a really good batch. This is all right, not the best, but it works." Lee points to the pool on her plate. "My grandmother, I tell you, she makes the best sauces in town. And trust me, I've had a lot of bad stews over the years." Lee extends her spoon, dripping with red and green chile. "Just try this, you might like it." Megan waves her arms in the air. "No, no thank you. Trust me, if I taste that, I promise you, I'll get sick."

Lee places the spoon on her plate. "Fine then. You don't know what you're missing." Licking her lips, slow and sensuously.

Megan feels herself flush as she crams food in her mouth, trying not to show her sudden nervousness. Lee glances up from her meal.

"You okay?" Squinting her eyes. "You look a little red. You weren't kidding, if just talking about the pepper does this to you, then maybe you should stay away from it," Lee jokes.

Taking a sip of water, Megan wipes the tear drops forming in her eyes. Damn-it, why did she have to react this way. She has no control over her emotions when it comes to women.

"I'm fine. I think I just swallowed some bacon down the wrong pipe."

Returning to her breakfast, both women listen to the clangs and bangs of the restaurant.

"So, do you want to go up to the hospital?" Megan breaks the quiet.

"Yeah, as soon as we finish here."

"Would you like me to wait after I drop you off?"

"No, you can just let me out in front."

Disappointment filters through Megan, believing she would go in with Lee to meet her
grandmother. "Oh, yeah, sure, no problemo," her words dripping with sarcasm.

Lee, misses the undertone. "I'm sure you have things to do today, and I've taken up enough of your time as it is."

"To be honest, my slate is clean for the whole day. So if you want some stranger's support, I'm your girl." Megan knows she sounds silly.

"I don't think that'd be such a good idea. I don't want you to get in the middle of my situation."

"What can it hurt?"

"I don't know. What I do know is that I don't want to take a chance." Pushing her plate away. "I'm sorry, Megan. I really like your company, but it's just not the right time to hang. Maybe after I get all of this figured out, we can get to know each other. But not now. Okay?"

"Yeah, I guess. I really don't have a say anyway."

"No, you don't." Lee pats Megan's hand. "I'm sorry, I don't mean to be so harsh."

"That's okay. I guess we should get going then." Slipping

her hand out from under Lee's, she reaches for the check, but Lee snaps it up first.

"I told you, this is on me."

"No, I don't think so."

"Listen, you've been overly kind, letting me crash at your house, and now driving me to the hospital. I just want to show my appreciation, okay."

"All right, but don't make a habit out of it. I'm a woman who likes to go Dutch."

Laughing, Lee steps over to the cash register. Megan watches as she digs into her pants pocket and pulls out some bills. Megan doesn't know why, but something is drawing her to this woman, and she wants to figure out, *what*!

❋   ❋   ❋

"I'm going home and that's that," Calvin spits, tossing the rest of his clothes into an aged suitcase. He pulls out a crinkled piece of paper from his shirt pocket with his confirmation number scribbled on it. His plane takes off in less than two hours, and if he misses this one, he won't be able to leave until tomorrow.

To hell with his job, Calvin's rants continue bouncing in his head. There is no way Lyman will fire him, unless the scientist wants him to tell the newspapers everything. So, all in all, he, Calvin Kramer, has Lyman Stone by the short hairs.

Euphoria sifts through Calvin as he surveys the room, making sure he isn't leaving anything. Seeing his cell phone setting on the night stand, Calvin picks it up, turns it off and slips the device into his pants pocket. What he doesn't need is any interruptions.

Seeing the red light blinking on the room phone, Calvin ignores it, and heads to the lobby to pay the balance on his bill. The day is cold and miserable, and Calvin wonders how anyone can live here.

Entering the office, Calvin's pushed forward as the door closes behind him.

"Mr. Kramer, what a pleasure. There's a message for you." The desk clerk holds out a piece of paper, and Calvin takes it from him.

Turning around, Calvin unfolds the telegram, and begins to read the disturbing words.

Thinking she hears the telephone, Jane Conner sticks her head out of the shower to listen. Stepping out, she studies herself in the mirror, and smiles. Her sixty-three-year old body hasn't started to show its age yet. It takes a lot of discipline to maintain her still firm, and tight athletic physique.

Lately though, she seems to forgo her routine, and instead, finds herself lifting a cocktail more often than her nine pound weights. She knows why, too.

It's Jed's fault. His infidelity is driving her to drink.

What more does she need?

Reaching for her Bloody Mary, Jane takes a sip and then begins rubbing lotion on her body. She'll show Jed. When he gets home he'll see how much she loves him. Who else will take such good care of their mother in-law.

Smiling to herself, she spreads lipstick across her lips and smacks them in a kiss. She'll be at Clair's side until the old woman doesn't need her anymore.

Yeah, that'll show her husband, Jane convinces herself as she climbs into her Mercedes Benz.

❂   ❂   ❂

Lee lumbers up to the information desk in the lobby of the hospital, and asks for Clair Conner's room number. The receptionist gives it to her, but won't let her go any further until visiting hours, which don't begin for another thirty minutes. Suggesting to Lee that she go to the cafeteria and get a cup of coffee, she pretends to head along the arrows pointing to the first floor. Glancing over her shoulder, Lee notices the woman's head is bent over some papers, and quickly dashes to the elevators, figuring she'll take her chances at getting caught.

Pushing number three, Lee listens as the ancient metal box squeaks from floor to floor. Giggling to herself, Lee believes she'll age a year by the time the ride is over. As the doors whoosh open, Lee sticks her head out, and seeing nobody in sight, steps onto the shiny-lime-green-tile floor, and cat-crawls toward Clair's room.

Everything is quiet, save for the occasional coughs coming from behind shadowed curtains. Lee stands in front of room 312 and listens for a sound.

"Grandma?" She whispers, opening the door a crack. "You in here?"

"Birdy?" A soft, weak voice rises from the bed against the

wall. "Is that you?"

Stepping forward, Lee knocks her knee for a second time, on a darkly cloaked chair, and covering her mouth, stifles a scream. There will be a bruise tonight.

Maneuvering around the obstacle, she stands beside Clair's bed. Reaching for her hand, Lee holds it in hers, and looks at her grandmother, all small and helpless.

"Grandma, how are you feeling?"

"A lot better now that I know you're all right. I'm worried sick about you. Jane doesn't know squat, thought you were at their house," Clair giggles. "It's kind of funny how upset she got."

"I'm sure it is." Lee rolls her eyes. "I decided not to stay there, figuring that'd be the next place this guy will go."

"Did you stay at a motel?"

"No, as a matter of fact, luck was with me last night. I went and had a beer, and this woman sat down next to me and we started talking. She's very nice, and I ended up sleeping on her couch."

Clair scrunches her face. "Don't you think you need to be a little more careful?"

"I was fine. Like I said, she's a really nice lady, and I felt safe, and was." Lee strokes Clair's forehead. "Now, when are you getting out of here?"

"I believe this afternoon. They couldn't find anything to keep me in this germ-infested institution."

"Well, you look great, maybe not great, but good."

"Thanks! You certainly know how to compliment a person."

"Any time."

The two women stare at each other for a moment and then Clair breaks the silence. "So, what's your game plan?"

"I'm not sure. I'm thinking about trying to find this guy and see what he really wants. Maybe it's nothing. He could just be a nobody."

"Don't take any chances, it's not safe, there's more to the situation than what you know."

"Will someone please just be straight forward and tell me what the hell is going on." Lee's voice rises.

"You might be in danger."

"From what, or for that matter, whom?"

Clair doesn't want to say anything right now. This isn't the place or time, but Lee is starting to talk crazy. Going after this guy; she doesn't realize how perilous her circumstance really is.

"Why don't you wait until after I get home, and we can discuss this together."

"What if we're running out of time?"

"I'm sure this man is still around, and will be until he gets what he wants." All Clair desires is to come out with the truth. Tell her granddaughter the real reason this assailant is after her, but she has to talk to Jed first, and as of this moment he's still missing.

"Why don't you meet me at my house later this afternoon. I'm sure Jane won't be sticking around for very long, after she leaves, we can figure out a plan. Maybe by then, we'll at last hear from your father, and we can see what he has to say. Okay?"

"Yeah, I suppose," Lee's voice sounds crushed.

Clair pats her hand. "Don't worry, sweetie, we'll get to

the bottom of this and then we can all get back to normal."

"Whatever normal is." Lee smiles. "Listen, I should probably get going. I don't want anyone to see me, and I'm sure Mom's going to be showing up soon."

"You're right, but thanks for coming by, you don't know how much this means to me."

"I think I do."

"Okay then, you'd better get going."

Lee leans over and hugs Clair. "I love you Grandma."

"I love you too, Birdy. Now, I'll see you later. In the meantime, lay low, all right?"

"Yeah, I will. Maybe I'll go to a movie."

"Good idea."

Hearing footsteps in the hallway, Lee turns toward the door. "I better scat, I'll see you around three, is that good?"

"That's great, honey."

Lee scoots down the hallway, and out of sight. Deep down Clair knows she has to tell Lee the truth, with or without Jed. There's so much at stake though, and she knows it will change the course of all of their lives.

Scurrying out of the hospital, Lee is surprised to see Megan still parked in the same spot. Jogging over to the car, she taps on the window. Megan leans over and opens the door.

"What are you still doing here?" Lee asks.

"I thought you might need a ride to wherever you're going." Megan smiles. "Plus, I don't have anything else to do."

Hawk-eyeing the area, Lee notices everything is covered with a spring snow, and the air is kind of cool for her light jacket. She'll freeze to death before she gets across the street.

"Okay, yeah sure, I guess. But I really don't know where I'm going."

"Well then, that makes two of us."

Smiling, she hops into the VW, closing the heavy door behind her. "Then away we go."

"Stupid dip wad!" Jane Conner screams at the tiny VW Bug pulling out in front of her, almost hitting the Benz. The puttering car scoots past her, and Jane sees Lee duck down, trying not to be seen.

"Burtrum Lee Conner," Jane yells through the window, wagging her finger at them. The car takes a sudden right, and Jane loses sight of them.

Wheeling the Mercedes into a parking spot, Jane gets out, and wobbling on her high heels, rushes toward the hospital. Clair will know where her daughter is going.

She wonders who the woman is Lee's hanging out with. Jane can't place the face. Maybe a new found friend, heaven only knows she can use a couple, maybe get out of the trance Clair has her in.

Jane still finds it peculiar, Lee not stopping and all. Everything's getting a little strange, she thinks to herself, as the elevator chugs up to the third floor.

Charging into the room, Jane screams. "She was here, wasn't she?"

"For crying out loud, Jane, you need to control yourself and stop yelling. There are sick people in this place." Clair leans over and grabs the glass of water sitting on the bed stand. Taking a sip, she sets it back down and glares at Jane. "You look a mess. Now tell me what you're babbling about."

"I saw them."

"Saw who?"

"Don't play coy with me, Clair Conner, you know perfectly well who."

"Honest Jane, I don't know what you're talking about."

Jane moves closer to the bed. "Lee, she was here with that funny looking woman."

"What funny looking woman? Yes, Lee was here, but she was by herself. And what's the big deal. She has every right to come and see her grandmother."

"During visiting hours. Why is she sneaking around like this?"

"Who knows. Maybe she's trying to lay low for a while. Keep off the radar of that man who seems to be following her."

"Why don't we just call the police. I mean Lee could be in harm's way and we're just sitting back doing nothing."

"What are we supposed to do, Jane? There's no way we can involve the officials, not with the past looming over us. I don't think there's any statute of limitations when it comes to baby stealing."

"Shhhhh," Jane hisses, making sure they're alone. "Lower your voice." Sitting down in the chair next to Clair's bed. "What do you suggest we do?"

"I don't know, maybe talking to Jed might help. Did he call you last night?"

"No! He must've gotten in too late and didn't want to wake me."

Clair's forehead wrinkles, as she studies her daughter in-law. "Jane Conner, are you lying to me? Is there something going on between the two of you that I should know about?"

Jane sighs and smirks at the frail woman lying in bed. "Well, all right, if you must know. Jed and I haven't been getting along so well lately. I think he's having an affair. He denies everything when I ask him about it. But by the distance he's put between us, I'd say that there's definitely something going on."

"So you haven't heard hide, nor hair, from him since yesterday?"

"Nope!"

"Wonderful! Just when we need him the most, he pulls a Houdini on us. Great, just great."

Clair is getting agitated and Jane knows it isn't the best thing for her. Standing, she reaches for her mother-in-law's frail hand.

Patting the boney knuckles, Jane says. "Clair, don't get worked up, it's not good for you. I'm sure Jed will call today. He doesn't want to lay down any more suspicion than he already has. You know?"

"I don't know anything anymore. What I do know is that my granddaughter is in trouble, I'm laid up in this hole, and you and Jed are on the fritz. Let me tell you, things couldn't be looking any worse."

"Clair, you're blowing things out of proportion."

"Am I? Think about it Jane. We know this man was sent by Lee's real mother. And we know when Lee finds out the truth about who she is, all hell will break loose. We might lose her. Did you ever think of that? She might get so angry with us for what we did that she won't want to have anything else to do with us. Can you bear that? I can't."

"Clair, you shouldn't be getting so excited. I'm sure it's nothing. And Lee loves us too much to ever abandon her family."

"Don't be too sure about that. This is major. How would you feel if you found out you were stolen from your real mother as an infant?"

"We didn't steal her, we saved her. That poor thing would've died out there if we hadn't rescued her."

"Like her mother."

Jane snarled. "We thought they were both dead. Jed even checked for pulses." The two women stare hard at each other. "Help me up," Clair orders. "They'll be here any minute with the wheel chair, I need to get dressed. We'll discuss this at home."

Without saying a word, Jane helps the elderly woman out of bed and into her clothes, just in time as a stout nurse's aid wheels a chair in, and assists Clair into the vehicle. She has to get in touch with Jed, and fast.

12

Dazed and frozen, Jane almost walks right past Burtrum, who lies broken in the snow. Red oozes from beneath him, coating the white, reminding Jane of a cherry snow cone. Easing closer to the still body, she nudges the torso with her numb toe. Stiff! Plopping down next to the still man, the cold of no importance, Jane pats his overcoat and feels a lump. Slipping her hand into the inside pocket, she fumbles with his wallet, and pulling it out rummages through it.

"Dr. Burtrum Lee, San Francisco, California." She stuffs the leather case back into his pocket. "My, my, my, Dr. Lee, you're a long way from home," announcing out loud.

An unclear rationality overtakes Jane's insanity as she gets to her feet, and, in a trance, stumbles to where Katie lies. Noticing a splotch of blood spreading from between the woman's legs Jane realizes she's having a baby.

Lifting the bottom of Katie's dress, Jane sees an infant

lying there, not breathing. Quickly lifting the child, she pats the back, trying to get it to inhale. At first Jane believes her efforts are too late, until suddenly the little girl begins to whimper, and then howl. Instant love, that's what Jane experienced at that moment, and in her heart she knew she'd never give up this baby.

Remembering her discarded son, Jane leers down at Katie, who lies tangled like a fractured puppet. 'She's dead.' Jane's inner voice tells her. 'Just rip the cord and switch the babies, who'll ever know?'

Lost in her demented thoughts, Jane doesn't hear Jed sneak up behind her, but then senses his presence when she hears his cries of disbelief.

Trotting over to his freezing wife, he wraps the blanket around her and the baby she's holding, thinking that it's still his son, until the child begins to cry again.

"Jane, what the hell, where'd that infant come from?"

"Jed, oh look Jed, we've been given a second chance." She holds the newborn in the air. "A baby girl, Jed, just for us."

Jed glances down and sees the dead body of their son lying between the unknown women's legs. "You've got to be kidding me, Jane. What are you thinking?"

"No one will ever know, Jed. We can take her home and then you can come back with the authorities. Just tell them you were out walking after the birth and came upon this death scene. You saw the baby boy and cut his cord in an attempt to save his life, but it was too late. The whole family dies, and we have a child."

"You're talking insane!"

"No, Jed, just take a look. See how beautiful she is." Jane holds her out for him.

His heart melts!

Jed notices the infant is shivering. "Okay, for the time being we'll take her home, and out of the cold while I go fetch help."

Jed knows he doesn't stand a chance with Jane and this decision, he can see it in her eyes, plus, *who would* ever know?

"Let me just turn off the headlights, we don't want to attract any hungry animals."

Jed crunches away toward the car. For a second, as Jane waits she thinks she hears the woman moan. Holding her breath, she waits for another sound.

Nothing!

Taking a deep breath and shivering, Jane assumes it's the storm.

Darkness engulfs them as they trudge through the deepening snow. Jed's large arm swallowing his wife and newborn like a Condor covering a chick.

13

Katie Lee sits back and listens to Wanda's soothing voice as she reads a poem by Walt Whitman. It is her favorite collection and she knows every word by heart. The sonnet had been hers and Burtrum's favorite piece.

I am the poet of the woman the same as the man,
And I say it is as great to be a woman as a man,
And I say there is nothing greater than the mother of men.

"Wanda, please, will you stop for a minute?" Katie raises her hand.

Glancing over her eyeglasses, Wanda stands up and moves closer to Katie. "Are you all right? You look a little pale."

"I'm fine. I think it's just the movement of the RV."

Wanda sits back down after feeling Katie's forehead. "I told you this wasn't a good idea. I don't know why we just didn't take the Lab's jet."

"You know perfectly well, I don't like to fly, and this is fine. I think driving a motor home is the best way to travel. You get to see the lay of the land and everything Mother Nature has to give."

"Yeah, but all in three days?"

"My word, Wanda, we've only been on the road for a day, how terrible is it. We'll be there before you know it, watch."

Wanda glares down at the book she still holds in her hand. "You know what would be a big help, don't you?"

"No."

"Letting me read from a different literary masterpiece." Wanda tries to ease the tension building.

Smiling, Katie reaches out for the worn covered manuscript. "Now, you know Wanda, how much these words mean to me. Burtrum used to read me passages from these pages, and it's all I have left of him."

"I tell you Katie, you're a better person than I am. Personally, I would've thrown everything out of his, try to get rid of all memories of him after what he put you through."

"Yes, Wanda, but none of that matters now. Soon I'll be in the arms of my daughter. My daughter Wanda, do you know how excited I am?"

"Why, after all of these years of knowing she was out there, you want to find her now?"

"I don't know. For some reason I suddenly feel the importance of us meeting. Tell her who she is, where she came from. Maybe I made a mistake all of those years ago, agreeing with Clair Conner to let them raise my little girl. And there have been many times that I've regretted it, but all that despair is gone, now."

"Yes, okay, but don't you think you should've contacted them before leaving. I mean, do you plan on just showing up at their doorstep?"

"No, Wanda. When we get to Santa Fe, I'll call Clair, after all, she is the one who informed me of the true circumstances back then." Katie pauses for a moment. "That's why we need to get to Burtrum before Lyman does. Heaven only knows what that lunatic will do if he gets his grubby hands on her."

"Well, Katie, I hope you know what you're doing."

"Me too." Katie stares out the window.

Sensing Katie's desire to be alone, Wanda says. "Listen, I'm going to go get us something to eat, you know a little snack."

"We just had lunch."

"Yes, I know. But hey, you drag me to the Southwest and I get hungry. Deal with it." Wanda struggles out the door giggling. A little more lighthearted, Katie turns her attention once more to the scenery flying by her.

Santa Fe, NM 1960

Katie Lee lifts her head. Her brain pounds so intensely she thinks her skull will split. Instinctively, she reaches down and feels for her baby. He lies cold and sticky. She drags him up her body and studies the still, pale face. Tears begin to drizzle down her numb cheeks. If she had not passed out, her son would still be alive.

Howls shake her whole being causing mercury pain to rip through her every nerve. Catching sight of Burtrum slumped against a tree, Katie thinks he looks like he passed out from drinking.

"Bastard!" She curses as she holds her child closer to her breasts. "See what you did! I hope you rot in hell." Sobs overtake her, sending searing swords ripping across her crippled body. The blackness on the horizon eases her agony as she falls into the comfort of unconsciousness.

Santa Fe, NM 2004

Katie recalls the accident, and how grief stricken she'd been at the loss of her husband and baby. She didn't want to live, but there was something deep down inside driving her spirit. A belief that she'll be needed, somehow, somewhere.

Then a few months later Clair Conner calls, telling Katie her baby girl, not boy, is alive and well. There was no mention as to how the child got into their care, or whose baby she held so desperately that night.

Clair had offered to return the child, but all Katie could do was plead with the stranger to take care of her baby, because there was no way she could raise a daughter in her condition. Clair was hesitant, at first, but then agreed, only on the condition that Katie Lee never contact them.

In the hollows of her gut, she's never forgiven herself for abandoning her daughter, but now she has the chance to make it right, and she's going to.

Katie hears Wanda padding down the slim hallway, and

wipes the tears off her cheek.

In a couple of days, four decades of pain and anguish will diminish.

❊   ❊   ❊

Calvin slams the cardboard door shut as he throws himself on the bed, yelling into the pillows. "No, no, I don't want to stay here," he screams. Thrashing around, he begins to cough as he tries to gain some composure. "Damn, Lyman." Calvin was almost out the door, and then the telegram arrives. Katie Lee is on her way to Santa Fe? By the contents of the note, Lyman is ordering him to stay until she arrives, and watch her every move. So, now, not only does he have to tail Burtrum Lee Conner, he also has to keep tabs on the CEO of Lee Laboratory's. "Must be my lucky day," Calvin hisses to himself, tearing the contents out of his suitcase, and flinging shirts and underwear across the room. What he needs is a drink, Calvin thinks to himself, recalling a place he saw at a mall. Rushing out of his room, his only thoughts are of getting a load on.

❊   ❊   ❊

"Oh, my lord!" Lee yelps, as she ducks down on the seat.

"What? What's going on?"

"Nothing, just nothing, keep driving. That's my mother in the Mercedes you almost clipped."

"Shit!" Megan careens her neck, hoping to catch a glimpse of Mrs. Conner, but the car disappears into the visitor parking lot.

"You can sit up now, I don't think she saw you."

Lee slithers slowly up the seat, peering through the window, making sure her mom is out of sight. "Whew, that was close."

"Why don't you want your mother to see you."

"It's a long story," Lee says, glaring out the window again.

The silence continues for an uncomfortable amount of time until Megan, getting a little perturbed, asks, "Hey, Earth to Lee. You there?"

Giggling, Lee answers. "Yes, I'm sorry, I just have a lot of things on my mind, and I can't figure some of it out."

"Maybe I can help."

"You already are." Lee touches Megan's arm as she drives.

Tingles coarse through Megan as Lee rests her hand there. Slightly choked up, Megan croaks. "So, what do you want to do now?"

"I'm not sure. It's way too early to go to my grandmother's house." Glancing at her watch. "I wonder what time the matinees start at the DeVargas Mall." Lee points ahead. "Stop at the corner and I'll get a newspaper."

Megan pulls over in front of a yellow box, and watches as Lee jumps out and retrieves a paper. Slipping back into Megan's VW, she smiles at her new friend.

"How does that sound. Maybe a movie to bide the time away."

"Yeah, sure, what's playing?"

"Well, the earliest one is *The Motor Cycle Diaries*. Do you think you might be up for that?"

"Anything really!"

Lee squints at Megan. "Is everything okay?"

"Yeah, why?"

"You just sound a little different."

"No, everything's fine. I just wish you'd tell me what's going on."

"I'm not sure myself, that's why I'm going over to Clair's this afternoon, hoping she can clear this mess up. Because to tell you the truth, I'm getting a little tired of it. All I want to do is get my life back the way it was before Friday afternoon. Is that too much to ask?" Lee's voice rises in agitation.

"Okay, okay." Megan shakes her head. "Hey, maybe this isn't such a good idea, you know, you and me hanging out."

"What do you mean? I'm sorry, I didn't intend to go off like that, I truly enjoy your company. It's nice to have someone around right now. Someone outside of a family member. So, come on, it's all right."

"Are you sure?" Megan begins to feel a little weary. Maybe this woman she picked up last night is really a nut job. After all, what proof is there of anything she's said. Maybe the hospital was just a rouse, part of the plot. What if this lady is some psycho, wandering the streets searching for the perfect victim, and she, Megan Masterson, is it!

"Yes, I'm sure. Now, come on. The movie starts in a half hour. Are you still game?"

"I don't know. Maybe I should get going, you know, let you get on with your life."

"Whatever you decide, Megan. You know I don't want

to keep you." Lee falls silent for a while, wondering what kind of person is she dealing with. She senses a slight attitude emanating from Megan, and to be honest, Lee isn't sure she likes it.

❀   ❀   ❀

"Listen, Clair. I need to go to the bathroom real fast, I'll be right back."

"Well, hurry up, I want to get out of here."

Jane scrambles down the hall, and whips into the restroom. Finding an empty stall, she slips into the chamber and closing the door, sits down on the toilet.

Breathing deeply, she fumbles in her purse, rescuing the flask from the bottom. Twisting the cap off the sterling silver decanter, Jane toasts the air, and takes a long hard pull. The bourbon burns all the way down. Tossing a breath mint into her mouth, she waits for a moment, letting the tablet dissolve slightly, before getting up.

Observing herself in the mirror, she notices her eyes are blood shot and pulls the tiny bottle of Visine out of her jacket pocket. Dripping a few drops in each eye, Jane feels instant relief.

Wiping the excess liquid off her cheeks, Jane prances out the door and down the hall. She'll take the old bat home, and then go spend some time alone where she can figure out how to rid her life of these sudden obstructions.

14

Dr. Lyman Stone squeezes the pink spongy exercise ball between his fingers and then throws it at the wall. The toy plops against the wood, and falls to the floor. "Damn-it Calvin, can't you do anything right?" Cursing out loud.

Pacing back and forth in his dimly lit office, Lyman can't believe the sudden circumstances arising. He'd hoped to have Burtrum Lee back here at the lab by now, but Calvin can't find her, and now Katie is on her way to Santa Fe. "Things can't be more messed up," he yells to himself, pounding his fist on his desk.

Lyman recalls the night he found out Katie Lee's daughter was alive. The feelings of success racing through him, sensations he's never experienced before, nor since. His experiment was a success. The fetus had survived the crash.

Dr. Stone wondered throughout the years what happened to the baby girl. He knew the infant boy wasn't Katie's; she'd been pregnant with a girl.

His girl.

Lyman's plan was full proof, switch the children at birth in the hospital, replace his child with an unknown boy. He'd even arranged it with the nurses. It was an iron-clad scheme. Until Burtrum, lunatic that he was, took them to New Mexico, and the rest is history.

Now, at last, if Calvin doesn't blow it again, he, Dr. Lyman Stone, can finally meet his daughter.

Strolling over to the bar, Lyman pours himself a shot of Chevis, and then sits down on the couch gazing out the window. The mid-afternoon California sun is bright against the sea blue sky. Spring dances in the air, ruffling scents of blooming fruit trees, and fresh salt air.

Dr. Stone smiles to himself. Soon, he thought, soon all will be right in the world.

Santa Fe, NM

Megan waits by the refreshment stand as Lee disappears into the bathroom. The theater is almost empty, and Megan feels a little awkward being here. She still has a funny feeling about Lee, like there is more to the situation than meets the eye. A part of her says to run as fast as she can, but she can't, something is drawing her to this woman and she wants to find out what it is.

The tantalizing scent of fresh popcorn makes Megan's mouth water, and she thinks about ordering a bucket, even though she just ate breakfast a couple of hours ago.

"Don't tell me you're still hungry." Lee grins as she approaches Megan.

"Well, you know, a movie isn't a movie without popcorn." Megan searches her pocket for some money. "You'll eat some, right?"

"Maybe a little, but don't get too big a size, I'm still full from this morning."

"I think we're the only ones at the early matinee," Megan whispers, as she waits for the concession guy to drizzle butter on the corn.

"Yeah, it's nice." Lee's beginning to feel relaxed with Megan. For a while she felt slightly uncomfortable, but now the air is more at ease. "You ready?" Waving toward the back.

"Yup, I'm right behind you." Following Lee, neither woman noticing the man staring at them from across the hallway.

❊   ❊   ❊

Calvin can't believe his luck. He just came from having a burger, deciding to eat instead of getting plastered, when he sees them. Burtrum Lee and that lesbian she was with last night. He watches as they enter the movie theater, figuring he'll wait around for the flic to end and then he'll make his move, whatever that's going to be.

Realizing he's standing in front of a pizza joint, Calvin glances at the magic-marker menu and notices a list of their desserts. Maybe he'll treat himself for his good fortune while he waits the two plus hours for the movie to end.

❊   ❊   ❊

"Well, it's about time you came back. I thought you left."

"If that's what you want, it's not too late."

"Oh, Jane, why do you have to be such a crab bucket?"

"Maybe it's the company I keep." Leaning against the door frame. "Are you ready?"

"As ready as I'll ever be."

Jane maintains a straight face. She isn't about to indulge in Clair's lame attempt at being funny. "So, is that a yes?"

Clair glares at Jane. "It'd help if you got behind the chair and pushed."

Jane eases the wheelchair out of the room and maneuvers it through the hallway, at last coming to the exit.

"Stop Jane," Clair demands. "I can walk from here."

"Are you sure? You seem a little shaky."

"I'm fine. Just hand me that cane they gave me to use."

Jane does as Clair requests, deciding to retreat from the bashing, figuring Clair is too weak to give her much of a fight anyway. And what fun is that?

"Why don't I go get the car, while you wait here. I'll pull it around and then you can hop right in."

"I don't think I'll be doing much hopping in the near future," Clair says, still annoyed with Jane.

"Just the same. I'll be right back. Don't go anywhere, I don't have time to be looking all over for you."

"Trust me, I'm not going anywhere. But will you hurry up, I'd really like to get home."

Clair studies Jane as she squirts across the parking lot. What is wrong with her? There really must be something big going on between her and Jed, and the timing can't be worse.

The sun is bright on Clair's face as she closes her eyes and inhales the fresh spring air. Deep down she can smell the first scents of fruit blossoms, lightening her heart. A slight smile creases her lips as memories flood her thoughts.

❋ ❋ ❋

1969

"Birdy, sweetheart, it's time to come in now."

"But Grandma, I want to stay out and play with the lizards."

"Come on honey, it's getting kind of late for a little girl to be outside playing."

"I'm not a little girl anymore. I'm nine." Lee stomps toward the newly constructed house. "I don't know why you have to live up here in the mountains, there's no one else around." The small child trying to think of a good complaint, maybe convince her grandma to let her stay outside just a little longer.

"You don't think it's beautiful?"

"Yes, but still. I don't have any friends up here."

"I like it. You and I can spend a bunch of time together. Isn't that nice?"

"Yeah, I guess so, Grandma." Lee sidles up to Clair and wraps her arms around her waist. Clair, leans down, kissing the top of her head. She smells like Pinon.

"Come on then, I have some hot chocolate for you."

"With marshmallows?"

"Of course."

Clair Conner reaches for the child's hand, and starts out toward the house, wondering if sheltering Lee this way is such a good idea.

"I love you Grandma."

"I love you too, Birdy."

"Clair, Clair!" Opening her eyes, Clair sees Jane hovering above her. "What, are you just falling asleep outside? Are you crazy?"

"I'm not dozing, I'm thinking. Now please, don't make a scene and just help me into the car."

The two women are completely silent as the sedan races across town and up the mesa to Clair's house. Jane pulls in front of the small mansion and slams the gear into park.

"Do you think you can make it into your house on your own?"

"Sure! I certainly wouldn't want to bother you." Wrapping her fingers around the door handle, Clair tries to pull the latch up, but finds it difficult.

"Oh, for heaven's sake," Jane whispers, whipping out of the Mercedes S Series. Stomping to the other side of the car, she flings Clair's door open and bracing her under the arms, hoists the frail woman out of the vehicle.

"You don't have to be so rough, Jane. I just got out of the hospital, show some compassion."

"Listen, Clair, I'm sorry, but I'm just tired and a little worried about Jed and Lee. I guess the stress is starting to get to me." Jane can feel herself lying, as her face flushes.

What she really wants to do is go to the Bullring for a drink, or two. Hanging on tight, she leads the way up the path, as Clair unlocks the door.

Opening the portal, the two women are greeted by desperate meows coming from Lucy. Clair tries to bend over to pet the feline. "Oh, Lucy, didn't any one feed you?" Clair glares back at Jane, who shrugs her shoulders.

"Hey, don't look at me. I didn't even know the cat was here."

"Come on Jane, use some common sense, will you?"

"Well, listen, I'll be on my way. You seem to have things under control. I'll call you later, okay?"

"You don't have to run off, it's still early," Clair tries to sound sincere.

"No, I'm gonna head home and try to contact Jed. I still don't understand why he hasn't called."

"I'm sure he has a good explanation."

Jane and Clair stare at each other for a moment, before Jane concludes.

"With that being said, I guess I'll be on my way, then."

"Good!"

"If you need anything, please feel free to call."

"I'll do just that," Clair retorts, thinking the only way Jane will be happy to hear from her is if she's lying on the floor dying.

"I'll let you know if I get a hold of Jed."

"Fine!" Clair is getting tired, and knows she needs to take a nap before Lee shows up. It's almost three o'clock, and Clair believes her granddaughter will be here anytime now.

Jane bolts out the door. "Bye, Clair."

"Bye." Closing the door even before Jane gets to the car, Clair shuffles over to the couch and lies down. Closing her eyes, she falls quickly to sleep, as Lucy, happily fed, and purring contently, snuggles next to her.

Calvin Kramer squirms in his chair, side-eying the waiter who's been glaring his way for the past fifteen minutes. Calvin's sure he's over stayed his welcome. He should step outside for a moment, figuring the movie will be another ten minutes or so. Standing, he then waves to the Spanish featured man, and saunters out. Glancing back at the theater, second guessing himself as to whether he should've stayed put.

Jed Conner steps off the small commuter plane at the Santa Fe Municipal airport. Stretching his arms above his head, he takes a deep breath, smiling at the spicy desert air. He loves it here in the Southwest. There is nothing like flying into New Mexico.

His trip had been a bust. Margy, the woman he's been seeing for almost a year now, is becoming very demanding, insisting Jed leave his wife and family for her, immediately!

But he isn't ready. As a matter of fact, Jed isn't even sure he wants to continue this affair. That's why he snuck away this morning, catching the first flight out of Los Angeles. He'd gotten lucky, and barely caught the plane out of LAX.

He's glad to be heading home, leaving this mess behind him, plus, there's been something eating at him, which he can't explain. He's been thinking about his mother a lot, and has a dreadful feeling something is wrong. He started to call Jane, after trying to reach his mom several times with no answer, which is very unusual, but decided against it, figuring there's nothing he can do while in flight.

Jed knows Jane has suspicions about his affair, and believes that in the best interest of his marriage, he truly needs to end it with Margy. It's just a fling, an itch, and if Jane doesn't bring it up, then he won't. Well, maybe later down the road when things between them aren't so fragile.

He just hopes it isn't too late to mend their relationship.

The town car lurches onto Airport Road. Feeling comfort from the sandy brown horizon, Jed sits back in his seat and studies the lonely landscape. His thoughts, as usual, return to Jane.

They've been in love their whole marriage, and then, overnight, the relationship changes. Jane becoming distant and less attractive to him. For a while Jed suspected she was having the affair, but knew better. Jane would never cheat on him.

The anxiety continues to race through him as they got closer to the Los Companos house. He doesn't know what's going on, he's never felt like this before. His chest tightens and breath shortens.

Opening the mini-fridge on the floor, Jed removes a bottle of water, and twisting the cap off, takes a long hard sip. Feeling better, after attributing his symptoms to dehydration, he gulps another swallow.

"The back or front, sir?"

The drivers voice shakes Jed out of his thoughts, and he sits up straight.

"Let's go around to the back this morning, Charles." He knows he needs to talk to Jane but wants to freshen up and have some coffee before the tongue lashing begins. Jed relaxes as the Lincoln disappears behind the massive adobe house. Glancing around, he quietly sneaks into the kitchen, removing his shoes on the glossy waxed floor. Tip-toeing up the back stairs, Jed's sinking feeling continues.

Calvin leans against the hot brown wall, wondering if maybe he should have gone in to the movie, but he didn't want to take the chance of being made.

The beating sun heats his face, producing tiny pellets of perspiration. A mother and daughter stroll by him, the young woman shooting him a laser look. Calvin flushes red for no reason, and lowers his head.

A small crowd gathers outside the entrance waiting for the next showing. At first Calvin has trouble seeing over their heads, but then finds a space in the back, realizing the movie hasn't let out yet.

Waiting patiently for what seems like hours, Calvin observes a flock of pigeons gathering on a power line, and wishes his life was that simple. Glancing at his watch, as the outside crowd slowly enters the theater, Calvin senses something's wrong. Strolling up to the man sitting in the windowed box, he leans over, and talks into the speaker.

"Can you tell me what time the last movie got out?"

"Hey, dude, that flick ended almost ten minutes ago."

"Ten minutes. Where did all of the people go?"

"We exit them through the back, like we always do when there's a crowd out here. I tell you, I don't know why so many people show up on Sundays, it's crazy."

"Yeah, crazy," Calvin whispers to himself, stepping back, his brain freezing in a haze. Unable to move, he can't believe it. He thought this would be his chance, the opportunity to at last approach Burtrum Lee Conner. But no, that's not how things go for Calvin. Now what is he going to do?

Storming out the door, Calvin searches the parking lot for the two women, but doesn't see them anywhere. Ringing his face with his hands, he snarls out loud and heads toward his car.

❉ ❉ ❉

"For Christ's sake!" Lee whines as she and Megan leave the theater. "I don't understand why they have to cattle us out the emergency door?" She continues. "The car's parked way over on the other side!"

"Yeah, it's odd. But what can you do?" Megan walks in silence for a moment as Lee follows behind. There seems to be a sense of tension growing between them, and Megan thinks maybe they're spending too much time together. After all, they just met, and even though Megan is growing very fond of Lee, there's still a slight uneasiness.

"So, what's on the agenda?" She asks.

Looking at her watch, Lee replies. "I should head to my

grandma's. It's getting late. Would you mind driving me?"

"No not at all. Where does she live?"

"Just a-little-ways up Bishops Lodge Road. Is that okay?"

"Yeah, sure, no problem." Megan thinks of her fume filled gas tank. Hopefully there's enough to get her there and back. She hates paying the two dollars and nineteen cents a gallon.

"That's not the vibe I'm getting," Lee said, noticing the scowl on Megan's brow.

"What are you talking about?"

"I don't know, there's a strange look on your face."

"It must be a look of hunger," lying.

"Well, I'm sure Clair will make us both something to eat."

"I don't know if I want to impose. She just got out of the hospital, and I'm sure she's not in the mood to cook for a stranger."

"You don't know Grandma. Now that you've mention it, I'm a little hungry too."

Megan tags along, wondering if she's made a mistake befriending this peculiar woman.

❋   ❋   ❋

"Turn here," Lee instructs Megan, who steers the small car onto the dirt driveway, spitting rocks and dust up behind her.

The two women pull up in front of the house. Megan's jaw drops at the sight of the adobe mansion.

"You've got to be kidding me. Your grandmother lives

here?"

"Yup, it's one of the first houses built along this road," Lee replies proudly, getting out of the car. "Come on, it's a little cold out here."

Shyly, Megan slithers up the walkway, keeping a slight distance between her and Lee. Feeling intimidated and a little out of her league, Megan wonders if it's the size of the house, or the realization that Lee's family has money.

"Come on," Lee waves to Megan to hurry.

Hesitantly, Megan steps into the pantry and is instantly hit with a sense of déjà vu. Stopping in her tracks for a second, she feels herself begin to spin. What is wrong with me, she thinks, bracing herself against the wall.

Realizing she lost Megan, Lee glances back. "Hey, you all right?"

Shaking her head. "Yeah, I'm just a little dizzy." Catching up with Lee. "I tell you, I just experienced a major déjà vu. I swear, I've been here before, or at least it feels like it."

"Well, why don't you come into the kitchen and sit down. I'll get you a glass of water and a snack, then I'll check on Clair. Okay?"

"No, you need to go say hello to your grandma. I'm fine, I'll just sit here until you return."

"Maybe you're right. Just relax for a minute while I run upstairs." Lee turns back. "You know, there are times when this place still overwhelms me, so don't worry about it."

"Hello, who's there. Birdy, is that you?"

Hearing her grandmother's voice, Lee disappears up the stairs. "Yes, Grandma, it's me and a friend. I'm coming right up?"

"No, don't, I'll come down."

Stabling herself on sea-legs, Megan slinks against the counter as Lee enters the room.

"Come on, sit back down, Megan." Lee pats a chair by the table, as Clair Conner appears in the archway.

"And who do we have here?" She approaches with the aid of a cane.

An unfamiliar pang beats in Lee's heart as she watches her grandmother struggle to get to a chair.

Rushing over to help the elderly lady, Lee wraps her arm around her waist for support as Clair sits.

Slapping Lee's hands away, Clair snips, "Quit making a fuss. I'm fine, just a little older than I was yesterday."

"Still, Grandma, you need to take it easy."

"You haven't answered my question."

"And what is that?"

"Who's your friend?"

"Oh, I'm sorry, how rude of me. Grandma, this is Megan, Megan, my grandmother, Clair Conner."

The two reach across the table and shake hands.

"Nice to meet you, Mrs. Conner."

"Nice to meet you too, Megan, but please, call me Clair."

"Okay, Clair."

"Well, why you two are chatting it up, why don't I make us some tea," Lee suggests.

"That sounds lovely, dear."

Megan's face begins to flush as she feels Clair's gaze upon her. She rubs her cool hands over her reddened cheeks.

"Have we met before?" Clair asks.

"No, not that I recall."

Noticing Megan's unease, Clair inquires. "Are you all right?"

"Yeah, it feels like I'm having a hot flash. I'm sure it'll pass in a minute."

"You look kind of young to be going through the change."

"I don't think it's that."

"Okay then dear," Clair continues. "Would you like some aspirin or a shot of brandy?"

The thought of having a drink makes Megan want to gag. That's what's causing this heat wave, but she doesn't want to admit it out of embarrassment. It's nobody else's business about her developing problem.

"No, no, just some water. That'll be great. And if you don't mind, may I use your bathroom?" Trying to be polite as possible.

"Just down the hall and to the left." Lee points.

"Great, then I'll be right back." Megan scurries down the dimly lit hall and finds an immaculate restroom at the end. She needs to splash some water on her face, try to cool down her core.

As she approaches the entry, Megan halts for a second as she hears Lee say her name. Sneaking up to the frame, Megan holds her breath and tries to listen.

"So, how much does this new friend of yours know?"

"Nothing."

"I can't believe you're hanging out with a woman who you just met in a bar. You know she's gay, right."

"What difference does that make?"

"None, it's of no concern. What matters is you not getting anyone else involved in this mess. I don't want someone we hardly know getting hurt."

"Don't you think you're over reacting just a bit, Grandma?"

"No, I don't Birdy. I believe we need to exercise extreme caution right now, and that means keeping a lid on everything." Clair sounds distressed. "And I'm worried about your father. Jane hasn't heard anything from him, and that's not like Jed."

"I'm sure it's nothing, Grandma. He's probably just tied up with something."

Feeling like an intruder, Megan knows she needs to get out of there fast, as she steps into the kitchen.

"Hey, listen. I'm not feeling so great, so I think I'm going to head home," Megan explains.

"You're not going to stay for dinner?" Lee asks, suspecting something is wrong.

"I don't think so. I really need to head out."

Megan stops in her tracks as all three women became immediately silent after hearing a noise come from the living room. Clair glances at Lee, who looks at Megan, putting her finger to her lips indicating for everyone to be quiet.

Grabbing the rolling pin hanging from a hook, Lee hides against the wall, waiting for the unknown visitor to come in. Soft padded footsteps approach them, and holding her breath, Lee raises the baking tool to a striking position.

"Jed!" Clair screams, seeing her son. She scampers over, hugging him tightly. "Where've you been?"

"Dad?"

Jed notices his daughter, raised roller in hand. "Honey, what are you doing? Put that thing down. What's going on here?"

"We thought you were that man coming back."

"What man?"

"Oh, Jesus. You don't know anything? You haven't talked to Jane?"

"No, I just flew in and she isn't at home, so I thought she'd be here. What's going on? And who is she?" Jed points to Megan.

"She's Lee's new friend."

Jed's face cringes as he glares at Megan. "Oh! Well, then, it still doesn't explain things."

"Jed, just sit down. We were about to eat when you came in, are you hungry?" Clair tries to lighten the tension floating in the air.

"Listen, I think I'm just going to take off," Megan announces, heading toward the door. She knows when someone doesn't like her, and Jed Conner isn't making any attempts to hide his distaste.

Reaching for Megan's arm as she wisps by, Lee pleads. "No, don't go. I'd really like it if you stayed."

"Hey, Lee, if the woman wants to leave, let her," Jed's voice is demeaning, and Lee can't figure out why he's acting like this.

"No, your father's right. Obviously there's something going on with you people and I think it's best if I don't get involved. You understand, right?"

"Will someone please tell me what's going on?" Jed is getting perturbed.

"They've come for Lee."

Clair doesn't need to say anything else as the look on Jed's face tells them that he knows exactly what she is talking about.

"When?"

"It started this past Friday. Her house was ransacked, and there's some guy stalking her. He showed up at the B&B, and came here twice. The first time he knocked me down, and then Jane came and scared him away, and then the second time, he frightened me so badly, that I fainted, and everyone thought I had a heart attack."

"But you're all right now, yes?"

"I'm fine. I spent the night at the hospital, but only as a precaution."

"Do you know what this guy looks like?" Jed snake-eyes Megan standing by the back door.

"No," Lee pipes in. "But I think we should let this guy find me. See what he wants."

"I don't think that's a very good idea."

"Why not? I'm tired of this mess. What's the big deal? So I'm one of the first artificially inseminated babies, who cares? I turned out fine, isn't that the most important thing?" Lee takes a breath. "I'll tell the guy that whomever he's working for needs to lay off. I'm not interested in what he's selling."

Sitting down next to his daughter, Jed takes her hand. "Listen, sweetheart, it's a little more complicated than that. But right now isn't the time to be discussing the situation."

Abruptly standing, Lee snarls at her dad. "Don't you think it's time I know the truth. After all, I am an adult."

Tears well in her eyes. "All of my life I've never felt like I fit in anywhere or with anyone. I figure I'm a little off because of the way I was conceived, but lately, I don't feel comfortable with who I am, and I want to know why."

"Let me find this goon and tell him to get lost." Jed pounds his fist in his hand.

"Yeah, that's a good way to handle it. Let's rough-house a stranger."

"Listen Lee, he's the one who trespassed in my mother's home and assaulted her. No, the gloves are off and the rules broken."

"You're being childish Dad." Lee's temper heating. "This is my life, and I have every right to find out the truth, and there's no one, nor nothing, that can stop me."

"Calm down Lee," Jed's words ring a little softer. "Let me see what I can find out before you do anything rash."

Lee doesn't appreciate the condescending tone in her father's voice. "Well, maybe we'll have to see what Mother thinks about this."

"Talking to Jane won't do any good," Clair chimes in. "She seems to be caught up in one of her own personal dramas and doesn't have time for this problem."

Plopping down in a chair, and rustling her hair with her hands, Lee pleads. "Stop, please, everyone just be quiet for a minute," She snaps. "All I want to do is get to the bottom of this, is that too much to ask? After all, it is my life, right? Plus, what could be so bad that they'd want to hurt me?"

Jed and Clair look at each other, and then quickly away before Lee or Megan notices.

Clair moves over next to her granddaughter, placing her

hand on Lee's arm. "Listen Birdy, you know we only have your best interest at heart, right?"

"Yeah, I guess so," Replying softly.

Megan, still standing by the back door, shuffles in her place, bringing attention back to her. "Maybe I should get going now," She says.

"It's getting pretty late. Why don't you just stay here tonight?" Clair invites.

To Megan it seems like an odd invitation, since she just met the Conner family. Are they trying to keep her here? "I don't know. I've already heard more than I should or want to. So I believe it best if I just cruise." Reaching for the door knob.

Lee moseys over to Megan. "Just tonight." Lee glances back at her dad and Clair. "You know, to play it safe."

"To be honest, I don't want to get involved."

"We won't let you. All we'll do is eat dinner and then hit the hay. We'll have our own rooms, our own baths, it's like staying in a palace. Come on, what do you say?"

Deep down, Megan is drawn to Lee, but it isn't that physical, sexual thing this time, which she doesn't understand.

Surrendering, Megan agrees. "Okay, but I'm leaving first thing in the morning, no if's, and's, or but's about it."

"Great!" Lee turns back to her grandmother. "Grandma, Megan has decided to stay the night. We can have a slumber party."

"Good then." Clair laser beams her son. "And you? It's getting late and we haven't eaten yet. Are you staying or going?"

Jed checks his watch. "No, I'd better go find Jane. I know by now she's probably climbing the walls wondering where I am." Shaking his head. "I'll come by in the morning or call. Until then I suggest you three stay in the house and don't open the doors for anyone. If something happens, call me immediately. Is that understood?"

Jed Conner's massive body hovers over the three women as he wags his broad finger at them.

"Yes, dear," Clair agrees, pulling on his coat collar to get him to bend down so she can kiss him good-bye. "I'll take care of everything, Jed. Haven't I always?"

There's an awkward silence in the air as mother and son stare at each other. Lee watches her father's eyes soften.

"Yes, Mother," Jed mumbles. Going over to Lee, he kisses her on the cheek. "You be careful, and do as your grandmother says. Understand?"

"Yes, Dad, you don't have to worry. I'm a grown woman now, and I know how to take care of myself."

"Well, in my eyes, you're still my little girl."

"Thanks Dad." Lee's eyes bubble with tears, as she quickly brushes them away.

"Okay then, I'm out of here." Jed gives Megan the once over, and doesn't say a word. There is no way he is going to be congenial to a woman he knows squat about, plus, there's something off about her. "I'll talk to you in the morning," he says to Clair, disappearing into the living room.

A cold wisp streams into the kitchen as Jed leaves through the front door. Megan, who can't believe he'd been so rude to her, smiles softly at Lee and announces.

"Hey, you know. I think I'm just going to crash. I'm

really not hungry. And I'm pretty tired."

"That's fine dear," Clair motions for Megan to follow her. "I'll show you to your room."

"Good night, Megan." Lee stands and unexpectedly hugs her. "And thanks. I'll make this up to you, I promise."

Flushing, Megan responds. "Think nothing of it. My life needs a little stimulation anyway."

All three women giggle as Clair slowly ascends the staircase, Megan following behind. Lee watches until she can't see either of them anymore. Sitting down at the table, she reaches for her almost empty wine glass and finishes the last sip. There's something funny about the way Clair and Jed are acting, and Lee wonders if there is more to the story then what meets the eye.

"Wanda, Wanda!" Katie Lee chokes, unable to breath. "Wanda," she gasps, trying to awaken the snoring woman sleeping in the bed across from her. Wanda stirs but doesn't wake.

Laying back, Katie tries to calm her racing heart. She needs to control her crazy thoughts, relax, and then she'll be able to breathe. Counting to ten, she gazes at the brown ceiling above her, slowly feeling herself mellow.

The excitement about seeing her daughter is driving her nuts. For forty years she's been allowing her child to be raised by strangers, but at the time she believed she was doing the right thing. Now, though, with Lyman sniffing around like a mad dog, trouble is on the horizon, and Katie blames herself.

"Oh, I can't wait to see you," Katie cries.

"What, huh, Katie, is that you?" Wanda rolls over and opens her sleepy eyes. "Are you all right?"

"Yes, I'm fine. I'm thinking, so go back to sleep."

"Are you sure?" Wanda sits up.

"No, not really. I can't get to sleep. My thoughts keep running wild."

Wanda hoists her legs over the side of the bed, and stands up, steadying herself as the Winnebago slightly jerks back and forth.

"I know I don't have to ask what you're think about, and you know I'm going to say the same thing I've been telling you for the past few days now. You need to get hold of yourself. It's not going to do anyone any good. See, we're both up because of it."

"I'm sorry, I don't mean to be such a bother," Katie's tone is sharp.

"Don't be getting snotty with me, I'm not the one who woke us up at three-thirty in the morning."

"You don't understand."

Wanda drops down on her bed. "I don't understand? I'm probably the only one who does. Now, in a day or two everything will be out in the open, and maybe the truth will be revealed. But you also have to keep the promise you made all of those years ago."

"All promises have been taken off the table, Wanda. My daughter is in trouble, and it's all because of me."

"You can't put the blame on yourself. There were many factors involved. You had no idea what Lyman and your husband were up to, and do you know what Katie, if things had turned out differently, you know, if Burtrum wouldn't have crashed and instead gotten you safely to a hospital, no one would've known the truth. So maybe, in a distorted kind of way, it's a good thing this happened."

"I can't believe what you're saying."

"Well, believe it or not, that's what I think."

"So you believe it's a good thing my child was stolen from me."

"Not stolen, rescued. If they hadn't been there, all of you would be dead. You should be thankful."

"Yes, but what about them leaving their deceased son between my legs. Don't you think that's a little demented?"

"Do we have to talk about this right now? I'm really tired, and getting a little agitated."

Katie closes her eyes. "You're right, Wanda. I shouldn't have woken you with my worries. Go back to sleep and I'll try also."

"Would you like me to get you a pill?"

"No, I think I'll be all right. Good-night, Wanda."

"Night, Katie. Just think, soon you'll be hugging your daughter."

"Yes, yes I will."

It isn't long before Katie hears Wanda's chronic snoring vibrating from her bed. She closes her eyes, knowing sleep won't be arriving anytime soon. Motherly worries race beyond sanity, as she seethes in anger over Lyman Stone's deviance. She'll take care of him, and take care of him good when this fiasco is finished.

15

Gusting winter winds rock Clair Conner as she shields her eyes against the crystallized flakes. They sting her frosted skin, as she gets closer to the accident. It was a deep thud that she heard, and at first couldn't figure out for the life of her what it could be. Almost like a sonic boom. For a moment she believed it might be Los Alamos. So, layering up, she dared the elements and trudged through the deepening snow to where the shining light beamed. Clair Conner never expected to see what she found. A horror show. Bodies and blood all around, with eerie shadows dancing to the blizzard's howl. Hearing a cry, she digs her way over to where a woman lies.

Examining the scene, Clair sees an infant lying in her mother's fluids, and reaches down for the newborn. She screams in thankfulness, her tiny voice muffled against Clair's fur coat. Studying the body, cracked and broken,

Clair leans over and checks for a pulse. Her veins pump still. She edges closer to her face and tries to feel a breath. Nothing! Signing the cross, Clair knows the woman is dead, and needs to get the infant to safety. She'll leave her at Our Lady of Sacred Hearts church down the road. They'll take care of the child. Freezing, Clair bundles the infant inside her coat, and begins her mile and a half trek to the sanctuary.

Los Alamos, NM 1960

"You listen to me, and you listen to me good, Lyman. You are to discontinue any further experiments dealing with cloning. My labs aren't about defying nature, but working along-side it." Dr. Lee wipes his brow. "I don't want to hear anything else about the subject, am I making myself clear?"

"But Burtrum." Lyman reaches for his arm, he shucks the grip away.

"My mind's made up, and now I have to go, the weather's worsening and I want to start out for the airport before we get snowed in. Plus, Katie's not feeling well."

"Katie's with you?"

"Yes, I wanted her here with me in case something happens."

Dread etches Lyman's face. "Burtrum, maybe you should just stay up here in Los Alamos for the night, let the storm pass. What's the hurry?"

"I want to get home." Dr. Lee stomps to the door, and turning around quickly, glares at his counterpart. "I'm serious about this, Lyman. I hear one word of you conducting any more tests, and I'll have your head on a platter." He whips out the door, as Lyman Stone stands frozen in place, worry furrowing his brow.

Should he call someone, maybe flatten a tire before they leave so they can't? Lyman didn't know Katie would be with Burtrum when he ordered the car to be 'taken care of'. Now, he's endangered the lives of her, and unbeknownst to Katie, *their* child. But then, with them both out of the way, he can proceed with his findings with no one to stop him.

Lyman Stone cracks a smile as he watches the Lee's sedan fishtail out of the lot.

16

Megan sits on the edge of the bed, trying hard not to breath too heavy, fearing Lee or Clair might hear her. She doesn't feel right about staying overnight, there's something odd about the whole situation, but the intrigue keeps her here.

What she needs to do, and needs to do now, is leave. She'll wait until she's sure everyone has gone to sleep and then she'll sneak out the back door, and pray her car will start. She's regretting not gassing up earlier.

Smiling as she lays back on the bed, she stares up at the deep red brown of the Kivas lining the ceiling above her. Megan tells herself she has enough problems of her own without diving into a stranger's troubles.

Wet winds scrape against the adobe home, reminding Megan of a dog scratching a post. Out of nowhere she hears, "meow, meow," and slightly startled, looks over to the door, watching as Lucy slithers through the sliver of an opening.

The cat wraps herself around Megan's legs and begins purring loudly. Reaching down, she pets the feline, feeling a sense of calm rush over her. She's a little surprised when Lucy jumps up on the bed and lays down next to her, like they're old buddies.

Continuing to stroke the cat, she closes her eyes, not realizing she's fallen to sleep until Lucy stirs a few hours later, and Megan wakes in a cloud of unfamiliarity. She slept way too long, and now her chances of slipping out might've been compromised.

Tip-toeing down the carpeted staircase, Megan scans the room before soundlessly exiting through the back door.

Concealed in the staircase shadows, Clair watches as Megan sneaks out the door. Her first instinct is to grab the woman and tell her everything, inform her she might be in danger herself, even though she knows nothing about what's going on. There's still a chance. But no, the best thing to do is to keep this trauma strictly in the family.

Calvin Kramer sits quietly glaring at the silhouetted wall. The thing he likes best about motel rooms is the curtains keeping the light out. And the Kelly green drapes hanging in front of him contain the cold darkness.

Lifting the almost empty Jack Daniels bottle to his lips,

Calvin sucks the last few drops out of the recently purchased fifth. Tossing the empty glass on the floor, he searches for more, but realizes he drank everything? How odd, he doesn't even feel drunk.

Calvin is scared, frightened of what the daylight might bring. According to Lyman's message, Katie Lee, who just happens to be Burtrum Lee's biological mother, will arrive in Santa Fe today and what is he going to tell her?

Not only that, but when Calvin tried calling Carla, all thirty-nine times, she never picked up. Are his suspicions true? Is his beloved wife cheating on him?

"This is ridiculous," Calvin hisses to himself. He needs to get back to San Francisco and fast before his whole world tumbles down. Who cares about this woman anyway, as far as Calvin is concerned, Burtrum Lee Conner is nothing but a freak show. And if he had the balls, he would say so to Lyman. The best thing the aging doctor can do, is leave the mutant alone and let her live out her unnatural life.

"Ohhhhh," Calvin moans, slapping his forehead. "I'm such an idiot."

Slipping his shoes off, he lies down on the bed, not bothering to get undressed. At this point Calvin doesn't care about anything. He can't figure out why his whole life is being turned upside down so quickly.

Sleep sucker punches Calvin as he falls into a semi-alcohol induced coma. Dreams wrestle inside of him, filling the black holes of emptiness.

❊   ❊   ❊

I'm with an older couple and we're going to this farm to see their daughter. The house is decrepit, and there's a funny stench around the yard. We go into the kitchen and the daughter sees her parents and starts hugging and kissing them. I presume they haven't seen each other in a long time. Suddenly, the daughter looks behind her as we all hear footsteps coming from the distant living room. She turns to us and whispers, "we've got to hide and quickly." I crawl between a table and a wall, while the old man tucks himself away beneath a rotting bench, and the old woman stuffs herself into a cabinet. We all hide just in time as this mean aged woman appears, spitting as she yells. "Where are thoses clones?" She bends over and looks right at me and the old man, but doesn't see us. She thumps out of the kitchen and the daughter hurries us out into the yard. We shuffle to a rusted out white stretch limo, and jump into it. The old man is driving, and I'm in the back seat. We're having trouble getting out because the limo is stuck in a snow drift, but finally the old man rocks us to freedom and we go peeling down the driveway. I glance behind me and watch as the old woman who is now walking behind the daughter, shoots her in the back of the head.

Lee bounces up like a dead woman revived. Shaking her head as images of her dream start to take form. "Oh, lord!" She whispers, flinging her legs out of bed and standing up, still a little shaky from her nightmare.

"Shoooo, where did that come from?" Tussling her hair with her hand, Lee scans the clock and sees that it's almost seven in the morning. She's going to be late for work, but decides she'll just call in sick. There is no way she can deal with the B&B today. They'll just have to understand, and it's not as though she does it all the time.

After hanging up with the owner, who isn't thrilled, Lee strolls out to the top of the illuminated staircase, and smells coffee drifting up from the kitchen. Clair is already downstairs and raring to go. She should wake Megan, but decides to let her new friend sleep for a little while longer while she goes downstairs and relives her dream with Clair, who's always been fascinated with the subconscious world.

"Morning, Grandma," Lee announces as she appears in the door. Slipping over to the elderly lady standing by the sink, she kisses Clair on the cheek. "How are you today?"

"I'm fine, but sit down dear, I'll pour you a cup of coffee."

Recognizing that, *something is wrong tone*, in Clair's voice, Lee inquires.

"What's going on?"

"Well, hopefully nothing. You see, your friend left earlier this morning, and I'm a little afraid for her safety. I mean she doesn't know a whole lot, but she knows something, and that might be enough for this mad man to go after her."

"What should we do?"

"Maybe go find her, explain the situation, and that the best thing for her to do is stay with us until all of this passes over."

"Grandma, I barely know the woman. What am I going to say? Hey, Megan, I think you might be in danger, so it's best if you stay close? I don't think so. If someone says that to me, I'm gone."

Clair is silent for a moment, trying to hold her tongue from telling Lee about the perils that lie ahead, and how their lives are in jeopardy if this secret ever gets out.

"You know, Grandma, I don't see what the big deal is. So, I'm one of the first inseminated babies from the sixties, so what. It's common place, now. Why are they still interested in me? I mean, I'm sure I'm just one of many from back then, why isn't he terrorizing them?"

"Lee, I don't know. What I do know is someone is after you, and you need protection."

"I should just go confront this guy, not wait for Dad, use myself as bait until he shows up. I'm not going to let this interfere with my life any longer. I'm already tired of the whole thing."

Clair grabs Lee's arm as she moves away. "We discussed this last night, and I still don't think it's a good idea. Let's wait to hear from your dad, and see if he's found out anything, okay?" Clair releases Lee. "And in the meantime why don't we go pay your friend Megan a little visit, see if she wants to hang out with us for a while."

"Why would she want to do that?"

"I don't know. It just seems like the two of you were hitting it off. It'd be good for you to have a friend after all of this is over."

Lee shakes her head. Her grandmother never stops. "Okay, I guess, but I'm driving."Recalling she wanted to tell Clair her dream, Lee tries to remember the details, but the events have already fallen into the black hole. Never to be recovered. She wonders why dreams disappear so quickly.

❂   ❂   ❂

Megan is shivering so badly she can barely drive. The

light spring coat she wore is no competition for the early morning cold. Plus, the Volkswagen's heater isn't any help. Maybe it's time to start thinking about getting another car.

Turning right onto Guadalupe, Megan's thoughts continue to veer toward Lee. Why is this stranger haunting her? Megan tries to think about work, and how she dreads going in today. She's afraid that after Friday, and the way she behaved, Danny will want to have a little chat with her, and she isn't in the mood.

Lost in her torment, Megan doesn't notice the orange Volvo pull up behind her, and glancing in her rear view mirror, sees Clair and Lee Conner right behind. A sudden sense of fear envelopes her.

Terror shakes her every nerve as her wild imagination goes hay-wire. Where did they come from? And why are they following her? Do they want to kidnap her, rough her up a little bit so she won't talk?

What do they want?

Now, Megan is truly creeped out. Deciding to ditch them, she quickly turns into the Border's Bookstore parking lot, and watches behind her as the Volvo speeds by, unable to stop in time.

Ditching her car at the edge of the lot, Megan scans all directions before dashing across the field through the Aspen grove, and to her flat. Crackling spring leaves ring in her ears as she rushes into her apartment, bolting the door behind her.

Out of breath, and totally exhausted, Megan trudges up the stairs and glances out the balcony window. Seeing no signs of the Conner women, she slinks into her bedroom and flops on the bed.

Two hours, that's how long she can sleep. Closing her eyes, a foggy cloud begins to cover her thoughts, and before she can count to ten, Megan Masterson is fast asleep.

❋   ❋   ❋

"Where did she go?" Lee questions, slowing the car down as they crawl through the Sanbusco Center parking lot.

"I swear I saw her turn in here, just cruise around," Clair insists, stretching her neck out the open window for a better view. Driving the car to the back parking lot, Clair suddenly yelps. "There it is!" Pointing toward Megan's car. "But she's not in it."

"Damn, now what do we do? She can be anywhere."

"I can't believe you don't remember where she lives."

"I wasn't really paying attention. We walked and it was dark."

"Well, do you know where she works?"

"Yes, but I don't think she'll be there yet. They don't open until eleven."

"Then I suggest we go home, and wait."

"There's no place you need to go? The grocery store, library, nursery?"

"Nope, just take me home."

"You don't have to be such a sour puss," Lee retorts, driving right past Megan's place.

❋   ❋   ❋

Jane Conner awakens not knowing where she is at first. She jumps up and the motion sends her head reeling. Slowly laying back down, Jane gently massages her temples. Reaching over to the nightstand she grabs the glass, and tipping it to her lips, takes a large swallow of the tepid water, replacing the crystal goblet to the stand.

"Oh, my gosh," she moans. "What did I do to myself?" Blankness fills her memory, as she whips the quilt off her body and rolls out of bed. Standing, she has to steady herself at first because her sea legs feel like they're going to give out at any moment.

Jane doesn't know what got into her last night. She never drinks that much in such a short period of time. It's as though she's been possessed by Ernest Hemingway, or Dean Martin.

Her over heating brain screams in agony as Jane dashes to the bathroom. Reaching for the green bottle of Excedrin, she shakes three into her palm, and tosses them down her throat.

Studying herself in the mirror, Jane doesn't recognize the face glaring back at her. Who is this woman with the sunken blood shot eyes, with deep brown bags sagging below the once hazel orbs. Running her hand through her dyed brunette hair, Jane can see slight strands of gray starting to show themselves at the roots.

Has it been that long since her last visit to Manuel? She needs to make an appointment for later today. Whether he's busy or not, he'll fit her in, after all, she is Jane Conner, and if it wasn't for her, Manuel would be nothing in this town.

Creasing pain rips through her head, and Jane figures a

little hair of the dog won't hurt. Stumbling to the living room, she moseys over to the bar and opening the mahogany paneled mini fridge, pulls out an ice cold bottle of Stoly. Reaching for the pitcher of Bloody Mary mix, she pours herself a cocktail.

"Don't you have anything better to do with your mornings than get drunk?" Jed's booming voice makes Jane jump, spilling some of the red concoction onto the pure white shag carpet. Whipping around and ready to kill, Jane yells. "Damn it Jed, look what you've made me do."

"You should be a little more careful when you drink." Swaggering over to the couch, he sits down, never taking his eyes off of his wife.

Jane, still feeling shaky, leans against the bar. "So, why are you here? I thought your *business meeting* was supposed to last until Friday."

"I would think you'd know why I'm here."

"Oh, you mean that crap with Lee," Jane sounds disconcerting. "I'm sure it's nothing. She probably pissed some guy off at a bar or something like that, and he wants to scare her a little. You know how she gets."

Jed sits on the edge of the cushions. "Jane, I don't think you're conceiving the magnitude of the situation. It's them."

"Them who?"

"You know perfectly well who I'm talking about."

Jane begins to pace back and forth. "Listen Jed, if it were *them*, don't you think they would've come after her long ago?"

"Maybe they just realized she's alive."

"But how? Lee seldom leaves Santa Fe, much less New

Mexico. It seems she's either at work, or looking for work, or hanging out at Clair's. No wonder she doesn't have a boyfriend."

"Jane, will you focus? Our daughter is in trouble, and we need to protect her."

"Why Jed? I mean seriously. Maybe this is for the better. Maybe we should just hand her over, give her back. It's obvious that Lee isn't happy, and she's always felt like she doesn't fit in. Maybe what she needs, is to be with the people who created her."

"You're talking nonsense. The booze must've gone to your head already. Do you realize what might happen to Lee if they find her?"

"I don't think it's as serious as you're building it up to be. Why don't we just chill and see what pans out. Who knows, I might be right, and it's just some weirdo guy with a fixation on Lee." Jane, finishing her drink, sets the empty glass on the bar. "Listen, I'm going to go shower and get dressed. Then I'm going to visit Lee at work and make sure she's all right. You can do as you please."

"Why don't we both go?" Jed suggests.

Still, very angry with her husband, Jane replies snidely. "No, Jed, I think I'll go by myself. I want to talk to her about something else anyway."

"What?"

"Oh, just some girl stuff." Jane heads back toward her bedroom, but stops in the archway, twirling back. "I'll let you know what's going on," she says, disappearing.

"Damn-it!" Jed hisses. His first reaction is to follow Jane into her bedroom, which used to be theirs, until she got a whim up her butt, and set him straight as to who is boss. A lot of good that will do, Jed chuckles, knowing who really wears the pants in this family.

Moving over to the door, he removes his coat from the hook. Wrapping it around his broad shoulders he steps out into the cool crisp morning air, and breaths deeply. He can smell spring waiting on the fringes, and smiles to himself. Who knows, maybe Jane is right, Jed speculates, getting into his Pathfinder. Could be this guy is just an ass trying to rattle Lee, and now that they're on to him, he'll leave her alone.

❀   ❀   ❀

Megan can't get warm. Her body trembles, waking her. Her teeth, chattering, bite her lip, sending waves of pain through her still sleeping brain.

The morning light streams between half open Venetian blinds, squirting Megan in the eyes with bright sunrays. Squinting, she looks at her clock. Seeing she still has a little time before leaving for work, Megan rolls over onto her side and gazes out the window. Water-dogs roll over the morning mountains, capturing the sun in their gray clouds. A shadow creases Megan's bedroom, and feeling tired and groggy, she closes her eyes and feels the sensation of nothingness float over her once again.

❀   ❀   ❀

"Now what do you suggest we do? It's only ten o'clock,

we still have a good hour and I'm starting to get a little antsy."

"If you'd like we can go out back and start cleaning the flower beds."

"No, it's too cold."

"You can vacuum."

"Nope, don't feel like doing that either."

"Why don't you go into the living room and watch TV."

"There's nothing on."

"My word, I give up, why don't you just sit there and complain."

"I'm already doing that."

Shaking her head, Clair wipes her hands on the dishtowel and hangs it on the loop.

"Why don't we head out, maybe grab a latte on our way to the Bistro."

"Do you think it wise, you drinking caffeine?"

"Nobody told me, I can't." Slipping into a jacket. "Let's go."

"Just like that?"

"Just like that."

Patting Lee's shoulder, Clair really just wants to get her granddaughter out of the house and doing something. The woman is beginning to drive her nuts. A cool breeze kisses their cheeks as Lee opens the car door for Clair. The old woman slides into the Volvo. A slight shiver races across Lee as she jogs to the other side and gets in.

"Are you sure you're feeling okay, Birdy, you're white as a ghost."

"I just got the weirdest feeling, I can't explain it."

Clair reaches out and touches Lee's forehead. "It doesn't feel like you have a fever. Maybe it's just the stress of the past few days. We haven't seen or heard from this guy since Saturday. Could be he's given up."

For a moment, Clair's breathing becomes harsh, and Lee glances over. "Grandma, you all right? You don't look too good."

"I'm fine, but I think I'm having second thoughts about that latte. Maybe I should just go back in, and lay down."

Worry creeps up Lee's spine as she helps Clair out of the car and back into the house.

Jane Conner slowly opens the shower door, not wanting the glass plate to creak. She listens intently for any sounds of Jed, and hearing none, steps out of the bath. Reaching for the cotton towel hanging on the rack, she licks her lips, and begins drying herself off, relieved that her husband isn't leering around the corner.

Feeling much better than she did fifteen minutes ago, Jane decides to have a second drink. After all, it's Jed's fault she's hitting the sauce so hard. She figures it's a way to dull the pain of her husband cheating on her.

After making herself another cocktail, Jane returns to the bedroom and lies down on the bed. Her muscles are tight and aching and she tells herself to remember to make an appointment at Ten Thousand Waves for a massage.

Thinking about what happened over forty years ago sends chills down Jane's spine. Maybe they did do the wrong thing, but at the time it seemed right. Who knows where Lee would be if they hadn't saved her.

But now the ghosts have emerged, and it's frightening.

Finishing her drink, Jane Conner gets up and dresses, figuring she'll catch her daughter at the B&B and have a little chat with her.

❋   ❋   ❋

Bluuuueeeee. Songs are like tattoos, you know I've been to sea before, crown and anchor me or let me sail away.

Megan increases the volume on the CD player and listens intently to Joni Mitchell as she sings. There is no one else whom Megan turns to as much, when she needs to think deeply. The musician's songs of love and life resonate with Megan's somber thoughts. A tear rolls down her face as the all too familiar melancholy enters her thoughts. Why is she feeling like this? She isn't anywhere near her period, and up until this past weekend she's been in a good mood. Megan wonders what the planets are doing.

Studying herself in the mirror, she slips her pants on. She's lost a good fifteen pounds since the breakup, and believes she's never looked better. Her pecan butter eyes, and slight reddish hair encompass a narrow, straight forward face.

Edging in closer, she outlines the scars framing her left eye. A few years back they removed a mole dangerously dangling on her lower lid, leaving tiny remembrances. Like the memory of the searing pain as they first sliced into her. Unaware the anesthetic hadn't taken, the razor sharp scalpel edged her skin until she shrieked in agony. To this day she still cringes when she recalls the experience.

"Ah!" Megan whispers, snapping her jeans after tucking her stained green shirt in. She dreads having to work today, and feels maybe it's time for another job. Something that isn't so time consuming, heartless. The money's good, Megan has to admit, plus, the hours are short. It's the, having to be there six days a week, that's grinding on her nerves.

Feeling her stomach grumble, Megan notices the time, and figures she can stop at the Chicago Dog Express, on her way in. She knows having a hotdog this early isn't the best diet, but hey, you only live once.

Stepping out into the warming air, Megan's spirits lighten slightly. She knows her mood is due to Lee Conner, and the fiasco she almost got caught in. Man, that would have been bad, Megan thinks to herself as she jogs across Guadalupe Street.

Standing outside, the small hut with a blue awning, Megan orders a breakfast burrito with no chile, instead of the dog she planned on. Figuring it'd be better for her.

Walking as she eats, Megan starts to feel better. Maybe after work, she'll try and call Lee, ask why she was following her this morning. Smelling apricot blossoms, Megan smiles and continues on her way.

17

Katie Lee is on the verge of blowing a gasket. If she has to stay cramped in this Winnebago for another moment, she is going to scream. And Wanda, well she's been of no help what-so-ever. Telling Katie to quit whining, and that this whole adventure is her idea. Katie just waves the old lady off, telling Wanda she wants to be alone.

"Fine with me, you old bat," Wanda spits as she leaves the room.

Shaking a fist at the closed door, Katie gazes out the window, her thoughts angry and frustrating. That fool Calvin is making things worse. Her daughter will never be able to trust her if she believes she and her family are in harm's way. Buffoon!

When Lyman called earlier this morning and filled her in on all the details of his lackey's mishaps, Katie was ready to fly through the roof. All he has to do is find out if this woman is truly who Katie thinks she is. Not scare her into hiding.

Thank goodness no one called the police yet, Katie sighs, imagining the chaos that would ensue. How could any of them explain what is happening?

Maybe she'll call Lyman back and tell him to get that slough out of Santa Fe before he ruins everything. She'll take over upon her arrival.

Pressing a button next to her, Katie Lee summons Wanda back to her quarters, knowing her friend will be upset that she's being disturbed once again. Even though it's her job.

Wanda stomps through the door, bouncing off the walls. "Now, what do you want?"

"Get me Lyman on the phone."

"Why?" Wanda seems agitated, more than normal.

"I want him to get Calvin Kramer out of Santa Fe, and then from here on out, I'll be in
charge."

"Really," Wanda's voice softens. "Do you think that's such a good idea, Katie. I mean come on, so the guy makes a couple of mistakes."

"A couple of mistakes. My daughter believes she's being stalked. What happens if they call the cops? I might never get the chance to see her, again."

"What are you talking about. You didn't do anything wrong. It's those people who stole your baby, who've kept her all of these years without even letting you know she's alive. I mean, please. Katie, think about it. They left their dead son in place of your live girl. What kind of sick people are they? From my stand point I think the whole clan should be sent up river."

Katie averts her eyes. "I knew she was alive."

"What?"

"Yes. Clair Conner contacted me, and I told her to keep Burtrum. Granted, what they did was terribly wrong, and I'm sure over the years the guilt has done more harm than good, but still, there was no way I could've raised a child in my condition. How could I take care of a baby if I couldn't take care of myself? And then when I figured out what Lyman had done, with the car and all, there was no way I was going to let him know my child was alive. I'm sure the Conner's have done a wonderful job with my little girl."

"You, poor woman." Love resonates in Wanda's words. "Why don't we wait and talk to Calvin when we arrive in Santa Fe. Find out what's really going on, and then we'll call Lyman. Okay?"

Exasperated, Katie sighs. "All right, if that's what you think is best."

"Yes, I do. Now why don't you take a little nap."

"I'm not tired. I think I'll just sit here and daydream."

"Okay then, suit yourself. If you need anything else just buzz, okay?"

"Yes, yes."

Wanda stands still for a moment studying Katie Lee as she looks out the window. Since the beginning of this little escapade Wanda has had doubts. She knows that in the end someone is going to get hurt, and she sure as hell doesn't want it to be Katie.

Peering out the window and wondering why Wanda won't leave, Katie is softened by the light green sage bushes surrounding an abandoned adobe structure blending in with the landscape. Katie's never seen anything so beautifully innocent.

Listening as Wanda finally departs, an unknown calmness soaks into Katie, making her smile. The idea of seeing her daughter for the first time sends shivers down her spine as she pulls her shawl tighter around her shoulders.

❂ ❂ ❂

Jed Conner can't believe Jane's behavior. To her, everything is hunky-dory. She needs a wake-up call, and to lay off the booze for a while. Has *he*, driven her to this?

Checking his cell phone for missed calls, Jed is curious as to why his lawyer/PI, Allen Ruiz, hasn't returned his call. He pays him plenty. You'd think he'd jump when Jed says jump. Jed wants the low-down on the jerk following his daughter, and that strange woman, Megan, who's mysteriously appeared out of nowhere.

This is all a big mess. They should've come out with the truth years ago when they first found out Lee's mother was still alive. But by then they'd become a family, and they thought it best for Lee to just be who she thinks she is.

Now, they can lose everything, end up in prison, never see Lee again. That would be the worst, because even though Jed knows she isn't his blood, he's always felt like she's his real daughter, and the idea of never seeing her again rips at his heart.

Pulling over to the side of the road, Jed parks his Pathfinder by the De Vargas Parkway. It's quiet here, all of the

Mexican men who gather in the morning looking for work are gone. Must be a productive day in Santa Fe, Jed Conner laughs, resting his head back, hoping Allen will call him soon.

❀ ❀ ❀

Calvin Kramer tilts his head over the porcelain toilet bowl and pukes for a third time. The coke he drank didn't help, neither did the last of the warm Beck's sitting on the table. He's really gone overboard this time, and now he's paying.

Shaking, he staggers back to the bedroom and kicks a glass bottle lying on the floor. Stinging his toe, he jumps around trying to ease the pain.

He needs to stop this self-abuse. He's beginning to lose control. Katie Lee is supposed to arrive today and Lyman has made it perfectly clear that if he doesn't meet her, then he can pretty much count on being out of a job. And Calvin knows that won't fly with Carla. She's gotten used to a certain life style.

So, all in all, Calvin Kramer finds himself stuck between a rock and a hard place. It seems that's where he's been anchored his whole life. People taking advantage of him because they know he'll never stand up for himself. He always wants to please his superiors, make them notice him. Well, they did, and here he is today.

Lifting his wrist, Calvin squints at his watch and sees that it's almost eleven o'clock. He has to get going, but has no energy, no drive. Calvin feels downright depressed. Lyman should've made this trip himself. He's the one freaking out over this woman, whomever she is. Maybe if he had a little more information about what's going on, he'd be more eager to complete this absurd mission.

Deciding a hot shower might lighten his mood, Calvin rolls off the bed and stands up as the room spins around him. Freezing for a moment, he takes a step, and stumbles to the bathroom.

❋　❋　❋

Megan Masterson's body jolts back to life as she savors every bite of her burrito. As the food sweeps through her stomach, she begins to feel better, but still can't rid herself of this nagging sensation gnawing at the back of her brain.

The Conner's have made quite the imprint on her, and she thinks about her own family, and how she herself will never be able to meet her real mom because she died at child birth. Megan was raised by the Masterson's, of Edina, Minnesota, since she was six days old. So, except for the DNA part, they are her true family.

Tossing the burrito wrapper into a trash can outside the Bistro, Megan counts to ten before pulling open the blue door. Danny is right there to meet her, as if he's been watching for her.

"We need to talk," he demands, as he whips past her and ducks into his smelly office.

"Well, hello to you, too," Megan whispers under her breath, as she follows him.

"Close the door," he orders.

Megan does as she is told and then leans against the wall. The stench from his work shoes and constant body order sends Megan reeling, and for a moment believes she'll lose her breakfast.

"So, we've got a problem."

"Oh, yeah," Megan says nonchalantly.

"Yeah. It seems I've been getting a few complaints about you."

"From whom?"

"Well, for starters, those women on Friday."

"What women?"

"You know perfectly well what I'm talking about. The dessert incident."

"They totally misunderstood me, and if that cow wouldn't have interrupted and let me finish, they would have heard me say, I'll be right back."

"That's not the point. They said you were rude to them."

"I was, after she smarted off to me. Listen, Danny, you know as well as I do that I'm not rude to people unless they're rude to me first."

"What you need is to keep your mouth shut and do your job."

Megan's temperature rises as she snake-eyes Danny. She can't believe he's talking to her like this. Who does this ass think he is? She can get a job anywhere, and probably one with more respect than she's ever getting here. Megan is nearing her third year of working for Danny, and has experienced a few outbursts from him. But lately, over the past couple of months, he seems to have keyed her out for his wrath.

"Listen, Danny, you have no right talking to me like that. I've been with you for quite a long time now, and have put up with more crap than at any other restaurant. But if you think you can stand there with your condescending attitude and tell me that I need to keep my mouth shut, well then, you can go to hell."

"You know, Megan, this is why you're not going anywhere in life. You always have to say something that gets you in trouble. Why don't you go home today and think about if you want to work here anymore, and let me know tomorrow."

"I won't have to let you know tomorrow. I quit today. You know what Danny, everyone thinks you're just this great guy who will do anything for anyone, but you're not. You do things for people so that you can hold it over their heads later, and in my book, that's pathetic." Turning around, she storms out of the office. "Ass-hole," she hisses.

"Get out, get the hell out of my restaurant," Danny yells at the top of his lungs, his face getting so red, Megan believes his head will explode.

Megan's anger rattles through her whole body. She needs a drink and needs one now, heading in the direction of Tiny's Lounge.

The bar is dark as she pulls open the wooden doors to the speakeasy style room. Once her eyes adjust, Megan notices she is the only patron, figuring she arrived before the lunch rush.

"Why good morning, young lady."

Megan flinches at the voice and peers in the shadows to see where it came from.

"Morning." Pulling out a stool, she sits down.

The elderly bartender boxes up in front of Megan and asks. "What can I get you today?"

"A Bass, please."

"Are you old enough to be drinking?" The old man teases.

Not really being in the mood, Megan says. "I was yesterday." Smiling slightly.

Sensing his only customer desires to be left alone, the man grabs the beer and says, "Would you like a glass?"

"No thanks, the bottle is fine."

Setting the amber ale on a coaster in front of Megan, he announces. "That'll be four dollars, ma'am."

Megan fishes in her pockets and pulls out a ten. Slipping the bill on the bar, she watches as he makes change, and places it in front of her.

"Thank-you," he says, walking away.

Dread floats into Megan's head as she takes a sip of the English brew. What is she going to do? Maybe now is the perfect time to bolt out of Santa Fe, maybe go back home to Minneapolis. She's sure her parents will welcome her with open arms, maybe even start to accept the fact that she's a lesbian. That will certainly make living near her family bearable. Being forty, she'd think by now they'd gotten used to the idea.

Or, maybe she should be bold. Head up to San Francisco, start living her dream. Try to be happy for once in her life, rid herself of the feelings of not really knowing who she really is.

Finishing the beer quickly, Megan slides her seat back,

and not seeing anyone, walks out of the dim, dark bar. She's blasted by the sun-light, dazzling her at first until she slips her sunglasses on.

The warm afternoon welcomes her, as Megan Masterson heads home.

Burtrum Lee Conner is beside herself. She can't believe Megan got fired. She doesn't seem like the hot headed type Danny described. Now what is she going to do?

She feels like calling the police. Take some of this distress off of her, but knows she can't. Clair's been pretty insistent, convincing Lee it's not practical getting the officials involved, but she's never said why.

Instinctively, Lee finds herself pulling into her driveway. She hasn't even been thinking about where she is going, or what she is going to do next, and is glad her homing device has led her here.

It'll be good for her to clean the place up a little, try to chill in the warm blanket comfort of her home. Rid the house of the sense of intrusion.

Stepping onto the back porch, Lee unlocks the door, suddenly feeling an eerie vibration float over her. Shaking her head, she attributes it to the recent events.

Sniffing as she lumbers into the kitchen, she smells something sour coming from the sink. Remembering she hasn't done the dishes since Thursday, she runs water over the crusty heap, squirting a healthy dose of soap within the crevices.

Before she has a chance to open a window, the phone rings, startling Lee. Drying her hands on the towel, she reaches for the receiver hanging from its cradle on the wall.

"Hello," she says, wondering how smart it is to be answering the phone.

"Birdy, oh, Lee, thank heaven, you're alive."

"You're being a little too dramatic, Grandma. Just calm down, take a deep breath and relax. I'm fine."

"When I woke up, you were gone, with no note. I thought you'd been kidnapped." Her breathing is deep and heavy. "I'm so scared, Birdy, why didn't you leave a note?"

"I'm sorry, Grandma. I didn't plan on being gone so long. I didn't mean to worry you."

"Where'd you go?"

"To find, Megan, who just got fired and left in a huff. I missed her by a few minutes."

"So, why are you at your house?"

"I don't know, I just landed here, and I feel good. I think I'm going to straighten up, open some windows, clean a little."

"Do you want some help?"

"No, Grandma, I need a little space, if you don't mind."

Her tone vibratos disappointment. "Oh, okay."

Changing the subject. "Hey, have you heard from Mom and Dad, yet?"

"Nope, nothing." Lee hears her grandma shake her head back and forth. "Go figure, the one time we really need them, they blow us off."

"I'm sure that's not the case. Why don't you just call them?"

"Why don't you?"

"Because this isn't my mess." A tense silence crosses the line, and Lee clears her throat. "It's our mess."

"No, you're right, Burtrum," Clair said, using her birth name, one which Lee hates. "I have to go."

Clair hangs up before Lee has a chance to rebuttal. "Grandma, Grandma," she bellows into the mouth piece.

Slamming the phone down, Lee takes a deep breath. The kitchen is gross. She'll be glad to get all the garbage out of her house.

※　※　※

Calvin Kramer feels a million times better as he steps out of the stale motel room. The sun is bright and the air crisp, as he walks to the parking lot. His light mood doesn't last long as Carla comes racing back to his brain. Where is she? Why hasn't she returned his calls? Granted she's mad, but her actions are a little extreme.

His face flushes as he ponders the possibility that maybe his adoring wife has moved out.

That will kill him.

Calvin knows he's working himself up for no reason. There has to be a simple explanation. She lost her phone, went to Tahoe to visit her mother. Trivial reasons why she hasn't called back yet.

"Damn-you, Sheila," Calvin hisses. His mother-in-law always seems to have some kind of ailment, requiring Carla to make the three-hour drive to Truckee. Sometimes she stays for over a week. Those times are hard on him. Being alone and having to take care of himself.

He can, of course. Calvin Kramer is no dummy. He just prefers it when Carla makes him dinner and does the laundry and housework. It seems so natural. They both having their little roles. Until Carla's mother interferes.

Snorting the air like a bloodhound, Calvin smells something spicy, making his mouth water. From across the street, tantalizing vapors rise and wisp into the breeze. Looking both ways before crossing, Calvin notices a train station behind the building, and meandering over to the stand housing flyers and brochures, he reaches for a schedule, and slips the pamphlet into his back pocket.

He's always been fascinated with trains, and knows the Santa Fe Railway has been around for a long time. It'd be a fantasy come true. It would make this whole trip worthwhile if he can go for a ride.

Katie Lee won't be arriving until later this evening, so that gives him the whole afternoon free. He's done with this PI business, he's going to start enjoying his little vacation, because it might be his last. When he meets with Ms. Lee, he'll turn over all the information he has, and be on his way home. But first, a little fun.

Heading back toward the restaurant, he feels like there's a jack hammer at work in his stomach, as he enters through the heavy paneled doors.

He is well ahead of the rush as a brightly dressed woman leads him to a small table against the wall. The place is empty, and Calvin's glad, because then he'll get fast service.

"Good afternoon, how are you?" A heavily laced Spanish voice booms in.

Calvin glances up from his menu and says. "I'm fine, thank you."

"May I start you off with something to drink?"

"Yes, I'll take a house margarita."

"With or without salt?"

"With."

"Do you know what you'd like to order, sir?"

Calvin scans the items, recognizing none of them. "How about the taco plate."

"Beef, chicken, or shredded carne."

"Which is best?"

"I'd recommend trying one of each."

"I can do that?"

"Yes."

"Then let's go for it."

"Will that be all?"

"For now."

"Great, so that's one house margarita, and the taco plate."

"Yes, thanks."

Satisfied, Calvin relaxes as the waiter quickly comes back with his drink. The light green liquid inside the clear glass reminds Calvin of Gatorade. The drink is probably poured from a faucet.

Sliding the plate in front of Calvin, the waiter announces. "This is pretty hot, so be careful."

As the server turns away, Calvin touches his plate, burning his fingertips. The man turns around and jokingly says, "Told ya!"

Calvin smiles, nodding his head.

He's more famished than he thought, as he finishes slopping up the last of the beans with a sopapilla. Still slightly hungry, he thinks about ordering more, but doesn't want to get too full, so he pulls out the schedule to check the times.

Discovering there's a train leaving at one o'clock, which is in fifteen minutes, he signals for his check. Laying a twenty on the table, Calvin shuffles between the now gathering crowd, making it just in time to the locomotive, as the whistle screams and the conductor bellows out. "All-aboard!"

Clair paces back and forth, forth and back, fuming with every step. Lee doesn't grasp the seriousness of this matter. Isn't she at all worried that at any moment she can be snatched up and they'll never see her again.

The whole situation is really starting to get to Clair, as she pours herself a Cabernet. The red wine soothes her nerves temporarily, but she feels the anger boiling inside her will eventually erupt.

How could she have let this happen? They'd been so careful over the years keeping her out of the public eye. Clair gathers Katie must've seen Lee's photo on the website for the B&B. She didn't even think anything of it, until it was too late.

Clair's disappointment in her son and wife, flares along with her fear. How can they be so complacent at a time like this? They should get Lee out of the city, maybe even the state. Leave town for a while until everything calms down.

But they've taken no action. She hasn't even heard from either of them today and it's getting to be well past noon. Shaking her head, Clair sits down on the couch, and rubs her face with her hands. What is she going to do?

"Clair, are you all right?"

Jane's voice makes Clair rise suddenly, she reaches her hand out for the arm of the sofa to steady herself. "Jesus, Jane, do you have to sneak up on me."

"I thought you heard me."

"Well, I didn't. I guess I'm just lost in thought. What are you doing here, and why haven't you or Jed called me?"

"I don't know why Jed hasn't called. But I just went to the Casa Magdalena, and Lee isn't there. Do you know anything about this?"

"Of course, she stayed here last night, and this morning she thought it best if she laid low, and I agreed."

"So, where is she?"

"At her house?"

"What? Doesn't she know it's not safe there?"

"She told me she doubts the culprit will return because she hasn't been around since Friday."

"That's nonsense. I'm going over there right now and get her. She shouldn't be by herself, and I can't believe you agreed to this."

Clair takes a deep breath, counts to ten and then exhales. "I didn't have much of a failed adventure. "So, I laid down on the couch and fell to sleep, while your daughter snuck out."

Jane flops on the couch in the same spot Clair just occupied. "What are we going to do? Heaven only knows what these people are like. If they get their hands on Lee, we might not ever see her again, do you realize that Clair?"

"Yes, and the fact that all three of us could wind up in prison. To be honest, I'm way too old to be doing any jail time. I think what we need to do is tell Lee exactly what's going on. We've been lying her whole life, maybe now's the time to come clean."

"Clair, are you crazy. Do you know what that could do to her?"

"It might help. For a long time now your daughter has been living her life in a cloud. Not knowing what she wants to be, or even attempting to start a relationship. It's as though she's lost, and I believe the only way to snap her out of this, is to tell her who and what she really is?"

"And are you going to be the one to do it?"

"No, Jane. I thought the three of us would tell her together."

"I don't know, Clair. We need to talk to Jed first. A thing like this could put Lee over the edge and we won't have to worry about her being kidnapped because she'll probably not want to have anything to do with us after that."

"That's a chance we'll have to take. Lee's a smart girl, just confused, and I truly believe that by being up front with her, it's going to help in the long run."

Jane, becoming adamant, quickly stands up and says. "Listen to me, Clair Conner. Until you get the okay from both me and Jed, I don't want you to mention any of this to anyone. Do you understand? This is *our* business and you have to learn to respect us."

"Don't be snide with me, Jane Conner, you made it *my*

business the moment you told me of the deed. The instant those words spilled out of your mouth, it became just as much of a responsibility for me, as you. And don't you forget that. Lee is the main concern here, and her welfare is at stake. I love that girl too much to just stand around and pretend everything will be all right. Because deep down we both know it won't be unless we start doing something about it immediately. Now, where's Jed?"

Clair is steaming, she can barely stand still. Her hands shake and face flushes. What she needs to do is calm down before she has another anxiety attack.

Jane comes over to her. "Clair, are you all right. Here, sit down. You shouldn't be getting yourself so worked up over this."

"Not worked up! Listen, Jane, this is serious, you both need to get more involved. The first thing to do is go get Lee and bring her here. She shouldn't be alone."

"Yes, you're right about that. Why don't you just lay down and rest while I go get her. Should I call first?"

"No, just go over there. If you call her, it might scare her off, and she'll run. You know how stubborn she can be."

"Okay, Clair, I'll do that." Jane pats the older woman's shoulder, trying not to get her anxious again. What they don't need is for Clair to kick the bucket. "I'll be right back, okay."

"All right, Jane." The two women stare at each other. "And listen, I'm really sorry if I snapped at you, I'm just worried."

"Yes, I know, and I apologize too." Jane bends over and kisses Clair on the forehead. "I'll only be about a half hour, okay?"

"Good!" Clair watches as her daughter-in-law walks out the back door. Even though over the years the two have had their scuffs, Clair knows Jane is a good woman and at times feels that what she did so many years ago affects her relationship with Lee.

Jane wheels out of the driveway and onto Bishops Lodge Road. Unsnapping her purse, she fumbles for her flask. Twisting the cap off, she takes a long hard pull, feeling courage flow through her. She's never been good at handling stress, and right now Jane Conner can't think of a more stressful situation.

Megan's mood isn't getting any better as she scampers through the rail yard listening to the cat calls coming from the drunken bums. A shrill whistle pierces her ears as the antique locomotive announces its upcoming departure.

Struck by an idea, she decides to go to Lamy. She's never been out to the tiny town, and figures the adventure will surely lift her spirits.

Barely making it on time, Megan boards the old-west style car, and is suddenly hit with scents and odors reminding her of the 1800's. The train jerks forward, tossing Megan against a man sitting in the aisle seat.

Slightly giggling, she apologizes. "Oh, I'm so sorry."

The man side-eyes her and growls.

"Nice," Megan whispers to herself, wondering if maybe this isn't such a good escape after all.

Bouncing down the row, she spots a mini-bar at the end of the cabin and heads in that direction. Another drink won't hurt. What else does she have to do?

After ordering a vodka and tonic, Megan slowly heads out to the open flatbed. The train bounces back and forth, as it chugs along the tracks, sending Megan swaying. Feeling a little off balance, she sits down and takes a sip of her cocktail. A sudden ease begins to envelope her as she senses that everything is going to work out. After all, don't things happen for a reason?

Reaching in her coat pocket, Megan draws out a cigarette from a crumpled pack of Camel Lights, and digs deeper for some matches. The first three blow out before she can even get them to the tip, but then the forth catches hold and Megan inhales deeply, feeling the tingle of nicotine coarse through her veins.

She seldom smokes and the rush makes her head spin, as the train picks up speed. For a moment Megan believes she's going to upchuck, and stomps out the cigarette on the wooden floor boards. Tossing the extinguished butt into a trashcan strapped to a metal pole, she licks her briny lips, and spits over the rail.

Shivering, Megan wraps her arms across her chest and waddles back into the warmth of the cabin. Most of the seats are occupied as she scans the car.

Eyeing an empty spot at the back, Megan heads toward it, this time trying not to knock into anyone as the train rocks. She recognizes a man, but can't place his face. Probably a customer from the Bistro, she thinks, sliding into the cold leather bench.

Resting her head on the metal bar behind the seat, Megan closes her eyes and listens to the soft rumbling of the train's wheels on the tracks. The sounds are hypnotic, as Megan Masterson drifts into sleep.

❋　❋　❋

Calvin Kramer can't believe his eyes. Is that really the woman who was with Burtrum Lee Conner? But where is she? Calvin studies the girl. Her red hair, and porcelain skin, makes her quite attractive.

He'll have to keep an eye on her.

The train moves in rhythmic motions. This isn't so bad, Calvin thinks to himself, as he watches the brown landscape pass him by.

❋　❋　❋

Jed Conner is pissed. Jane told him Lee will be at her house, and she isn't. Allen, his lawyer/PI warned him that he needs to find his daughter and find her fast, before these people kidnap her.

That whole night back then seems dreamy now, like it never really happened. The accident, just a figment of his imagination. To this day, Jed Conner has never regretted his and Jane's decision in the woods. Standing there shivering as he surveyed the scene. How Katie Lee ever survived was beyond belief. He had checked for pulses, and found no beating hearts on either of them. Maybe the cold had slowed her rate down, Jed figured, when he first heard Katie Lee was alive.

It was all over the newscasts in New Mexico back then. For almost a week, the air waves were filled with the tragic story. Maybe that's when they should've done the right thing, given Lee back to her real mother. But by then they'd become so attached, they couldn't let her go, *wouldn't*, let her go!

Trying the front door again, Jed peers through the window, but sees no movement. "Damn-it!" He hisses, kicking an imaginary stone off the porch.

Fumbling for his cell phone buried in his pants pocket, Jed pushes the speed dial, and begins talking.

"She's not here either." He's silent, as he listens.

"I don't know," his voice irritated.

"Well, we can't waste much more time, we've got to find her before they do."

Jed stammers in his place. "Don't tell me to relax. Do you know what's on the line here? Everything!"

"Yeah, yeah, I'll call you later." Flipping the cell off, he tosses it back and forth in his hands, shaking his head in disgust. His wife is useless, telling him to relax, ha!

Maybe she's at Clair's, Jed thinks, returning to his car. The sun is higher in the sky, and a reflection from the chrome bumper clips Jed in the eye. Stumbling off the curb, he catches himself before falling to the pavement.

"Shit," he mutters, standing up straight and brushing himself down.

18

Lee careens her neck over the window sill and watches as her father drives away. She has no desire to see or chat with anyone. Especially, her parents. They've been hiding a secret from her all these years, and what could be so bad that would cause this much commotion?

At first she believed the chaos was the consequence of her scientific conception, but then, as the situation developed, and her family became tight lipped, Lee concurred that there is something more than meets the eye.

Flustered and annoyed, Lee knows she and only she has to get to the bottom of this. Somehow she'll find Megan, and ask for help. Even though they're barely acquaintances, Lee senses a bond between them.

Jetting out the door, Lee hopes Megan's ex-boss will give her an address. Spring winds kick in as she slides behind the wheel of her grandma's car. Yup, it's time to start playing Nancy Drew, Lee chuckles to herself.

178 • MARY MAURICE

❋   ❋   ❋

"Go to hell, Jed." Jane tosses her cell phone on the seat next to her. "It's bad enough that I have to deal with your mother, much less you," She curses out loud, speeding down Paseo de Peralta, paying no attention to the posted limits.

Deciding to just go home, Jane feels her head begin to pound, creasing pain rips through her left frontal lobe, and she wishes she hadn't taken that sip of Vodka. What was she thinking?

Cruising past the Veterans Cemetery, Jane heads out to Los Companas. Hoping to take a nice long hot bath when she gets home. Relax these muscles, give herself a chance to unwind, think about everything that's happening. Maybe find a solution in the bubbles floating around her.

A crooked smile creases her lips, as Jane realizes this was bound to happen sooner or later. After all, isn't that one of nature's laws, everything comes back to bite you in the ass.

❋   ❋   ❋

Megan wakes up, hitting her head against the window. Waving her hands in front of her face, she tries to grasp her surroundings. The growl of the cars stopping puts Megan back into perspective as she remembers she's on the Lamy Train. Regrouping, she tries to recall her dream, but can't conjure up the memory.

"Man!" She whispers, wiping her sweaty forehead, and checking the time. She only meant to close her eyes for a second, give them a little rest, but thirty minutes later she re-opens them, and here she is in good old Lamy.

"Lamy, all out for Lamy," the conductor announces as he sailor steps up and down the aisle.

Feeling a little groggy and sick to her stomach, Megan hopes the fresh air and solid ground will help her feel better.

The soft breezes wisp around the newly budding trees, as she steps off the train. Spotting a refreshment stand on the other side of the platform, Megan beelines over to the shack to buy a bottle of water. Her body is totally over heated and needs to chill, she diagnoses, as she sits under an old Cottonwood tree, gulping the cool liquid.

Calvin mills around the platform of the small train station, trying not to be conspicuous. The one thing he doesn't want to do is bring attention to himself. He doesn't want the girl to spot him. Well, she's more like a woman, but dresses like a boy. She must be one of *those*, he snickers.

The sun beats down on his unprotected head, as Calvin starts to sweat uncontrollably. This can't be good, he thinks, spotting a shady area across the tracks. Plopping down on a rickety bench, Calvin licks his lips with a parched tongue, and surveys the grounds for a drinking fountain. He sees none, just a lean-to with an attendant selling goods. Shaking his head, Calvin feels the accommodations have a lot to be desired.

Leaning over and peering into Megan's apartment window, Lee sees nothing. Danny had no issues with giving her Megan's address, which she thought odd. Usually employers are a little more private with employee information.

Sitting on a cinder block by the door, Lee contemplates waiting, but has no idea how long she might have to. And being exposed like this, isn't the smartest thing to be doing.

Lee's stomach begins to growl, as she remembers she needs to eat.

Heading to the Zia Diner for a sandwich, Lee figures she can get the food to go, and then come back here to stake out the place. What else does she have to do?

Katie Lee breaths deeply as she rolls out into the New Mexico sunshine. The Southwest beams glare brightly on her face, as she reaches for her sunglasses dangling around her neck.

"Oh, Wanda, this is so beautiful. I don't remember it being like this."

Wanda stumbles out of the RV behind Katie, not really impressed by the scenery. "Probably because it was so long ago when you were here, that things are a lot different than what you remember? Plus, it was winter and you were about to have a baby."

"Yes, yes, I know." Katie wheels her motorized chair around. "But you can't deny that these mountains are something special?" Katie Lee gazes at the still snow capped Sangre de Cristo mountain range and feels a sense of peace. A sense of familiarity.

"Let's go for a walk," Wanda suggests.

Sensing something is wrong with her long-time friend, Katie puts on the brakes as Wanda shuffles beside her.

"No, wait a minute. What's going on? I thought you'd be glad to take a little break from home?"

"I am, I just wished it wasn't here."

"I don't understand, Wanda, you've never been to the Southwest before. Why don't you like it?"

"Maybe because of what happened here all those years ago."

"Yes, but none of that will matter once I see my daughter. Right?"

"I don't know, Katie. I'm just a little weary, that's all."

Katie turns her head around so she can see Wanda. "You don't have to worry about anything, it's not like we're going to stay long. I'm just going to meet with Burtrum Lee, and ask her if she'd like to come and live with me for a while in San Francisco, and then go from there. That's all. It's really no big deal, right?"

Wanda stiffens her jaw. "I suppose," she says, patting Katie's hand. "You don't even know if it's really her."

"Yes, I do. A mother has these feelings."

"Something I'll never know about," Wanda whispers with regret.

"What did you say?" Katie asks, unfolding a piece of paper.

"Oh, nothing." Wanda starts walking again. "Shall we check out the plaza?"

"Yes, that sounds like a grand idea." Katie Lee studies

the printout of the B&B's web- site where she first saw her daughter's picture. The resemblance is uncanny. Even Lyman was taken aback.

When she first saw the photo, she wanted to go immediately to New Mexico, but Lyman suggested he send someone down first, just to check things out, to make sure it is her. "After all, the situation is very fragile," he said. "Why don't you let me handle it."

Why she said yes was beyond her, especially after finding out the truth about what Lyman did to their car. She thought he'd changed after all of these years, but apparently, it was all a rouse. How could she be so stupid?

She'll be damned if he ever gets his hands on her daughter!

The calming earth tones of the small city comfort Katie, as the dry air helps her breath. The high altitude must benefit her respiratory system, she believes, breathing more freely here than at home. She might want to think about having a second house in the Southwest.

Clair Conner closes her eyes and presses the cold washcloth against her temples. The splitting headache Jane brought on, isn't going away. Even after taking three aspirin.

Telling herself maybe she should lie back down, Clair tiptoes to the living room and gently stretches out on the couch. Her heart is pounding hard as she rests her hand on her chest, trying to slow it down.

She knows the stress from the situation is getting to her,

and she's trying to remain calm. It's not like she can just ignore what is going on.

Shutting her lids for a moment, Clair is quickly swallowed into the black hole of sleep.

❋   ❋   ❋

The water revives Megan, as she watches the people buzzing around on the platform. Few, if any, have dared to wander through the deserted town, nothing of interest sparking their imaginations.

Suddenly, out of the corner of her eye she spots a man coming toward her and recognizes him from earlier. Shivers splatter across her body as goose bumps appear on her arms. A sensation of someone trouncing over her grave vibrates her nerves.

Scared, Megan rises, moving away from him. She doesn't know what it is, but he creeps her out. Maybe it's the forceful way he is approaching her, or the crazed, overheated penetration gleaming in his eyes.

Does this have something to do with Lee Conner?

Behaving cautiously, Megan boards the train, feeling safer by surrounding herself with people. He won't try anything in front of a group, she hopes. The question is though, what does he want with her?

Shaking her head, trying to rattle the paranoia growing, she glances behind her and sees him eyeing her through the window. Sweat begins to drizzle down her body, as Megan swallows another mouthful of water, hoping it'll cool her down once again.

Hearing footsteps thump along the flatbed, Megan looks behind her, and starts shaking. Man, this guy really has her spooked, but why?

Paying close attention to his progress, she sees him enter the door to the car behind her, and moving to the exit, Megan jumps off the train, and darts to the caboose. Ducking into a seat, she slumps down, hiding in the shadows of the afternoon.

The bellowing train whistle relieves Megan's mind, as she prays the stranger won't come searching for her back here. The locomotive chugs forward, banging Megan's knees into the hard wooden bench in front of her.

Calvin Kramer watches as Megan leaps off the locomotive. He tries pushing his way through the crowd gathering at the bar, but they don't let him pass. He loses sight of his prey, and isn't sure if she got back on or not.

He's hoping to find her and inquire about Lee Conner, but instead it seems the Conner's have filled her head and she is frightened of him.

Calvin means no harm.

All of his instincts tell him she's on the train, and that he'll have to become invisible if he wants to speak with her. He'll wait for the perfect time when they reach Santa Fe. Find a corner he can pull her into, and then get the information he needs to impress Katie Lee. After all, it's really *her* he has to answer to.

Smiling to himself, Calvin watches the empty landscape pass by, still unable to see any beauty in the starkness.

❂ ❂ ❂

Lee hears the shrill train whistle as it pulls into the Santa Fe rail yard. The station consists of a ticket office, and a small snack bar. The tiny building is decorated in white adobe, with a red brick slate roof.

Children, playing on the flatbed, scream and wave at her as the train rattles down the track. Smiling back, Lee experiences a sense of euphoria. Freedom floats in her heart, as the gleeful sounds tantalize her.

Waiting for the carriage to pass by, Lee watches the faces lining the windows, and seeing Megan's pressed against a glass pane, starts waving and yelling out her name.

"Megan, Megan!"

Jogging along, Lee waits at the exit ramp for the passengers to disembark.

Searching over the crowd, she sees no sign of Megan, as the last person gets off.

"*Pisssst, pissssst.*" Lee turns to where the hissing is coming from and notices Megan hiding behind an old box car, motioning her to come over.

Looking around, she dashes over to where Megan remains hidden. Out of breath, and a little anxious, Lee rounds the corner of the car.

"Megan, what are you doing? How did you get off? I watched everyone leave out the same door."

"I snuck out the back when no one was watching. Listen, there's some really weird guy stalking me. I think it's your man, but I'm not sure. Anyway, he followed me when we were in Lamy, and I almost missed the train coming back when I tried to ditch him."

"Where is he now?"

"I don't know. Somewhere close, I'm sure. We've got to get out of here." Suddenly, Megan looks puzzled. "What are you doing here?"

"Searching for you. I went by the Bistro earlier and they said you got canned. Then, I stopped by your apartment, but you weren't there. So, I decided to go get some food from Zia, and here I am."

"Why are you looking for me?" Megan's suspicious.

"I need your help?"

"With what?"

"You know, figuring this whole mess out." Lee searches the tracks. "Where is this guy, what does he look like? If you point him out to me, then I can go talk to him and get things settled once and for all."

"Whoa, wait a minute. First, I'm not even sure if this man is who we think he is, and second, I don't know if I want to get involved, and third, do you really think it's safe to go up to a guy who's trying to kidnap you?"

"I don't think he wants to hurt me. He probably just needs to ask me some questions."

"I don't trust him."

"We don't even know him." Lee bows her head. "I'm just glad you're okay." She play-punches Megan in the arm. "Hey, I'm starving and need to eat."

"Yeah, me too. Why don't we go back to my place and I can make us a couple sandwiches, I think I have some turkey."

"That sounds good. Then you can tell me everything that happened to you on your field trip."

The two women are silent as they stroll through the abandoned field surrounding Megan's apartment. The afternoon sun has melted away the chill of the morning, and at last the day is warm.

Inhaling deeply as they walk past an apricot tree, Lee says. "It sure is a nice day."

"Yeah, I just wish I was doing something else besides getting fired and followed," Megan giggles, feeling a little better with Lee at her side.

"Well, maybe your afternoon will get better." Lee pats Megan on the shoulder as she unlocks the door.

Stepping into Megan's apartment, Lee remarks, "I really like your place, it feels homey."

Megan turns toward Lee. "No pun intended?" Megan chuckles.

"What, huh? I'm not sure I know what you're talking about.

"You know! Homey, homo."

Lee begins laughing as Megan slips into the kitchen. "No, no, that's not what I meant. I mean it feels very comfortable, like a home, and not just a house like my parents live in."

"I know. I'm just messing with you." Bumping hips with Lee, Megan turns and opens the fridge, scavenging inside, she picks items up and then sets them back down. Tossing a glad bag full of turkey onto the counter, Megan looks up and asks. "What would you like on your sandwich. Lettuce, tomato, mayo, mustard?"

"My, you certainly are prepared."

"Hey, you can take the waitress out of the restaurant, but not the restaurant out of the waitress."

Lee studies Megan. "So, what happened at the Bistro?"

"I couldn't take it anymore. I was on the verge of slapping someone and that wouldn't have been pretty. You know what I mean."

"Kind of, not really. But in answer to your question, you can make my sandwich like yours."

"That's easy enough."

Lee watches Megan meticulously construct two sandwiches with chips and a pickle. The whole process taking about five minutes at tops.

"I'm impressed," Lee compliments, sitting down at the table next to Megan.

Biting hungrily into her lunch, she sits there chewing, while smiling at Lee.

"So, may I ask you a personal question?" Lee breaks the silence.

"I've been gay all of my life, but I've only known about it since I was twenty-four," Megan chimes in.

"No, that's not what I want to ask."

A little embarrassed, Megan lowers her head, nibbling on the crusts. "Oh," she mutters. "Well, then yeah, sure, what's your question?"

"Do you sense some kind of connection between us? I don't mean sexual, either. I'm straight, and there's no two ways about it."

A slight spark of disappointment flickers in Megan's eyes. "Yeah, I guess. I haven't really thought about it." Liar. It's all she's thought about since they met.

"I'm not sure what it is, but I feel very close to you, like I can tell you anything, and you'll always have my back."

Megan notices sincerity in Lee's words, bringing pools of tears to her eyes. "Yeah, I know what you're talking about. I feel the same. It's like we're related in a way."

"Yes, yes, that's it. But there's no way. I'm an inseminated child."

"So, that rules out us being sisters," Megan chimes.

The two are silent for a moment, Lee pretending to concentrate on her meal, while Megan gazes out the window.

"Yes."

"Yes, what?" Lee inquires.

"I'll help you."

Jumping up, Lee wraps her arms around Megan, and hugs her tight. "Thank-you, thank-you, thank-you," she jubilates, planting a kiss on her cheek.

Megan, face blazing red, playfully pushes Lee away, and standing, picks up her plate and sets the Cornell in the sink.

"We should head back to the rail yard, could be he's still there," Lee states.

"I still don't think that's such a great idea. He might be dangerous."

"Between the two of us, I'll take my chances. I need to get to the bottom of this and nothing's going to stop me. I want to know the truth," Lee's voice cracks.

"Okay, we'll start there, and then see where time takes us." Reaching into the fridge, Megan grabs a couple of waters, and tosses one to Lee. "Here, take this."

Lee juggles the plastic container at first, and then catches it.

"Nice," Megan teases, walking past Lee and opening the door. "After you, Mademoiselle."

Bright sun rays pierce Lee's eyes before she has a chance to put her glasses on. Florescent ameba float in front of her, jellyfish like, in a sea of gray.

❋   ❋   ❋

Calvin Kramer is miffed as he turns from side to side and back and forth trying to catch a glimpse of Megan, but she is nowhere to be seen.

Is there another exit he didn't know about? He thought for sure she'd be coming out the same door everyone else did. He can't believe this has happened a second time. Now, here he stands all alone on the red brick platform; mad, sweltering, and steaming hot.

Winds whirl around him as a sudden gust raises dust into tiny tornadoes. He covers his mouth with his sleeve, but is too late as he swallows the tan sand. Bending over and hacking, Calvin spits, while wiping his mouth with the back of his hand.

He loathes Santa Fe!

Thirst, swelling his tongue, he shuffles to the coke machine and slides three shiny quarters into the slot. Listening as the slugs jingle down, Calvin lifts his finger to the plastic button and pushes. The can tumbles into the black holder, and reaching for the cold beverage, Calvin licks his lips.

He's never tasted anything better in his whole life, he thinks, taking a second swallow, and then burping out loud. What would life be like without Coca-Cola? He asks himself, finishing off the soda and tossing the tin into a trash barrel.

"Ahhhhhh!" He sighs, thinking another one might be good, but decides against it. Recalling his promise to Carla to lay off the poison. Calvin doesn't see what the problem is, it's just soda pop.

At first he thinks it's a mirage, one of those hallucinations a person gets when they're over-worked and over-tired. Squinting, Calvin leans slightly, angling himself for a better view, but staying out of sight.

Could his luck be changing? Has Madame Fate finally turned a kind hand and put Burtrum Lee right in front of him? And she's with that woman.

Suddenly, turning his way, Calvin ducks around the corner of the ticket booth. Peeking out, he watches as the two enter an empty field. Sneaking behind freight cars, and small bushes, Calvin follows them, and watches as they enter an adobe apartment.

His breathing is heavy, his out of shape body not used to such physical activity. He'll have to start working out again when he gets home. Maybe that's one of Carla's reasons for becoming distant toward him.

Realizing that they aren't coming out right away, Calvin scans the area, and seeing an old chair by an abandoned garage, decides to have a seat and wait for them.

Sitting down in the radiating sun, Calvin removes his sports coat, and reaching into the side pocket, retrieves his cell phone. Flipping the casing open, he turns the device off. The last thing he needs now is his phone to ring. Nope, he's too close, and he isn't going to blow things this time.

19

Jed Conner is extremely annoyed with his daughter. He can't find her anywhere. He even went to the Bistro that woman works at, and wasn't surprised to learn she'd been fired. He guessed her character from the get-go. Just another loser, but worse yet, a lesbian loser, whom he is certain is after Lee.

Contemplating the situation, he sits in his car, deciding to head up to Clair's. Maybe everyone is there. Her home has become control central all of a sudden, sneering to himself.

"This whole affair is getting out of hand," he mutters, checking his phone for messages. There are none. Thinking he should call Jane, he listens to his better judgment, and doesn't. He'll wait until he gets to his mom's. Turning onto Bishops Lodge Road, Jed races up the hill, neglecting the thirty-five mile an hour speed limit.

❋ ❋ ❋

Katie Lee is dizzy and a little woozy as she sits in her hotel room waiting for Wanda to get back with her blood pressure medicine. Katie swears she had the bottle last night, but today she can't find it anywhere. She doesn't know what happened. One minute she's feeling like a young girl of eighteen again and the next, she's back to being the crippled sixty-six-year old she is.

She feels like screaming, as her heart begins to palpitate. Rubbing her chest with her hand, she prays this isn't her time. God can't be *that* diabolical to let her get so close to meeting her daughter, only to take her away.

"Is that too much to ask?" She hisses at the ceiling. "You've certainly rained on my parade quiet often in my life, all I ask is just this once, you let the sun shine."

"Katie, Katie, breathe."

Hearing Wanda's voice float over the clouds surrounding her thoughts, Katie feels a hand touch her shoulder.

"Take these, you'll feel a lot better." Placing two pills in Katie's mouth, Wanda holds up a glass of water for her to drink. The frazzled woman sips out of the straw, swallowing the tablets.

"Thanks, Wanda," Katie whispers.

"My word, Katie. I can't believe you lost your heart pills."

Feeling a little more composed, Katie replies. "I swear they were with the rest of my medications last night when we went to bed. I don't know what happened to the bottle."

"Well, you wouldn't need them if you wouldn't get so excited."

"Excited!" Katie tries to scream, but her voice is still a

whisper. "I have every right to be agitated. I'm on the verge of seeing my daughter for the first time, and that Buffon, Calvin Kramer is going to blow it. I can't believe we haven't heard from him at all. I mean, what could he be doing?"

"I'm sure as soon as he gets the chance he'll contact you."

"I think we should call Lyman, see if he's heard anything."

Shuffling over to the window, Wanda pulls the curtain back and stares out. People bustle around on the streets below, like tiny ants with nowhere to go. The sound proof glass keeps the honks and street noise from seeping in.

"We need to be patient, and wait for him to get hold of us." Wanda turns back toward Katie. "Okay?"

"I don't know, Wanda. I've got a feeling something's gone wrong, and I don't know what."

"Katie, honey," Wanda lumbers over to her dear friend and reaches for her hand. Holding it, she says. "You know things will work out, Lyman won't let anything happen. He knows what he's doing and this Kramer guy, I'm sure he's not the duffuss we think he is, after all, he does work for you, right?"

"Yeah, I suppose." Katie wishes Wanda would leave her room, she wants to be alone, not have her standing there trying to make the situation better. The only thing that's going to change Katie's mood, is to see Burtrum. That and only that, will release this anxiety overwhelming her.

"Now, I want you to stay put while I go out for a minute."

"Go out, where are you going? I need you here."

"I'm going to get us something to eat. I'm starving, I thought I'd buy us a couple fajitas from the venders on the Plaza. I'd planned on surprising you, but no, Miss Busy Body had to blow it," Wanda tries to sound mad. "So, what kind do you want, chicken or beef?"

"Neither, I'm not hungry, I'm too upset to eat."

"Well, I think you're being a fuddy-duddy and I'm going to get you one whether you like it or not." Wanda moves toward the door. "I'll be back in about ten minutes, and I'd appreciate it if when I return, your demeanor is better." She smiles at Katie and leaves. At first, Katie feels a sense of relief as the silence of the room comforts her. But then, the dooms day gnawing returns, like an ominous cloud darkening her outlook.

Wanda stops at the front desk to asks the concierge where the pay phones are. When he suggests she use the hotel phone, she insists she'd rather not.

Spotting the row of the almost extinct Ma Bell boxes hanging lonely on a distant wall, Wanda sighs, figuring with the erupting cell phone craze, there'll be no need for land lines much longer.

Digging into her dress pocket, she feels around for her calling card. Squinting in the dim light, Wanda picks up the receiver and begins dialing the 1-800 number, then her pin and finally the number she wants to call.

Maybe a mobile phone would be easier!

She listens as the line rings six times before a perturbed

voice answers. "Hello!"

Wanda squawks. "Lyman?"

❂   ❂   ❂

Shaken by the forceful winds greeting her on the drive home, Jane Conner holds tight to the steering wheel as she turns into her driveway. She's experienced the desert gales before, but these, these are the worst. Whipping the Mercedes back and forth, almost forcing her off the road a couple of times. Granted, she's a little buzzed and her head still aches, but she is in control of her car, that's one thing Jane Conner prides herself on, her ability to drink and drive safely.

Parking, she gets out, and finds the sudden stillness peculiar, kind of eerie. Opening the door to an empty dwelling, she is swallowed in a sense of loneliness; a feeling of lost times when the house was filled with activity. Lee, always scampering around, with Jed stomping through the house searching for some blueprint he's misplaced.

Her home was alive!

Now though, everything has changed. It's just she and the maid who only works three days a week. No wonder she's turned to the bottle, instinctively heading over to the bar and pouring herself a scotch.

Downing the amber liquid, Jane plops down on the cowhide couch that Jed demanded they put in the living room. Leaning her head back against the antler armrest, Jane wonders where Lee might be. She could at least have the courtesy to call, just to let them know she's all right.

Jane believes the best thing to do is for everyone to sit down and talk about this. Clear the air, bring light to the dark times. These people are making a big deal out of nothing. Once they meet Lee, they'll see what a good job they did raising her. Then maybe they'll leave us alone and in peace, and we can get back to being a family.

Jane closes her eyes. A cool relief spills into her. She needs to plan a meeting, get the ball rolling, rendezvous in a safe, neutral space. That's the best solution, Jane decides, wondering at what point did her life become so complicated, as she reaches for her phone to call Jed.

Clair Conner snaps awake, and for a brief moment, her foggy head will not allow her to register where she is. Rubbing her eyes, she sees slight scenes from her dream tip-toe through her memory, suddenly vanishing.

Shivers cover her aged skin as she reaches for the glass of water setting on the end table. Shaking under the strain of the glass, Clair grasps it with both hands and slowly raises it to her lips, swallowing deeply.

Standing on wobbly legs, she slips down the hallway. Panting, she balances herself against a counter in the kitchen. Reaching up, she opens the cabinet, and scrounges around to the back of the shelf. Sliding an old tin can into her hands, she sets it down, and opening the make shift safe, sees the past rush before her eyes.

Worry floods Clair as she removes aged yellow newspaper articles, and a weather worn brown wallet. She can still smell the scent of the leather. Her stomach grumbles tensely, as she hears the crunch of car wheels on the gravel drive-way. Stuffing the evidence into her apron pocket, she prays it's her granddaughter.

❋　❋　❋

Minneapolis, MN 1960

The Masterson's cradle their newborn girl, excited that the adoption was so quick. Sister Beatrice said the child was from New Mexico. The baby had been abandoned on the Alter of a church just days before, with no note or anything.

The newly ordained parents snuggled the baby tighter, deciding to name her, Megan.

❋　❋　❋

Santa Fe, NM 2004

"Oh, darn," Lee blurts, as they stroll down the driveway. "I forgot to use the bathroom, do you mind if we go back?"

"No, not at all," Megan replies, turning around.

Unlocking the door, the two women enter, and Lee rushes in while Megan waits. A sudden knock startles her, and wondering who it could be, she looks out the peephole, but it's covered.

❋　❋　❋

Calvin, hearing voices, ducks down, peeling back the over grown bushes to see who it is. He watches as Megan and Lee head out, and then back to her apartment, apparently they forgot something. This is his chance, now or never.

Standing, he slithers across the small parking lot and perches himself in front of Megan's door. Covering the peephole with his palm.

❂   ❂   ❂

Megan, believing it's her friend Steven, who always does that, opens the door and is greeted with a fist to the face. There's no pain, just this blinding white light, and a warm liquid dribbling down her chin. She feels nothing as she folds to the floor. Waves of rippling consciousness roll over her as everything seems surreal.

Did somebody cold-cock her?

Her eyes, barely open, watch as Lee, unaware of the intruder, sees her sprawled on the tiles, and dashes over to her. Her knees buckle from the blow to the back of the head, as Lee Conner drops down next to Megan.

❂   ❂   ❂

Calvin's sweating like a pig as he carries Lee across the parking lot, hoping no one sees him. Huffing and puffing, he squeezes through a small fence opening and into the abandoned field where he sat earlier, waiting.

Setting her down by the condemned garage, Calvin crawls beneath the mangled door to inspect the space. The stench burns his eyes as they adjust to the darkness.

This is perfect, he thinks, returning to Lee outside. Dragging her into the dirty crypt, he swaggers to the far wall, and sitting her against the cracking brick, removes a roll of duct tape he cleverly snatched from Megan's apartment. Wrapping her feet and hands, he then places a strip along her mouth. Reaching for his tie, he tightens it around her eyes. Figuring no-one is going to come in here any time soon, Calvin sneaks back out and returns to Megan's apartment in hopes of finding her car keys. He'll take Burtrum back to his motel and then ditch the car somewhere.

Smiling to himself, Calvin ponders fate. It's almost as if good fortune is suddenly upon him, making up for all the crap he's endured over the past few days.

Stepping over Megan, who still lay unconscious, Calvin searches for the keys, and sees them in a soap dish. Leaving quickly, he hurriedly shuts the door behind him.

Maneuvering Megan's VW up to the garage door, he drags Lee out, and stuffing her in the back seat, covers the limp body with a blanket. Hopefully no one will notice the mound.

Squeezing into the oval vehicle, Calvin giggles as he feels like a Shriner in one of those small cars they drive in parades. All he needs is a Fez!

What he'll do is turn the tables on Lyman Stone and Katie Lee. Find out how important this little package really is. He'll hold her for ransom, and then with the money, he and Carla can leave the country together. Live happily ever after.

Pulling into the parking lot of his motel, Calvin turns into the closest spot to his room. Waiting to make sure no one is coming, he slips out of the car, and keeping the cover around her, carries the small woman to the door. Fumbling with his keys, he barely unlocks the portal before hearing voices rounding the corner.

Tossing the still unconscious woman onto the bed, Calvin leaves to dump the car. Across the street, he sees a lot stretching out at least a half mile, with trees and dark shadows.

"That'll be as good a place as any," he tells himself, driving over, and ditching the Bug in a far corner. He quickly wipes for prints, and scurries off before he's seen.

It's funny, he thinks, strolling back, how everything seems to be falling into place once he started working on his own.

Sliding the key into the door, Calvin realizes this is probably one of the few motels left that actually uses keys. Most of them have switched to plastic cards.

"Whatever," he mumbles, as he steps into the stale smelling room.

Lee moans and groans, as she starts rolling back and forth on the bed.

Trying to quiet her, Calvin shuffles over, and raising his hands in front of him, he says, "Relax, it's okay, I'm not going to hurt you." Reaching out to Lee, she pushes herself back against the headboard, trying to avoid his touch.

"You don't have to be afraid of me, like I said before, I'm not going to hurt you." He takes a step closer. "Now if you promise not to scream or try anything funny, I'll take the tape off your mouth, but one mistake, and on it goes. Got it?"

Lee shakes her head up and down. Her hair wiping in her

eyes. Calvin grabs a corner of the gray tape and pulls hard.

"Ouch," Lee screeches, as she licks her red, raw lips. Guess she won't be needing electrolysis any more, she thinks to herself. Her sense of humor never failing.

"Sorry!" Calvin apologizes.

"Yeah, right, if you're that sorry, you'll let me go. It's not too late and I won't tell anyone."

"It doesn't work that way, Burtrum. I'm sure you've watched enough cop shows to realize that, and whomever said television isn't educational, is wrong"

"I seldom watch TV," Lee replies snottily.

"Well, aren't you the hotty-totty of the intellectual world." Calvin's beginning not to like Lee and contemplates replacing the tape so that he doesn't have to talk to her.

"Hey, Mister, I have to go to the bathroom, do you mind."

"Already? We just got here. And didn't you just go back at your friend's house."

"Sorry, must be all the coffee I drank this morning."

"Okay!" Calvin reaches a hand out, helping her up. "Now, no funny business."

"Aren't you going to untie me?"

"You're kidding, right?"

"No! How will I pull my pants down?"

"I'll do it."

"What? I don't want you down there."

"I promise, I won't look. I'm a happily married man and there's only one woman I want. So it's either that, or you wet yourself, take your pick."

"I tell you, if I feel anything odd, you'll be sorry."

Calvin carefully slips Lee's shorts down, turning away as he does so. "There, was that so bad." What he didn't want to do is piss her off any more than she already is. He'd rather have her on his side when it comes right down to it. "I'll be right outside, so let me know when you're finished." Calvin exits the bathroom and closes the door, but not all the way.

It's not long before he hears, "I'm done." Feeling confident about his kidnapping abilities, Calvin isn't expecting Lee to be behind the door, and when she rams his gut with her head, he falls back, gasping for air.

"What, what are you doing?"

Lee doesn't get far as Calvin rolls over and snags her feet as she tries to shuffle by him.

"Help, help," she screams. He covers her mouth with his hand.

"I said be quiet." Reaching for the tape, he replaces the strip over Lee's mouth and stands up, leaving her lying on the floor.

Pacing back and forth, Calvin tries to *Zen* himself down, an expression Carla uses. His heart is beating out of control and his anger is flaring. "Damn-it, I thought I could trust you." Glancing at Lee, who still has her shorts around her ankles, Calvin goes over and lifts her to her feet, yanking up her pants as he does so.

"Listen Burtrum," Calvin begins. "I wish you would just cooperate with me, and believe me when I tell you that I don't want to hurt you. You're my ticket to a new and better life, that's all. So, you don't have to worry about anything, and if you knew what this is all about, or maybe you do,

204 • M<small>ARY</small> M<small>AURICE</small>

then you'd be upset too, and might even see my side of the situation." Calvin continues to pace after sitting Lee down in a chair, and taping her ankles to the legs.

Noticing her heavy breathing, Calvin stands by the chair. "Okay, why don't we try this one more time, all right. I'll take the tape off and you be good."

Shaking her head up and down and grunting, Calvin removes the gag.

After a short silence, Lee asks. "First, I like to be called Lee, I loathe the name, Burtrum. Second, what in the hell do you want with me?"

"You're going to help me get some money."

"How?"

"I'm holding you for ransom."

"My family doesn't have any money."

"Not your family, although come to think of it, that's not a bad idea. Anyway, I'm talking about the people I work for."

"Is one of them, Katie Lee?"

"Yes. You know about her?"

"Just lately. I overheard something." Lee recalls the conversation Jane and Clair were having, and how the name Katie Lee came up a couple of times, but that's all she heard.

"Yes, your mother is behind this."

"My mother, you mean Jane?"

"No, your real mother."

Lee begins to feel nauseas.

"What are you talking about, you must have me confused with someone else, my mom is Jane Conner."

Calvin moves closer to Lee, enjoying the moment. Leaning in, he whispers, "No, Katie Lee is."

❋ ❋ ❋

Megan awakes, her face pounding in pain. Reaching up, she touches her nose, it doesn't feel broken, just a little swollen and sticky. Her brain is groggy as she climbs to her hands and knees, and suddenly begins to relive what happened.

"Lee?" She yells. "Lee, where are you." Staggering to the bottom of the staircase. "Lee?"

Glancing through the front window, she notices her car is gone, and rushes out the door. He must've kidnapped Lee, Megan concludes, as she leans back against the frame, her head still splitting.

Her instincts tell her to call the police, but decides to contact Lee's family first and tell them what's going on.

Searching her mind for Clair's phone number, Megan can't remember it, and figures she'll just ride her bike up there. It'll be faster than walking.

Night-time arrives like an unwanted guest, as clouds gather, threatening rain. The winds begin to blow so heavily that Megan is having trouble riding up the road. Dismounting the bike, she jogs beside it.

Making the sign of the cross as she sees Clair's driveway up ahead, Megan can't believe the past couple of days she's had. And even though she's never experienced anything as crazy as the Conner's, it all seems so natural. Like it's supposed to happen.

Clair's house is a comforting sight as Megan leans her bike against the fence. Trudging up the path, she sees Clair and Jed arguing in the kitchen. "That doesn't look good," Megan whispers to herself as she raps three times on the screen door.

Turning, Clair sees Megan, and lumbering over, lets her in. "Megan, are you all right. I've been worried sick about you. Do you know where Birdy is?"

"Yeah, have you seen her?" Jed interrupts his mother.

"Jed, don't harp," Clair disciplines him like a little boy.

"Clair that's okay, I know he's worried, just like all of us. Yes, Lee and I ran into each other at the rail yard, and when we went back to my apartment for a moment, that guy appeared and punched me out cold. Then he kidnapped Lee."

"Where did they go?" Jed rushes up to Megan, but Clair stops him with her arm.

"Now, just hold on a minute, Jed. Let Megan catch her breath." Clair pulls out a chair. "Here dear, have a seat."

Megan remains standing. "Thanks Clair, but I don't think we have time for me to be sitting. I have no idea where he took her, but I do know that maybe it's time we call the cops. It's getting a little dangerous, now."

"We can't call the police. They'll mess everything up."

"What are you talking about. You don't expect to find this guy by yourself, do you?" Clair and Jed eye each other and then turn back to Megan. Clair begins. "It gets a lot more complicated, and we think we know who we're dealing with."

"Who are these people?"

"We can't say, all we can tell you is that we know they

won't stop until they have Lee, and then we might never see her again."

"I don't understand what in the hell you're talking about."

"We stole her, that's what we're talking about. And now the real mother is coming after her child," Jane's voice rings out from behind Clair and Jed as they both spring in surprise.

"Jane, don't say another word." Jed rushes over to her, but Jane pushes past him, tear faced and red nosed.

"It's true Megan. That's why they don't want to call the police because we'll all end up in prison. All of us!" Jane glares at Clair.

"Jane, you're being hysterical, just calm down."

"Calm down. How can I calm down when I'm on the verge of losing my daughter, a daughter that was never really mine?"

"Jane!" Jed yells.

She turns back toward him. "No, no, Jed, it's all right. I think the truth needs to come out, needs to be set free from the lie that's been holding it down all of these years."

Megan stands in awe, not really sure what is going on, all she knows is that is seems like Lee's mom is having a breakdown. She whips back to Megan.

"See, Megan, me and Jed did have a baby together, but he was stillborn. I went crazy, ran out into a blizzard and stumbled upon a car accident down the road. To my surprise the woman had just given birth to a baby girl who was alive. I decided to switch the infants, believing that no one would ever find out. But now they have, and we're all in trouble."

Jane plops down in a chair and begins bawling. "My dear lord, please forgive me for my sins."

Clair rubs her shoulders, trying to comfort her daughter in-law. "There, there, Jane, you thought you were doing the right thing. Both of you believed the mother was dead. You don't know what kind of life she would've had if you didn't rescue her."

"Well, it doesn't seem like the right thing now."

"You're drunk," Jed hisses from where he's standing. "Why don't you sober up for once and look at life through clear eyes?"

Jane raises her head and glares at Jed. "Because then I'd see what my life is really like." She stands up and races into the living room, plopping down on the couch and crying hysterically. Clair starts to follow her out, but Jed grabs her arm.

"Leave her alone, Mother. She'll cry until she passes out. That's the best thing she can do right now."

Clair studies her son. "Jed Conner I didn't raise you to act like this. You need to start showing some compassion for your family." Clair shakes her arm out of Jed's grip.

"We don't have time to argue right now, we need to find Lee."

Megan, still in a state of disbelief. Is it true what Mrs. Conner declared? Did they really switch babies forty years ago?

20

Lee feels the tear soaked tie wrapped around her eyes take on a chill as the room drops in temperature. She can't believe this is happening. It's like a bad dream you can't wake up from. Nothing makes sense anymore. It's as if her whole life is insignificant. Everything she's accomplished, which isn't much, has no meaning. All of her feelings, are useless. Maybe this is the reason she could never find her nitch in life, because she's living the wrong one.

Anger swells in her heart as sensations of betrayal race through her veins. How could Clair not tell her? Lee believed they'd always had more than a grandma/granddaughter relationship. Now, they don't even have that.

Lies!That's all she's been told her whole life and now look where it's taken her. Lee tries once again to wriggle loose, but the tape holds tight. She can feel her circulation slowing down as her fingers begin to go numb.

That jerk-off better get back here soon before I lose a

limb, Lee screams in her head, feeling more tears roll out of her eyes.

❀   ❀   ❀

Calvin Kramer perspires like a pig. Seems he hasn't stopped sweating since being in Santa Fe. He has to make a move and make it fast. He is wasting valuable time. Spotting a pay phone at the gas station, he looks both ways before carefully crossing the street.

Skipping up to the oblong box, Calvin jingles some coins in his pocket before retrieving two quarters. His first course of action is to call Clair Conner and tell her he has Burtrum, and that he wants a half million dollars in cash for her release. He wasn't going to at first, but when Burtrum mentioned her fake-family, he figured, why not hit them up too.

He'll ask for half a million from the Conner's and the same amount from Katie Lee. Leaving him a cool million to live out the rest of his life.

Digging in his trouser pockets, Calvin finds the slip of paper he jotted Clair's number down on, and squints as he tries to read it in the fading daylight.

Pressing the right buttons, Calvin stands there as the phone begins to ring.

"Hello?"

He isn't ready for someone to answer so quickly, and freezes. He can't think of anything to say, so he slams the receiver down and walks away.

A sudden chill in the air sends shivers racing across his body. He wraps his arms around his chest, as his muscles tighten. He feels spacey, as if he's been drugged. He shakes his head and slips the two quarters out of the coin return.

Sliding them back in, he dials again, this time with a game plan.

"Hello?" The same old voice answers.

"I've got your granddaughter, and if you want to see her alive again, I want five hundred thousand dollars in cash by tomorrow."

"What? Who is this? Where's Birdy?"

Calvin hears a rustling and then an angry man's voice comes over the line.

"Who is this? I tell you if you harm my daughter you'll live to regret it."

"Mr. Conner, you need to calm down or I'll hang up. Threats don't help," Calvin puffs with power. His tone, strong and even. "Now listen to me, your daughter is safe, and will be, as long as you do as you're told," He recites a verse he's heard a hundred-plus times in movies or on TV.

"I want five hundred thousand dollars by tomorrow afternoon and you'll get Burtrum back."

"I can't come up with that kind of money so fast."

"Oh, I think you can, and it needs to be in cash. I'll call later with more details, and let me advise you Mr. Conner, if I sense any sign of cops, you'll never see her again." Hanging up, Calvin quickly wipes all the areas he believes he touched.

Dashing away from the phone he ducks into a convenience store. He'll buy some snacks and then go back to the motel room. Wiping his brow, he opens the soda cooler, the chill of the fridge sends shivers down his arms.

❀ ❀ ❀

Clair stares at her son standing statuesque with the phone still in his hand. "Jed, Jed, what did he say?"

"He said he has Lee, and that if we don't come up with half a million dollars by tomorrow, we'll never see her again."

"Don't you guys think it's time to call the police?" Megan suggests.

"This is no business of yours, I don't even know why you're here."

"She's here because she wants to help Lee, just like all of us. Now, Jed, I don't want to hear another peep out of you, do you understand?" Clair is livid, her son is acting like a pompous ass and this isn't the time.

"We all need to relax so that we can think clearly. Now, Megan you have no idea where this guy might've taken Lee."

"I think somewhere close. He took my car, so he won't get too far."

"I can't believe this has gotten so out of hand," Clair agonizes, sitting down at the table as her legs become weak.

"Mother, you're getting yourself worked up, and that's the last thing you need. I'm sure all this guy wants, is money and then it'll be over. I'll see what I can do about getting the cash by the morning. I mean all my money's tied up in land, so maybe we can put that up as collateral. We'll think of something, and he's not going to harm Lee, she's his bread and butter," Jed tries to comfort Clair.

"I'm just worried how Lee's going to react after all of this is said and done."

"I guess we'll just have to wait and see. In the meantime, I'm going to go meet with some people. You two stay here with Jane and if the phone rings answer it and try to get as many details as possible. I won't be long." Jed kisses Clair on the forehead and walks to the door. "Mother call me if anything happens."

Glaring at Megan as he passes by her, Jed Conner sweeps out of the kitchen, leaving a

brisk breeze in his wake. Once again, Megan wishes she'd never met the Conner's.

❊ ❊ ❊

Katie Lee throws the plastic water bottle across the room. The empty container bounces off the wall and falls to the floor, rolling under the couch.

"Why haven't we heard anything yet, Wanda."

Katie's whining is driving Wanda to the mad house. "In due time. Just be patient. I'm sure we'll be hearing from Lyman soon."

"No, there's something wrong, I can feel it. I think we need to take action, and right now."

"What are we going to do, Katie? We know absolutely nothing. It'd be like running in a wild goose chase."

The phone begins to ring, and before Wanda has a chance to pick it up, Katie snatches the receiver, and holding it up to her ear, says, "Hello!"

"I need to speak to Katie Lee."

Not recognizing the voice, Katie thinks it must be the

front desk. "This is she, how may I help you?"

"If you ever want to see your daughter alive, I'd suggest you get a half million dollars in cash by tomorrow afternoon."

"Who is this?"

"You don't need to know that. All you need to be concerned about is your daughter."

"Okay, the joke is over. Tell me who you are right now before you get yourself in deeper trouble."

"Listen lady, this is no joke. Just do as I say. I'll be calling back with more details."

Katie is unable to get in another word as the kidnapper quickly hangs up.

"Damn-it!"

"What, what is it, Katie?" Wanda rushes to her chair.

"He has Burtrum."

"He? Who?"

"Calvin! He says that if I don't come up with five hundred thousand dollars by tomorrow, then I'll never see her alive."

"What are you going to do?"

"Get me Lyman on the phone," Katie insists, telling herself that Calvin Kramer is dealing with the wrong woman.

Calvin shakes from head to foot, he didn't like the tone of Katie Lee's voice. He knows how powerful she is, how many influences she has, on both sides of the fence. You don't get to her position in life without having a lot of resources.

Is he making a mistake? Should he think his plan through a little more before he takes action, or is it too late? Maybe he'll just set her free and leave Santa Fe, and hope everyone will forget about the whole incident.

No, that's not going to work. Whichever way he looks at it, his life is ruined, so he has nothing to lose. Plus, Calvin has no idea where Carla is, she hasn't answered the phone or responded to any of his messages. When he asked Lyman if he knew of his wife's where- bouts, the scientist said he'd heard that she drove up to the Russian River for a week-end spa.

Well, once this is over and he has his million dollars, Carla can spa as much as she wants, as they bask in the soothing sun on some small island in the pacific.

Smiling to himself, he trudges back to the motel room, figuring all he has to do is get through tonight, and then in the morning, it will be the beginning of a new life.

Lee's eyes are coated with dry crusty tears. The lids are cemented shut. She still can't believe this is happening. All of the events of the past few days have sent her into a whirl-wind. Finding out the truth about herself, how she was sto-len as an infant and raised by her kidnappers. What kind of people do that?

Lee loves the Conner's, or did, right now though, she doesn't know what to think. And Clair, of all people, Lee sulks, hiding the truth from her. She thought she could trust the old woman.

Her body feels hollow, like a deflating balloon. Is it because she isn't who she thinks she is?

Now what? Here she is, gagged and bound by some crazy man who doesn't seem to know what he's doing. Lee tries to devise a plan of escape. Maybe there'll be that right moment when she can kick him and run, but not as long as her feet stay taped together.

Right now there isn't much she can do, outside of waiting to see what's in store for her.

One thing she knows for sure, her life will never be the same.

Jane keeps still as she listens to Jed talking on the phone, and then to his mother. A half million dollars. Where are they going to get that? It'll break them, they'll never be able to recover. Even though the Conner's put on airs like they have a lot of money, they don't. A few bad investments by Jed and they are barely staying afloat.

Of course, Clair doesn't have a clue about her sons lack of business skills. Jed will never sink so low as to ask his mother for money, even if they lose their house. Jane doesn't know why. The old hag is loaded.

But now!

Jane hears Jed leave and wonders what he's up to. She needs to follow him, see who he's going to intimidate into lending him that kind of cash. In the back of her mind Jane fears that Jed might split, take off, disappear until the storm passes.

After all, this *is* her fault. She's the one who insisted they switch the babies. She was the one who convinced Jed that nothing would ever happen and that they were doing the right thing.

It had all been her doing.

Quietly standing, Jane tip-toes out the front door without Clair or Megan noticing. If she hurries she might be able to catch up to Jed and follow him.

Slipping into the sedan, Jane starts the Mercedes and listens as the engine clatters. She hates that sound; it always makes her think of a death rattle.

Speeding down Bishop's Lodge road, Jane spots Jed's tail -lights a few cars ahead and slows down. She'll tag him, but from a distance. Digging into her purse, she pulls out her silver cased flask.

"Jane, Jane." Clair switches on the lamp in the living room and searches for her daughter-in -law, who is nowhere to be found.

"Damn-it," Clair curses as she returns back to the kitchen. "Jane's gone. She must've snuck out the front door. I wonder where she's going. She better not screw-up things any worse than what they already are," Clair is fuming.

Megan, knowing the recent history of Clair's medical condition, tries to ease the elderly woman's tension.

"Clair, you need to chilax." Megan pulls out a chair. "Here, have a seat and I'll get you a cup of tea."

"I don't want any tea, Megan. Why don't you pour me a little glass of wine, the bottle is on the counter?" Clair feeling slightly dizzy, sits in the chair Megan has pulled out for her. "I don't know what that crazy woman is thinking, taking off without a word."

Megan places the glass in front of Clair, and sits down across from her. Taking a sip of her own wine, she begins. "You know Clair, maybe it's time you went to the police. I mean, Lee has been kidnapped and now the man is asking for a ransom. Do you really think she's safe without the authorities, who know how to handle cases like this?"

"Darling, you don't understand. There's so much at stake."

"What could be more important than your granddaughter's well-being?"

"Megan there are things that you don't know, and I can't tell you. Right now, what we need to do is sit tight and wait to hear from Jed or the kidnapper."

Rising, Megan prances to the counter. "Why can't you tell me? I think I'm in this pretty deep right now, after all, who was the one that got punched in the face?"

"The more you know, the more danger you'll be in. This way if you're asked any questions you can be honest and play dumb. Trust me on this one, sweetie, I know what I'm talking about." Exhaustion envelopes Clair, all she wants to do is lie down and take a little nap, but she can't, she has to be awake for Birdy.

"Clair, are you all right?" Megan walks over to her.

"Yes, yes, I just had a slight tired spell."

"Maybe you should go lie down."

"No, I'm fine. Just sit down Megan and finish your wine." Clair motions with her hand.

"I can't Clair. I can't just sit around and do nothing. I have an idea though. Why don't you wait here by the phone, while I take Lee's car and drive around? Maybe I'll see something. It can't hurt."

"Do you really think that's such a great idea? I mean really, what could you possibly see?"

"I don't know Clair, but it sure beats the hell out of hanging out here and doing nothing. Trust me, I'll be very careful."

"That's not the point. What if I need you here for something?"

"I'll call you every half hour, how's that?"

"How long do you plan on being gone?"

Megan is getting annoyed. "I don't know, not that long, maybe an hour, hour and a half. Please, Clair, I feel like we're wasting time."

Clair studies the woman and wonders if she can trust her or not. These days it's kind of a hit and miss with people.

"Okay, I guess it'll be all right. The keys are on the hook in the pantry, just be careful, and keep me in touch."

Megan kisses Clair on the forehead and trots to the back door, lifting the key off the ring. Turning back to Clair she says. "Make sure you lock the door after I leave."

"I will."

"I'll see you in a little bit."

Clair watches as Megan disappears into the dark. It's weird with that one, Clair contemplates. It's like she knows her from somewhere, but can't pin-point where. Standing,

Clair forgets to latch the bolt and slowly moves into the living room. Lying down on the davenport, she immediately falls to sleep.

❖   ❖   ❖

Megan Masterson doesn't have the slightest clue where she is going. She keeps driving around Santa Fe looking for something but doesn't know what. Suddenly an idea comes to her.

She should go check out Lee's house. Maybe this jerk accidentally left a clue that no one found yet. After all, as far as Megan knows, no one has really been over there looking. The only problem is she doesn't know where Lee lives.

Parking in front of the Shed Restaurant, Megan quickly gets out and rushes through the entrance. Her appearance takes the hostess by surprise, as her disheveled clothing startles the young woman.

"May I help you?" She says sternly.

"Yes, do you have a phone book I can borrow?"

Studying Megan for just a moment longer, the woman reaches down behind the podium and hands her the telephone directory.

Megan turns around and plops down on the bench in the lobby, waiting customers sneer at her in disgust. Megan is unaware of how tangled she appears.

Flipping through the white pages, she prays Lee is listed, and doesn't know what her next plan of action will be if she's not.

Her hopes being answered, Megan finds her address and

phone number, and closing her eyes for a moment, memorizes the info. Handing the book back to the woman, who seems a little more at ease, Megan races to her car.

The night turns dark and cold as she pulls onto Santa Fe Avenue. Driving slowly along, she has a hard time seeing the addresses, and then catches sight of what she believes is Lee's house.

Getting out of the car, Megan feels a sense of eeriness as she cat-crawls up to the unlit house. Following the driveway into the back, she notices that on each side of the yard looms a tall wooden fence, hiding her from the neighbor's sight.

Stepping up onto the porch, Megan first tries the knob, but it's locked. Deciding to just break in, she wishes she had a flash light as the moon slips behind the clouds, eliminating the glow.

After a short search, she finds a rock, and wrapping her shirt around the crag, slams the small boulder into the corner of the door. Muffled glass cracks and breaks behind her blow.

Looking around to see if anyone heard the noise, she cautiously opens the door, and steps in. Standing still for a moment, Megan lets her eyes adjust before she moves. She notices that all the blinds are closed so she flicks on a light and is bathed in brightness.

At first her eyes can't handle the shock and she closes them instantly. At last, daring to reopen them, she scans the kitchen, not seeing anything out of the ordinary. The drawers are pulled out and tossed, and the cupboards are ajar.

Scouring the floor and counter, she doesn't spot anything. Retreating to the living room she turns on a reading lamp, this time closing her eyes first before flicking the light on.

Megan is astonished at the trashed room. Cushions and chairs flipped over, papers, blankets, magazines strewn about, as though a Midwestern tornado ripped through the small adobe. Foreboding wavers on the horizon, as a flicker catches Megan's eye, but when she turns, there's nothing there. Shivers run up and down her spine.

Retreating to Lee's bedroom, Megan finds it to be the same as the living room. Sitting down on the bed, she places her head in her hands. This is senseless, she's not going to discover anything. What is she thinking?

Gazing at the hardwood floor through tear pools, she blinks a drop out, and watches as the water splashes right next to a toothpick wrapper. Retrieving the white strip of paper, she twirls it between her fingers and stops when she sees the engraved ad, *The Travel Lodge Motel.*

Her heart beat increases with every wild thought, as every nerve feels like heated pricks.

Can this be where he's hiding Lee?

Should she go over to the Lodge and see if she can spot her car?

Or, should she call Clair, tell her what she found. But what if it's nothing, just a speck of trash.

She has to do something!

Turning off the lights as she leaves, Megan locks the door behind her, hoping the broken window goes unnoticed.

❁ ❁ ❁

Calvin Kramer charges into the motel room, the key slipping from his hand and falling to the carpeted floor.

Lee groans as she hears him come in.

Rushing over to her in a fit of frustration, Calvin rips the tape off of Lee's mouth. "Don't you dare make a sound, do you hear me?"

"Yes," she chokes out. "Just don't hurt me, my family will get you whatever you want."

"We'll see about that." Calvin shuffles away. "Now, I'm tired and need to sleep, but first I'm going to take a shower. Do you need to use the bathroom?"

"No."

He blares the TV full blast. "Just in case you try to do something stupid."

By the sound of it, her captor is in a foul mood. Great, just what she doesn't need. Breathing deeply through her chapped lips, Lee tries to think fast, there has to be a way to over-take this guy.

She smells soapy vapors as he enters the room.

"Ah, much better."

Lee can hear him toweling his hair dry.

"Nothing like a hot shower to take the aches away."

"It'd be nice if I can take one," Lee croaks, her throat dry and parched. "A drink of water would help, too."

"Yeah, sure, sorry."

Lee listens as Calvin fumbles with one of the plastic wrapped cups, and then pouring water from the faucet, he holds it up to her lips.

"Here, drink this."

Normally, Lee would refuse, Santa Fe tap is nothing to write home about, but under these conditions, she decides to swallow.

"Water, yes, shower, I don't think so." Calvin jumps into the bed next to her. "You hungry?"

"No." She's starving, but will be damned if she'll take any food from him.

"Good, then. I'm going to sleep. If you behave, I'll leave the tape off, if not, it goes back on. Choice is yours."

"That's it, you're not going to tell me anything?"

"There's nothing to convey, trust me. Now, goodnight." Calvin turns down the TV.

There's nothing she can do tonight. He's sleeping, she's tied to this bed and can't get free. It's senseless to scream out, so she too, may as well go to sleep, if she can.

Taking a deep breath, she continues to twists her wrists, trying to loosen the bonds.

Megan pulls into the Travel Lodge driveway and cruises through the parking lot. Not seeing anything suspicious she turns around and drives to the Allsups gas station on the corner. She's getting tired and figures if she's going to pull a stakeout, she'll need stimulation to keep her awake, and a cup of bad coffee is her best bet.

Getting out of the car, Megan spots a row of pay telephones lining the side of the building. Should she just take it upon herself and call the police? Report Lee's kidnapping. Obviously, the Conner's aren't thinking straight, handling this mess themselves.

Is it really her place though? She's only known the family for a few days, and to be honest, she really doesn't know what kind of people they are. Right now, they all seem nutty. But then, who is she to judge?

Walking into the deserted store, Megan's wafted with the scent of stale java, all hopes of a fresh pot dashed. Paying for the sludge, she gallops out the door.

Leaning against the cooling sand wall, Megan hears one of the telephones ring once, giving her the creeps. Is this a sign? Should she contact the cops? That's the most logical thing to do.

Pitching the barely touched crappy coffee into the trash, Megan moseys over and picking up a receiver, wipes it off before holding it to her ear. Sliding two quarters into the box, she waits for a dial tone and then punches in 911.

"This is 911, how may I help you?"

"Yes, I'd like to report a kidnapping."

"Who's missing ma'am?"

"A friend of mine has been abducted. She's not missing."

"Hold on ma'am, let me connect you with a detective."

Megan stands there for a moment shivering from head to toe.

"This is Detective Sanchez. How may I help you?"

"Yes, I'd like to report a kidnapping."

"Who's been kidnapped, ma'am?"

"Her name is Burtrum Lee Conner."

"And how do you know for sure that she's been kidnapped?"

"I was there."

"When did this all take place?"

"This afternoon at my apartment. A man has been stalking her since Friday, and he finally found her."

"And what is your name, Miss?"

"I'm not saying. I'm just calling to inform you of this crime. Maybe you can do something about it."

"Why haven't you called us sooner if you say this guy has been following your friend since Friday."

"I was told not to."

"By whom?"

"Listen I've got to go," Megan fears they're tracing her. "Will you just investigate this, please?"

"You're not giving us much to go on."

"The only thing I can tell you is to check out the Travel Lodge Motel on Cerrillos."

Hanging up the phone, Megan dashes to Lee's Jetta and jumps in. Quickly driving across the street to the rail yard, she parks the car behind a tree, hoping to hide in the shadows.

She'll wait a little while and see if the cops come and check it out.

❁   ❁   ❁

Clair groggily opens her eyes, and at first can't focus on what is in front of her. Sitting up, she reaches for her glasses setting on the coffee table and wraps them around her eyes. She can't believe it.

"Katie Lee?" Clair stands up. Even though she's never met the woman, she knew instinctively who she was. "What in the world are you doing here?"

"How do you know it's me?"

"Who else could it be?" Clair smiles, trying to deduce

how the woman found out where she lives, much less breaking into her home.

"I think you know why I'm here. It's time Clair, time to set the tables straight. I made a big mistake all those years ago giving up my child, and now I think it's time the truth comes out."

"A lot of people are going to get hurt."

"That's only a part of it. This is not a decision I've just arrived at. The idea has been roller balling through my head for the past couple of years, and then when I saw Burtrum on the web site, and realized how much she looks like me, I just couldn't turn away this time. I'm getting weak, Clair, and I don't know how much time I have left. All I want is this one piece of small happiness. Can you understand?"

"I do, but my lord, Katie, don't you know what this will do to Birdy?"

"We don't have a choice. I believe if we all do it together, she'll respond better. Don't you think it'll be easier if she hears the truth from all of us?"

Clair stares at Katie. "You don't know?"

"Know what?"

"Lee's been kidnapped. We thought you, or Lyman Stone were behind it."

"What?" Katie plays dumb, wanting to hear what Clair has to say.

"Yes, this afternoon while she was at a friend's house. We think we know who it is too. That goon you sent out to spy on us."

"Calvin Kramer. So, he's asking you for a pay-off, also?"

"So, you know?" Clair seems a little baffled.

"It doesn't matter." Katie rubs her face in her hands. "Listen, all I instructed him to do was to find Burtrum, and get me an address. Wanda!" She yelps.

Clair watches as a hefty, stout woman lumbers out of the kitchen. That's how they must've gotten in. She forgot to lock the door, even though Megan reminded her right before she left. And by the way, Clair wonders, where is Megan?

"What? What's the ruckus?"

"I need you to get me Lyman. I don't care if he's in a meeting, on a date or taking a crap, I want to talk to him now or else heads are going to roll."

Clair is torn between being impressed and being a little scared as Katie Lee's tone turns vicious. She knows this woman is very powerful and has been on the Fortune Five Hundred list for a couple of decades now. Her laboratories lead the world in curing diseases. She's successfully dedicated her whole life to her research.

"Where's the phone?" Wanda asks.

"There's one in the kitchen you can use," Clair answers, watching as Wanda returns to the other room. "Why are you calling him?" She inquires.

"He's the man in charge of the labs, *for now*. When I first discovered Burtrum's picture, it was he I went to for help. See, Lyman is the scientist who fertilized me with Burtrum. At the time we thought we were going to have a boy, but he must've switched the embryo or something. I don't know, and would've never known had you not contacted me all of those years ago. I never told him I knew, because I figured the day would come when he'd have to pay the piper. Believe me, you, when all is said and done, his career will be ruined."

"Listen Katie, I'm only looking out for the safety of Birdy, the poor child. And I believe your decision to let my son and his wife raise your baby was a very noble and selfless act. She's had a good life, but there was always something missing for her, I could see it in her eyes, and I knew she felt it too. There have been so many times when I thought of our pact, and didn't let myself dwell on it."

"Well, our agreement is off the table. I don't want to waste any more time not being a part of my daughter's life."

"I understand perfectly well, but we still have to consider how Lee's going to react to the news that she's a clone. I mean, that's one pretty hefty admittance. What if she runs away or something? Tells us she never wants to see us again."

"Clair, do you really think she'll do that?"

"I don't know."

"Jed and Jane don't know, do they?"

"No," Clair lowers her head, and then raises it, staring directly at Katie. "I haven't told a soul."

"Good."

"Katie, Lyman's nowhere to be found and they can't get him on his cell?" Wanda announces, taking a bite out of an apple.

"This is unbelievable, where could he be. I instructed him to make sure I can always get in touch with him. What's he thinking?"

"Maybe he's on his way here," Wanda puts in.

"That would not be a very good idea." Katie scrunches her face. "I told him he was to go nowhere near my daughter, and I meant it. Part of this is his fault, and I know he wants to get Burtrum for himself and make her into a science project. Show her off as the first cloned human."

"We're not going to let that happen, but I'm not sure how much we can get done tonight." Clair checks her watch. "It's getting late, and I'm not feeling very well. Why don't we all get together in the morning and see what the day brings. Who knows, this could all turn out for the better," Clair tries to sound reassuring.

"Yes, you're right, Clair. I'm tired too. We'll just go back to the hotel and then talk in the morning." Katie wheels her chair around to the kitchen as Clair stands up and follows behind.

Placing her hands on Katie's shoulders, Clair leans over and whispers. "Everything will be all right. You just watch and see."

Burtrum Lee Conner can't sleep. Her attempts to set herself free haven't worked, and all she's done is rub her wrist till they're red and raw. Her assailant snores loudly, and she can hear him passing gas since the minute he fell asleep. It's grossing her out.

Is anybody even looking for her? Has her fate been determined by this buffoon? She'll be damned if that is the case.

She begins wriggling again, but her skin is so chapped, she stops immediately. She'll wait. There has to be an opportunity when she can run for it. People always make slip ups.

Listening as Calvin rolls over and lets out a measure of farts, Lee shakes her head and lies there, plotting her escape.

❊   ❊   ❊

Megan is freezing cold. The temperature must've dropped thirty degrees in the past fifteen minutes, she attests, not wanting to turn on the car for heat and bring attention to herself. She watches intently as the hour grows later. She's only seen one patrol car pass by the motel and they didn't even slow down.

"This isn't working," Megan announces to herself, trying to think of another course of action.

Suddenly, she comes up with an idea. She'll set off the fire alarm, that way all of the guests will have to exit their rooms and the police will be there to find Lee and her kidnapper.

"Great!" Megan yelps, opening her car door and stepping out into the bitter cold night. She should've brought a jacket. Racing across the street, she jets in and out of the stretching shadows. She'll act like she's staying there, and find the closest alarm.

Scanning the walls for a small red box, she spots one down the hallway near the ice machine. Dashing to the end of the corridor, she yanks down the metal handle, and runs in the opposite direction.

Sirens blare, making Megan's head ring, as she scampers away from the motel. Lucky for her, it took the attendant a few minutes to come out of the office, as she ducks into the darkness of the blooming trees.

Finding her car, she slips into the vehicle and watches as red trucks with howling alarms pull up to the motel, followed by several police cars. Megan stays slouched in her seat, paying close attention as the firemen lead the people out of their rooms. Megan has a clear sight line of the guests as they huddle around in a circle, but she doesn't see Lee anywhere. She is sure this is where her friend's being held captive. Fear floats around Megan as she continues her vigil.

Calvin shoots up, his head is groggy and his mouth dry. Licking his lips, he scratches his bristly chin and shakes his head trying to clear it of cobwebs. The screaming sirens vibrate the room, flashing lights everywhere.

Jumping up, Calvin goes over to the window and peeks out from behind the curtain.

"Shit!" He screeches, rushing over to Lee, who pretends to be sleeping.

Grabbing the roll of tape, Calvin rips a piece off and straps it over her mouth. "Don't you dare make a sound."

"We've got to get out of here." Shoving everything into his suitcase, Calvin scans the room one last time, making sure he isn't leaving anything.

Surveying the parking lot, he sees the coast is clear, and assists Lee to his car. Easing her onto the floor of the back seat, he covers her with a blanket. Snatching a glimpse of the police cars and fire trucks lining the streets, he expects to see flames or smoke, but there isn't any.

Smirking to himself, Calvin knows something isn't right.

He needs to get out of here. Coasting his car onto the side street, while keeping the lights off, Calvin knows better than to stick around when trouble's brewing.

Totally unfamiliar with this city, Calvin has no idea where he should go, when suddenly, Lee's house pops into his mind. What a perfect place to lay low. No one's going to look for him there.

He's on the edge, as he takes the corner smooth and cautiously, no need to bring attention to himself. His mind is baked, frazzled, crispy around the corners. But he knows losing his composure, will be the end of his dream.

Taking a right on Paseo de Peralta, he drives toward north Santa Fe. It's quite late so there isn't much traffic as he whistles along the empty streets. His mood is a little better, he just needed to get out of that motel, he tells himself, dimming the lights as he pulls into Lee's driveway.

Anxious to get a better angle, Megan squirms out of the Jetta, sneaking closer to the scene. Scanning the dark end of the parking lot, she notices a man helping a woman into the back seat of a car. The strangeness, like a bird in a house, catches her attention, and she suddenly realizes it's Lee and the kidnapper.

Megan's paralyzed. She can't move, yell, do anything. As she watches them drive down Don Diego Street, she snaps out of it, and jumping behind the steering wheel, tries to catch up to them.

Rounding the curve, she sees nothing, no tail-lights, cars,

nothing except her missed opportunity. "Shit!" She screams, banging the dash with her fists. A tear slips onto Megan's cheek as defeat slams her heart. She had them, her plan worked, but she didn't figure him slipping out the back way.

Going to the police is out of the question now. What would she tell them? That Lee and her abductor were in the motel and they just missed capturing them.

Tired and somber, Megan turns onto St. Francis Drive, deciding to go back to Clair's. There isn't much she can do right now. She has no idea where he took her.

21

Jose Sanchez stands shivering as a sudden sleeting rain begins to whip across his face. "Damn-it," he hisses, wishing he hadn't fielded that last call.

He was on his way home to his warm house and even warmer wife. Before he knew it though, habit invaded him and now here he stands investigating a false alarm, with his once hot wife turning frigid.

Normally this isn't Jose's territory, but when trace told him the phone call he received came from the gas station right next to where the alarm was sounded, Jose decided to check it out himself, believing in his theory that there are no coincidences.

But when he arrived and discovered nothing out of the ordinary, Detective Sanchez questioned his instincts. He can't be that off.

Noticing a driveway at the back of the motel, Sanchez motioned to a uniformed cop.

"Conrad, hey Conrad, come here."

The shivering officer forges over to him and leans against the car. "What up, boss?" Jose frowns and pulls the rookie off the sedan. "Stand up straight will you, and get off my car."

"Sorry." The police officer cowers away.

"What's going on with that back outlet." He points to a dark portion.

"I don't know?"

"Why isn't there anyone guarding it?"

"What would be the need, sir?"

Pushing past him, Jose stomps away disgusted, almost tripping on his trench coat slipping between his legs. "Get out of my way. I'll check it myself."

Coming up empty, Sanchez returns to the front of the motel, listening to the disgruntled moans over the false alarm, as the fire engines begin to pull away. Waving to his comrades, he scratches his bristly chin with his fingers, and turns his head toward the front desk.

A scrawny, fuzzy red head teen-ager, digs in his ear while flipping through some comic book. He is by himself now, and figures a few questions can't hurt anything.

The glass door squeaks as Jose pulls it open, the attendant looks up, then back down.

"No vacancies, sorry."

Reaching into his coat pocket, Sanchez retrieves his badge, and whipping it open, says. "That's good, because I don't need a room. I'm here to ask you a couple of questions about this incident."

At last paying attention, the delinquent raises his arms,

and cries. "Hey, buddy, it wasn't me, and I don't know anything about it. Probably some runts, you know, they run wild every night, causing havoc."

His eyes are bloodshot red, his words, long and thick.

He's high, the detective deduces. "Did you see anyone lurking about."

"Nope, nothing, not even on the cameras." He points to the monitors with four squares of different views of the motel. "Just the normal tenants."

He's not going to get anywhere with this kid. "What's your name, son?"

"Kirby, why? Am I in some kind of trouble?"

"No." Handing him a business card. "This is my phone number, if you think of something, give me a call."

"Will do, officer."

"It's detective."

"Will do, detective."

"Youth," Jose whispers to himself as he leaves the lobby, but stops when he hears.

"Wait, wait a minute, Detective Sanchez, now that you mention it, I did see something strange when I was taking out the trash. I guess I forgot."

Taking out the trash, my ass, probably burned a fat one. Jose snickers as he wheels back toward Kirby. "Okay, go ahead."

"Well, I don't know if it's anything, but I saw this man helping a woman into the back seat of a car. I couldn't see very well, because the light is out in that section. Could be she was sick and he was just helping her. I don't know, but that's it."

"Okay, great, Kirby?" Jose's annoyance level rises.

"Probably some John, stashing his whore," Kirby chuckles.

"If you think of anything else, let me know, okay?"

"Yes, sir."

Jose sees Kirby's reflection in the door, and watches him mock salute the detective.

"Jerk," he hisses as he stands on the landing buttoning his coat.

A sudden banging freezes detective Sanchez in his tracks. Slowly unlatching his holster, he lays his hand on his gun and turns around meticulously.

Slipping into a shadow, he sneaks behind a post and glancing down the hallway, watches as a door slams open and shut. Cat crawling up to the flapping brown portal, Jose draws his revolver and steps into the open passage, aimed and ready to fire.

"Anyone here?"

Darkness echoes off the solitary beam of light streaming out of the bathroom. Detective Sanchez surveys the room, noticing that whomever was staying here must have left in a hurry. They didn't even take the time to shut the door.

Kicking empty food containers as he walks across the carpeted floor, Jose looks down and notices a driver's license lying in the heap. Bending over, he picks up the laminated card, and reads the name.

"Holy Madonna!" Jose exclaims. Racing out the door and back to the motel office. He has to find out who was renting this room, and fast.

✷ ✷ ✷

Lee stifles her anguish, thankful her kidnapper didn't see her drop her driver's license on the floor before leaving the motel. She knows it's a last ditch effort, after all, no one will find it until tomorrow morning, and then it'll disappear after a while when the ID goes unclaimed.

At least she's making an effort.

Tears well up in her eyes as tiredness slaps at her brain. She feels fuzzy, a little cranky as her sleepless mind begs for mercy.

Feeling the car pull over and stop, Lee's heart begins to race out of control. It doesn't seem like they've driven very far, as she tightens her body against his grasp.

"Come on, get up," he orders, his sour breath brushing against her face. "What's your problem," the gruff voice demands. "Get up."

Yanking her, she cracks her head against the top of the door. "See what happens when you don't participate?" Dragging Lee out of the car and standing her on numbing feet. Stumbling up wooden steps, she breaths deeply, recognizing the scents.

He brought her home?

A spark ignites in Lee's heart; advantage her. What a blunder he's made, returning her to secure turf. She just has to wait for the right moment, and then pounce.

Pushing her through the front door, and onto the couch, her shoulder knocks against the back wall, igniting a creasing pain. Fear fills Lee, as she senses her assailant is becoming more aggressive.

"Now, just sit here and don't move, got it?" He instructs. "We'll stay the night, and once I get my money tomorrow, then I'm outta here. As for you," Calvin moves closer to Lee. "I don't give a rat's ass what happens to you. From the first time I heard your name I knew there'd be trouble."

Calvin shuffles in his place like a three-year-old who has to pee. "I don't know why you had to put that damn picture of yourself on the internet. Everything was going just fine until then. After Katie Lee saw your photo and the resemblance, she had to find you. Even after all of those years of never seeing you or hearing from you. See Burtrum, Katie knew you were alive, but she relinquished you to the Conner's after the accident because she didn't think she could take care of you, her being in a wheelchair and all."

Lee is stunned. What is this guy talking about?

He continues his rant. "I told Lyman, I told him this is a bad idea. He needs to let sleeping dogs rest, but he insisted I come down here, says he has more at stake than anyone, and do you know why?"

Calvin paces back and forth, stopping for a moment just long enough to rip the tape from Lee's mouth without her suspecting it. The pain is excruciating. Desperately, she licks her shredded lips with her dry tongue.

"I don't have the slightest idea what you're talking about," Lee gasps.

"I know, that's what makes it even better. You see my dear, you're a clone. Not just any clone, but the first human clone to still be alive."

Lee laughs. "You're not serious? Who are you? Where'd you come from?"

"I'm the only one who can save you." Calvin removes the tie from around Lee's eyes, while slicing the tape from her wrists and ankles. "The only reason I'm freeing you is because I know you won't run after I finish telling you everything."

Lee rubs her sore hands, stomping her feet, trying to regain circulation. "I don't know what you're talking about. Yes, I'm one of the first artificially inseminated babies, but Jane Conner is my mother, not this Katie Lee woman. I know all of this. I think you have the wrong person."

"No, Burtrum, there's no mistaking this." Calvin moves over to his sports jacket hanging on the back of a chair and reaches inside, pulling out what looks like a photograph. "Here, see for yourself."

Calvin hands Lee the picture. At first she doesn't want to trust him, but then curiosity overtakes her and she glances down at the aged still life. She can't believe her eyes, it's as though she's looking at herself. The resemblance is uncanny.

"Who is this?"

"Your mother, Katie Lee."

"This is some kind of trick you devised, maybe doctored up the photo so it looks like me."

"You see it, don't you? This is your true mom."

"This is ludicrous. I don't believe you."

"Well, you should because that's the reason I'm here to find you, but then I decided since everyone's being a jerk to me, I'll take things into my own hands and hold you for ransom. Then I'm gone, never to be heard from or seen again."

"And what about me?"

"That's up to you. I really don't want to hurt you. You

seem like a very nice lady. If you just go along with every-thing, then you'll be all right, but cause me trouble, and there's no telling what I might do." Calvin tries to scare Lee, but she only smirks at him.

"Yeah, right, you don't seem like you could hurt a fly."

Calvin raises his fists. "Oh yeah!" Shaking them piously. "Just don't push me." He plops down in a chair. "Now it's late, and I'm exhausted. Can I trust you?"

Lee shakes her head up and down.

"Then I'll leave the tape off."

"Don't worry, I won't try anything," Lee promises, not really wanting to see any of her family.

"Excellent! Then I'll be saying good night."

"Wait a minute, aren't you going to finish?"

"No, you'll find out the rest of the truth from the people who've been lying to you all these years. I hope you don't hold this against me, I'm not a bad man. I just got caught in a corrupt situation, that's all."

Calvin stretches out on the makeshift bed he's devised on the floor. "Good night, Burtrum."

"Lee," She corrects.

"Good night, Lee."

Lee analyzes Calvin as he closes his eyes, diving into sleep within minutes. Reflecting on her latest information, Lee becomes more and more angry. Has she really been lied to all of these years? Is her biological mother truly alive and searching for her? Is she really a clone? After all, she can't deny how identical she is to Katie Lee.

Feeling her mind short circuit, Lee lays out on the couch and closes her eyes. She's going to put an end to this mess, and that's that, she tells herself, drifting off into a tormented slumber.

❋ ❋ ❋

Dr. Lyman Stone is about to blow a gasket, as he slams the phone down in its cradle. "Jack-ass!" He screams, swiping the papers off his desk and onto the floor. He should have listened to his reservations when it came to sending Calvin down to Santa Fe. How hard is it to locate someone and not screw up? He can't harp on that now. Unless he quickly controls the situation, everything will explode in his face. And he's worked too hard over the decades to have his life be ripped out from beneath him.

Pressing the intercom button, Lyman screeches into the plastic box. "Penny, tell the pilot to be ready to fly out in forty-five minutes."

"Yes, Dr. Stone."

The line goes empty as Lyman sits back in his chair. He knows he has to keep his cool, keep this little secret to himself until he reaches Burtrum Lee. He didn't realize his experiment had truly worked until the discovery of Lee Conner. The only one left, after all those implants.

Lyman, reliving that fateful night, waiting in Los Alamos for the Lee's to arrive. Burtrum insisted on an unscheduled meeting. He'd discovered Lyman's plot. The scientist had been sure of it. His newly budding career would be finished before it even ripened.

But he had taken care of things. Unfortunately, Katie was one of the innocent victims. By the time he found out she was with him, it was too late, the flood gates had already been opened. Much to Lyman's dismay.

The intercom buzzes, and Lyman Stone holds down a button. "Yes."

"Your car is here to take you to the airport, sir."

"Thanks Penny, that'll be all for tonight."

Lyman Stone takes a deep breath, and picks up the phone one last time.

❋ ❋ ❋

Jane's cell vibrates in her pocket, as she reaches for it. Seeing Jed's name on the tiny screen, she flips the top up and holds it to her ear.

"Are you going to follow me for the rest of the night?" He sneers into the phone.

"Probably! Depends on where you plan on going?"

"To find help."

"From whom, one of those goons you refer to as friends?"

"Do you have any other suggestions?" Jed becoming annoyed.

"To be honest, I think the best thing for us to do is call it a night, and resume first thing in the morning."

"Doing what?"

"Trying to get our daughter back, that's what. Maybe, we should just settle up with the guy, for Lee's safety."

"I'm not paying that ass anything. I know we can find her, if we just use our senses."

"No, let's just pay the ransom."

Jed's silent for a moment. "We don't have it."

"What do you mean, we don't have it. The amount is chump change. We have that much in our smallest account."

"Not anymore," Jed's voice is somber.

"Jed, I'm not sure I understand what you're saying." Knowing perfectly well what he means, she just wants him to eat crow.

"Well, my dear, the bottom line is, we're broke."

"You're kidding me, right? Well, this isn't the time to be making jokes."

"No, Jane, we have no money, even our house is on lean."

"I don't get it. What did you do, Jed Conner?" Jane screams into the phone. Unaware of how broke they truly are.

By now, both cars are pulled over to the side of the road, and Jane whips out of the Benz, stuffing her cell phone into her pocket as she stomps up to Jed's identical Mercedes.

Slapping the window, she yells. "Open up, now."

Jed lowers his head, shaking it back and forth. He knew this day would come, but he didn't expect it to arrive so soon. He'd hoped to retrieve some of his losses back before Jane found out.

He unrolls the window. "Jane, you need to calm down, and lower your voice. It's late and we don't want to wake anyone. Now, go around to the other side of the car and get in."

Jane does as she's told, and finds herself being closer to her husband than she has been in a long time. She smells his scent, an unusual one of fear and desperation.

"Okay, Jed, tell me what happened."

"A couple of bad investments, and before I knew it, we were in the hole. And the more I tried to dig us out, the deeper we got. You know how careful I am about the business."

"Yes, I know," Jane wants to bring up the fact that maybe his having an affair didn't help things, but instead, bites her tongue. "Well I guess we can't worry about that right now, we have to concentrate on getting her back. Don't you have a friend who can bail you out of this?"

"No." Jed wipes his brow. "I tell you, we have nothing."

"What about Clair, I know she has money."

"I don't feel right about asking my mother for money."

Jane's brain is about to blow. "Damn it, Jed Conner, I'm sure it's your pride that got us into this mess, and I'm sure that it's your pride keeping you from going to Clair. Well, I say it's time to swallow it, or quit sitting on it, or one of those clichés, but the bottom line is, we have to take action."

"I guess you're right. Maybe we should go back to Clair's and talk to her about things."

"I think that's the best idea yet. Do you want me to drive with you, or follow behind in my own car?"

"You should drive your car. We don't want to leave it overnight in this area."

"Okay, then, I'll meet you there." Jane leans over and kisses Jed on the cheek. "Don't worry honey, everything will be all right. You just wait and see." Jane gets out of the car and returns to hers.

Jed Conner feels a sense of comfort while at the same

time, dread.

❁   ❁   ❁

Megan hesitates before stepping up to Clair's back door. The house is dark and she wonders if Clair has gone to bed. Megan figures it to be well past midnight, so she understands why all the lights are out.

Maybe this isn't such a great idea, she tells herself as she reaches for the door handle, and twists open the unlocked portal. Stepping in, Megan listens to the quietness of the night. The low rumbles from the refrigerator are the only sounds she hears as she sneaks into the living room.

Exhaustion over takes her as she crawls onto a chair and closes her eyes. Maybe she'll rest here for a moment until Clair wakes up, she decides, drowning in sleep.

❁   ❁   ❁

Lyman rings his hands through his thinning gray hair. He just called Wanda. Still no word as to where Calvin has taken his daughter.

Now what is he going to do?

Standing, he goes over to the liquor cabinet and pours himself another scotch. Downing the amber liquid, he throws the glass against the wall and watches as it shatters like a star exploding. Tiny shards of splintered crystal cover the carpeted aisle.

Everything is falling apart. This isn't what he'd envisioned all those years ago. Burtrum Lee should've never taken his wife with him that fateful night. He should've never taken Katie to New Mexico.

Lyman knew all along what Burtrum wanted to speak to him about, and when he found out Katie was with him and that they were on their way to the lab in a car that had been tampered with, well, there was nothing Lyman could do.

He'd wanted Dr. Lee out of the way as much as the others. The CEO of the lab was about to put a halt to their newest cloning experiments, just when they were on the verge of a breakthrough. Burtrum believing they were tampering with nature in an unhealthy manner. So, when Lyman got wind of his intent, Dr. Stone took it upon himself to assure his research continued. He never expected the outcome to be so gruesome, or heart breaking.

Well, it's all coming to a head now, and it is time to meet his fate. Reaching for his suit jacket, Dr. Lyman Stone wraps the hounds-tooth around his shoulders and leaves his office for the last time.

Lee awakes in a cold sweat. Shivers rack her, as a tired mind cries out for relief. She can't stop thinking about what Calvin said.

He has to be making this stuff up about her being a clone and all. How is that possible? Were they even experimenting with genetics like that in those days? Then again, who really knows how long any of this new scientific technology has been going on.

Like stem cells, or impregnating a cow with a human embryo to help carry the fetus to term. She wonders how that kid turned out. Humans, and their egos.

What will they tell the child when it grows up? "Oh, honey, a cow was your biological incubator."

Lee moans to herself. "We certainly live in a strange time," she contrives, trying once again to doze, but is unable to.

She worries about Megan, and how she is. Lee briefly remembers seeing her lying on the floor before she herself was knocked unconscious. She hopes her new friend is not injured. It's weird the way they met, with Lee feeling that immediate connection to her. Kind of like a cosmic thing. Like in some way, shape or form, they are related. Who knows, could just be all the stress she's been feeling.

Lee's brain becomes fuzzy as she rolls over and lies on her side. It doesn't take long this time for the sandman to find her, as Lee slowly dips into sleep, whispering Megan's name out loud.

❀　❀　❀

The Conner's pull up to Clair's dark house. "She must be in bed," Jane says, leaning into Jed's window.

"Well, I don't want to wake her, why don't we just go back to our place."

"Okay, I guess that's a good idea, and are you going to stay?"

Jed looks at his wife and then reaches for her hand. "If that's all right with you?"

Jane feels herself blush at Jed's tone. It has been a long

time since he's spoken to her so gently.

"Yes, of course, it's your house too."

The couple fall into silence for a moment, and then Jed asks. "Do you mind if I sleep in our bed?"

Jane squeezes his hand. "If you'd like to, Jed," she answers. "Now, let's go home."

Climbing into the passenger's side, the Conner's drive away from the shadow cased house, holding hands.

Katie Lee listens as Wanda snores the night away. She is tempted to hurl a shoe at her, but thinks twice. Earlier, she partially over heard the conversation Wanda was having with Lyman Stone. What do *they* have to talk about? They barely know each other. The bits and pieces she made out, are senseless. She'll inquire about the call in the morning. Why hadn't he wanted to speak to her, unless the two of them are in cahoots. She wants to scream, but all she can do is remain silent and pray that the dawn will rise soon. She hates the fact that she is so close to her daughter, yet can't talk to her.

Did she make a mistake all of those years ago?

These thoughts are a constant beating Katie has given herself throughout the decades. Did she do the right thing? Was her little girl okay without her? There was no way she could have raised a child. She can't even care for herself.

A warm tear rolls down her cheek as Katie Lee hopes it isn't too late.

❋   ❋   ❋

Detective Jose Sanchez sits behind his desk studying the license he found. The name wasn't in the motel register, so why was it in the room?

The romantic evening he'd planned with his wife had been totally blown, and she is so mad at him, he decided to stay at work to avoid her wrath. Plus, this false alarm is really beginning to bother him.

Twirling the laminated ID between his fingers, he looks at the address. 714 W. Santa Fe Street. Right by the capital. Maybe he should go check it out, see if there's anything suspicious going on, but then decides to wait 'till morning.

Figuring eventually, he has to buck up and face his adoring wife, he turns the light out, and leaves his office. First thing in the morning he'll investigate Burtrum Lee Conner's house.

❋   ❋   ❋

Carla Kramer has never been so scared in her life, and now Lyman has her on a plane to who-knows-where, and he's well aware about her fear of flying.

When he showed up that evening, she thought he was just stopping by for a quick romp, but when he knocked her down and then threatened her at gun point to either come with him, or die, she really didn't have a choice.

Carla knew from the very beginning when they first started having this affair, that it would lead to trouble, and tonight her problems appeared at the door.

All along Carla wondered if Lyman was really interested in her, or whether he's just using her to get something. She never figured out what that something was, so she thought maybe he really does love her.

Tonight though, he's proving her wrong.

"Lyman, what are you doing, where are we going?" She cries out as he pushes her up the fuselage's staircase.

"Just shut up and get on."

The pressure of a gun jabs her in the back. "I don't understand, why are you doing this. If it's some kind of surprise date, you're certainly going about it the wrong way."

"I said, shut up," he screams and throws her to the floor.

Sobs ring out of Carla as she stumbles to get to her feet, afraid of what Lyman will do if she really pissed him off. "But I'm afraid of flying, Lyman. Can't we just take the car."

"We don't have time for that. Now sit down and buckle up, we'll be taking off shortly."

Carla watches as Lyman disappears behind the door to the cockpit. Not only is she about to fly, but she is about to take off in a tin-can no bigger than her walk-in closet.

Thinking of Calvin's desperate phone calls she ignored because she believed she and Lyman were going to run away together, makes her sad. She's been a fool, and realizes Dr. Stone's been using her to hold over Calvin.

Whomever this Burtrum Conner is, she certainly is ruining a lot of lives.

"Oh, Calvin, if I've ever needed you before, I need you more now," Carla whispers to herself as she hears her captor coming back.

22

Calvin Kramer jumps up like a Jack in a Box. Sweat trickles down his temples as he desperately wipes them away. Something isn't right, he thinks, shining the flashlight at Lee who lies sound asleep.

His breaths ease slightly as Calvin surveys the rest of the room. Everything seems to be the same as when he went to sleep, what is this agitation gnawing at his nerves?

It has to be Carla, something is wrong, he can feel it down to his raw bones. Stumbling to his feet, and trying not to wake Lee, Calvin tip-toes into the kitchen where earlier he saw a phone attached to the wall.

Picking up the receiver he sticks the tip of his thick finger into one of the holes of the dial. Twirling the device to the number of his home, he waits for Carla to pick up, and when she doesn't, he immediately tries her cell, but to no avail.

"Damn-it," he hisses, slamming the ear piece into the

metal hook.

What is going on?

Everything he is trying to accomplish won't be worth squat if Carla isn't there. Has she left him? Calvin has always suspected that she is seeing someone on the side, but doesn't really want to admit it to himself, because lately it seems like she's starting to return to him, not physically, but more on an emotional level, and that's why this trip has proven to be so destructive to their reuniting.

Calvin reaches for the phone again, this time dialing Lyman's number. Maybe he knows where his wife is.

Lee opens her eyes slightly as she hears Calvin shuffle into the kitchen. What is he up to? She listens as he keeps dialing numbers on the telephone and then slamming it down. But now, he seems to be talking in a rough, gruff voice to someone Lee is sure he's angry with.

Is he speaking with Katie Lee?

For a split second Lee wants to run over to Calvin and rip the receiver out of his hand, hear her mother's voice for the first time. Erase years of silence, decades of separation. But she knows that'll be a bad move. She's sensing Calvin is on the verge of snapping at any minute, and right now, Lee wants to stay on his good side, so she can find out more about her past. There are still a few things that don't add up.

Shutting her eyes as she hears Calvin's return, she's stunned when brightness surrounds her and she feels him pulling her off the couch.

"Get up. I know you're awake."

Lee tries to act like he's just aroused her from a deep sleep, but he isn't buying it.

"We're getting out of here."

"Why, what time is it? Can't we wait until dawn?"

"I said we're leaving, so put your shoes on and grab whatever you need. I don't want to hear another word about it."

Lee knows something's wrong. Has Calvin's plan taken a bad turn? His voice is shaky, yet determined, his body actions deliberate, yet hesitant. It's as though he's experiencing two separate sensations at the same time and doesn't know how to handle it. Figuring the best thing she can do is to play along with him, Lee puts her loafers on, and says. "Do you mind if I go to the bathroom first?"

Calvin shakes his head. "You might want to think about getting your bladder checked. Go ahead, but make it fast."

Lee disappears down the hall, glancing back into the living room before entering the bathroom. Calvin stands in place wringing his face with his hands, muttering something to himself. Lee doesn't like the look or feel of this at all and knows that it's too late to make a run for it.

Lyman glares at Carla as the phone stuffed in her pocket begins to ring. They just landed at the Santa Fe Airport and are about to get into their car when the familiar tune of *I Am Woman*, begins to jingle out of her coat.

Cramming his hand into her pocket, Lyman snatches the

cell phone, and not recognizing the number, lets it go to voice mail. Snarling at Carla, Lyman snaps. "You certainly are one stupid bitch."

"Lyman, why are you talking to me like that? I thought you said we'd be together forever, isn't that true?"

"Never believe what a man says, Carla, you should know that by now." Holding the phone up to his ear as he retrieves the message, he smiles richly. "It's from your husband. I want you to call him back, find out where he is, but don't you dare mention that you're here."

"No, I refuse. I'm not going to set my husband up so that you can hurt him. I already damaged our marriage, he does-n't need any more disappointments. Calvin's a good man, and the reason why he's in trouble is because of you, Lyman. You and only you. You pushed him too far and now he's flipped."

"Shut up and call him, or both of you will be sorry. You don't know what's on the line here Carla, and believe me, neither you, nor Calvin's life, is worth half as much as any of this." He twists her arm. "Now call him."

"What should I say?"

"Ask him where he is and how he's been doing, and make something up about why you haven't been answering the phone or returning his calls. You know, maybe tell him you went to one of your favorite spas where you're not al-lowed to communicate with the outside world."

"I should tell him about us. How you promised to run away with me and that's why I haven't been available." Carla yanks her arm out of Lyman's grasp.

Slightly taken aback by her surprising strength, he

reaches for it again, but this time she is able to avoid his clutch.

"Then what, Lyman? What's going to happen after you find him? You gonna kill us?"

"No, don't be ridicules, we'll just go back to normal, how it was before everything happened."

Carla can't tell if he is lying or not, up until this point his words seemed genuine. Something happened, though, that made him change, and right now Carla's receiving a bad vibe from her soon to be ex-lover.

"Okay, give me the phone."

Dr. Stone hands her the cell and watches as Carla looks at the caller ID number and punches it into the carrier.

He'll find out where Calvin is, and then take care of this nonsense once and for all.

Calvin shivers when he hears Lee's phone ring, wondering if he should answer it or not. Finally, walking into the kitchen, he picks up the receiver and listens.

"Calvin? Calvin, is that you? It's Carla."

Relief washes over him, like a tidal waved beach. "Carla, where are you? I've been trying to reach you for the past few days."

Glancing at Lyman, Carla flips him the bird, and continues. "I went up to the Russian River to think things out."

"To think what out?" Calvin's heart leaps in his chest.

"I don't know Calvin. Just stuff. I'm feeling a little confused about life and just wanted to try and get grounded."

"And have you?"

Carla can hear tension in her husband's voice, and the warm feelings of love she believed had died, spark to life. "Yes, I have, and when you get home we'll talk about things, okay. I think it's time we livened up our marriage somehow, you know, maybe we can figure something out that will put some juice back into us."

Silence passes through the line, and for a split second, Carla thinks Calvin has hung up.

"Calvin you there?"

"Yes, I'm just mulling," his voice is strained.

"I don't mean to worry you. Believe me when I say that you're the only person I want to be with, and whatever may happen between us, that will always ring true."

"I'm not sure what you're getting at."

"That's okay. We'll talk when you get home. When will that be, and where are you? This number on my phone isn't familiar."

"I'm still in Santa Fe. I've run into a little snag."

"How little? I thought this was supposed to be a cut and dry job."

"It was, but then things started to get complicated. I can't explain it right now. I wish you were here. Maybe you should fly down, and after this mess is cleared up, we can drive to Mexico for a little vacation before going back to Frisco."

"I don't know, Calvin. Why don't you just come home. Call Lyman and tell him to finish the job himself, that you've had enough."

"He'll fire me, honey."

"So what, you're a great scientist, you can get a job anywhere."

"Not if he black lists me."

"He won't do that."

Carla inspects Lyman, leaning against the car, patting his side where a gun is jammed into his belt.

"Don't be too sure."

"Well, where are you? I tried calling the motel you were staying at, but they said you checked out."

"Yeah, I had to leave fast, something came up. Now, I'm hiding at that woman's house. You know, the one I'm supposed to locate, well, I found her."

"What are you doing there?"

"Like I stated earlier, it's just too out of joint to explain right now. Listen, I really need to get going. I miss you sweetheart, and I can't wait to see you. Are you sure everything's all right?"

"Yes, Calvin, don't worry about anything. Just hurry up, finish, and come home, okay. I miss you."

"I miss you too, Carla, I just wish you were here. Things would be so much easier if I had you by my side," Calvin's voice cracks, and Carla detects something terrible is wrong.

"Honey, what's going on?"

"I don't know. I just think I've really messed up this time and I'm not sure how I'm going to get out of it."

"Calvin, please tell me what you're talking about."

"I can't. Listen I have to go. I'll call you later. Don't try to contact me here because I'm leaving, but you can call me on my cell phone. I love you Carla, and soon everything will be different. Bye."

"I love you too, Calvin." Carla listens to the phone click dead.

Calvin leans against the wall as he hangs up the receiver, and strokes his face with his fingers. Lee, coming around the corner, sees her captor grimace. Compassion arises inside of her, a kind of sorrow for this man who is obviously wrought with indecision.

"Is everything all right?" She asks, not wanting to over step her ground.

Calvin casts a glance up in surprise, not hearing her approach. "Yes," he chokes out. "Everything is fine." Straightening himself. "Have you packed? It might be a while before you return."

"I don't need anything. You know, we can work this out before someone gets hurt, don't you think?"

"No, I believe it's too late." Calvin keeps hearing the background noise from Carla's phone, and the announcement he heard for a flight about to leave the Santa Fe airport. Is Carla in New Mexico, and is she lying to him? Why? What reason does she have for deceiving him?

Lyman Stone is behind this!

Grabbing Lee, he swings her around and leads her back into the living room. Realizing he's made a mistake by telling Carla where he is. "We've got to get out of here fast. I'm not going to let him get you."

❋ ❋ ❋

Lyman rips the phone out of Carla's hand and throws the device into the yellow grassy field across from the parking lot. She watches it disappear into the weeds, as a cold fear penetrates her. "What are you doing? That's my phone. All my information is stored in there. Don't think you're not going to replace it."

"Shut up." Lyman raises his hand to her. "Where is he?"

Carla stands her ground. "He's at Burtrum Conner's house." She turns toward the knoll to retrieve her phone.

"What?"

"Yeah, he had to leave the motel quickly and he brought her home because he figured no one would think to look for them there." Carla smiles. "Kind of ingenious, if I do say so myself."

"That idiot." Lyman lowers his hand, and opening the car door, pushes Carla into the back seat. He points his gun at her head. "I don't want to hear one little peep out of you, do you understand?"

"My word, Lyman, you need to calm down before you have a coronary. Even if you are threatening me with a gun, you can't talk to me like that, not after what we've been through."

Carla doesn't see it coming, the motion is so quick. At first she's numb, until she hears the crunching of her cheek bone, as a throbbing pain echoes through her. She collapses on the seat, feeling warmth ooze out of her nose and mouth. Green and white stars waltz in front of her, as nausea hustles in her stomach. The blackness is a welcome comfort as she dreams of Calvin and how she might never see him alive again.

❖ ❖ ❖

Clair bolts up, her old bones complaining at the sudden motion. It takes her a moment to get her bearings, her mind fogged in from the deep sleep and disturbing dreams that flash in her memory. Something about a woman lying fetal in a mud pond, and sensing she is dead. Clair visualizes a purple shirt and green shorts worn by the unknown body.

Shaking her head, she hurls her aged legs over the side of the bed and checks the time. 6:42. How did she sleep so late?

Balancing herself against the bedpost, Clair feels weak, and out of energy, as if someone or something has pulled the plug on her life force. She won't be brought down. No way, no how.

Slowly shuffling to the bathroom, Clair splashes water on her face and studies herself in the mirror. What is she going to do? Her granddaughter is in trouble and there's nothing in her power that can help.

If she paid the ransom, what insurance does she have that Lee won't be hurt or killed, anyway. What guarantee is there?

Clair eases herself down the staircase, holding tight to the rail, wondering how much longer will she be mobile enough to climb up and down these steps.

Orange sun streaks crisscross through the kitchen window, as Clair stops for a moment to take in the beauty of the coming day. If there is one thing in the world that's constant, it's nature, and each and every day that Clair Conner can participate, is a blessing to her.

Filling the coffee pot and turning it on, Clair notices a piece of paper lying on the counter top. She goes over to the note and picks it up.

DEAR CLAIR,

I'M TRULY SORRY TO RUN OUT ON YOU LIKE THIS, BUT I'M TOO RESTLESS TO SLEEP, FEELING LIKE I SHOULD BE DOING SOMETHING, BUT NOT KNOWING WHAT, SO, I THOUGHT I'D HEAD OVER TO LEE'S HOUSE AND SEE IF I CAN FIND ANY-THING THAT MIGHT LEAD US TO HER. I'LL CALL YOU LATER. DON'T WORRY.

SINCERELY,

MEGAN

When did Megan return? And why is she doing something so dumb and dangerous?

She needs to call Jed, and have him meet Megan at Birdy's house.

Picking up the plastic phone, Clair struggles to punch in her son's telephone number, cursing at the smallness of the digits.

Megan pulls up in front of Lee's house and turns off the car. The street is quiet, tinted a gray/yellow hue. Dawn! A few birds twitter in the distance, songs fill the breeze. A perfect spring morning, almost feels like summer, Megan thinks, as she contemplates her next move.

Remaining in the car, she scan's the house. Is there a light burning? She doesn't recall turning any on when she was here. Is there somebody in the house? Quietly opening the door, Megan steps out into an unexpected cold wind, whipping her in the face, making her eyes shed a tear. So much for that summer sensation!

Closing the car door, but not all the way, Megan tip-toes across the street and to the side of the house, where she carefully peeks through an open curtain window. Astounded, she holds her breath. There, with only a pane of glass dividing them, stands Lee.

Pacing back and forth is her kidnapper, ranting about something. The situation doesn't look good, but Megan realizes that Lee isn't gagged or tied up. Has she gotten free on her own. The two seem like they're having a conversation. Are they commiserating together?

Megan has to get Lee's attention, but how? She'll wait until he turns around or something and then tap on the window. But she doesn't have to, Lee suddenly about faces and sees Megan squatting in the bushes. At first her expression is of pure disbelief, and she doesn't seem to recognize her, but then Lee makes a slight motion to Megan, directing her to go to the other side of the house.

Not knowing what to make of it, Megan sneaks around and waits.

❋ ❋ ❋

"Listen, I know you're upset, and that you want to get out of here right away, but I need to go to the bathroom just one more time, you know woman problems," Lee pleads with Calvin.

Not wanting to hear anything more about *women problems*, Calvin waves Lee away, saying. "Just make it quick. We don't have much time." Turning away from her, he peers out the same window Lee was just at, and hisses. "Women!"

Rushing to the bathroom, Lee closes the door behind her, making sure it's locked. She hurls the lattice open, and sticks her head out into the tinted orange morning. "Megan, Megan," she yells softly, glancing back at the latch.

"Lee!" Megan appears from around the corner and jogs up to the window. "My lord, are you all right?"

"Yes, yes, I'm fine, a little tired, but other than that, he's done nothing to me."

"Well, good. Then let's try to get you out of here, and then I'll call the cops to come arrest this guy." Megan begins to yank at Lee's shoulders. She pushes her away.

"No, wait, stop. I'm not going anywhere."

"What are you talking about? This guy's gonna hurt you, don't you see? You're just acting crazy. You know I'm right. What, do you have a case of the Stockholm Syndrome?"

"No! I've never felt so sensible in my life. This guy knows my real mother, and I think he can lead me to her, don't you see?"

"There are other ways of meeting your biological mother. Safe ways, without involving a lunatic."

"He's not crazy. He just got caught in something he shouldn't have. Trust me, this guy wouldn't hurt a fly."

"Yeah, well he certainly put a punch to me."

"Listen, I don't have much time before he starts to suspect something. Tell my grandmother and parents that I'm fine, and not to worry. Okay? And when this is over, we can all sit down and have a real family dinner."

Megan stares at Lee for a long time, and it's as though she's gazing at herself. They have some similarities. In a way, Megan believes, they could be sisters. But that's ridiculous. She's an orphan, how could there be any connection?

"Well, let me at least follow you so that I know where you're going."

"I don't think that's a very good idea. Calvin might notice you, and then it'll ruin everything."

"What are his plans, do you know?"

"I think he's asking a ransom from Jane and Jed, and then more from Katie Lee. That's my real mother's name. I'm not sure though. I just caught bits and pieces of what he was saying." Lee glances back at the door again, thinking she hears footsteps coming closer. "I gotta go. I'll see you later, okay?"

"Yeah, I guess so." Megan worries as Lee vanishes through the door. She can't believe Lee's is going to play along with that creep. She's not thinking straight. He's already done something to her. A kind of brainwashing.

Well, whether Lee likes it or not, Megan isn't going to just stand around and do nothing.

❋ ❋ ❋

Jane Conner opens her swollen eye lids and tries to recall what happened last night. Rolling over, she touches Jed's leg, and the memory of their love making comes flooding back. Did they truly re-connect?

Studying him for a while, not yet wanting to wake him, Jane realizes how much she misses their passion. A crease of pain sheiks through her brain, as a dull throbbing begins to pound. Once again she drank too much last night. Maybe now though, with her and Jed finding each other again, she won't depend on booze any longer.

Wanting to reach out and stroke Jed's face, Jane catches herself for a brief instant, recalling the feelings that they had shared so many years ago. Pure, undaunted love. They couldn't live without each other. They didn't want to be apart, be separated, everything in their world was perfect and they wanted it to last forever.

But it didn't.

Her stillbirth changed everything. And then stealing Lee like that. She knew what they did was wrong, but there was nothing she could do about it. She was out of her mind, and by the time she'd come to her senses, it was too late.

And now look.

Over the past few years she's noticed her and Lee growing apart, severing a close tie they shared as mother and daughter. There was always something missing. Jane wonders if it's the same for every mother and adopted child. Is the biological bond a key to truly feeling like a mother?

Jed moans, and rolls over onto his back. His eye lids flutter for a moment, and Jane thinks he's waking up, but he continues to lie there. She'll let him sleep for just a while longer, then she'll rouse him. There are too many things that need to be done.

Finding her daughter is one of them, because even if she and Lee don't share blood between them, they've shared their lives. Her and Jed are all Lee knows for parent's and even though it doesn't seem like they did a very good job, she turned out all right.

Granted, she isn't in a relationship, and has jumped from job to job most of her life. She had the opportunity to go away to any college she wanted, but chose instead not too. It seems like Lee lacks something, and it's not just her biological mother.

Jane continues to watch her husband, thankful that he is there lying beside her.

❋　❋　❋

Jed feels Jane staring at him. He wants to tell her to stop it, but then she'll know he's awake. He hasn't slept all night, and for that matter not very well since this whole thing began.

Nothing like fate coming back to slap you in the face.

That dreadful night keeps reeling through his mind, when he went back to the accident and discovered Katie was still alive, and then leaving her for dead. He's never forgiven himself for that, and when he found out she survived after all, he was relieved, but still damned himself for being a coward.

Things would be so different if he just would have been a man about things.

❋　❋　❋

The nightmare rages back. Katie swearing to herself as

her eyes pop open. What did it all mean? It had disappeared for many years, and just recently, when she arrived in Santa Fe, it re-appeared, not making sense this time either. Deciding to write it down before she forgets the new details, Katie Lee reaches for a pen and paper sitting next to her on the night stand.

I'm getting on a bus to return to San Francisco. The driver takes off so fast that I'm thrown to the back and have to hold onto the rails so as not to fall out the open emergency door. I notice he's driving east instead of west, and then suddenly I realize I've gotten on the wrong bus. In my fog, I'd stepped onto the number three, whereas I should've boarded number six. He keeps driving further and further away and I can see the Minneapolis skyline in the distance, even though I've never seen it before. The driver, unannounced, stops to let a couple board. They have two babies who are crying. I have a bad feeling about them and remain in the back of the bus. They immediately start killing the passengers and bus driver. I disembark and run, but don't know where I am going. All around me are acres of dried yellow corn, and snow- capped mountain tops. They look familiar. A few passengers, who also escaped, join me, and we start trudging through the fields until we reach a farm. They are bringing horses out of the stables, large plow horses, and for some reason everyone is relieved because they feel safe now, but I know differently. I worry about the twins, because I believe they're mine.

The sudden blast of the phone brings her back to reality. Katie listens as Wanda answers on the third ring. Sliding into the room, still garbed in her bathrobe, Wanda sits on the edge of Katie's bed and hands her the mobile phone.

"It's Lyman."

"Where is he?"

"He didn't say. He just wants to talk to you." She waves the black slim box in front of Katie. "Take it."

Snagging the cell out of Wanda's hand, Katie places it to her ear and speaks. "Yes, Lyman, hello. Where have you been?"

"Right here, at the lab, what do you think?"

"I've been trying to reach you for the past day or two, and you always seem to be too busy even to talk to your boss. So, tell me, what's been so important," Katie's tone is filled with tense dissatisfaction.

"I'll explain it when you get back."

"No, you'll explain it now, or I'll call security and have them escort you out of the building."

"You're too late, I'm not there. I'm in Santa Fe, on my way to claim my daughter."

"You're daughter, what are you talking about."

"It used only my DNA for our clone, don't you understand. There is nothing about your late, *so called*, great husband in the mix."

"What, what are you talking about, Lyman, why are you rehashing this? I know you contaminated the experiment with your DNA, you told me that a long time ago, and I'd thought we'd gotten past it."

"Yes, but you still don't get it. The embryo that I inseminated you with had none of Burtrum's DNA. It was just yours and mine. Burtrum Lee Conner is a combination of us. We're the lucky parents, and now I'm going to stake my claim, and there's no court in this country that will have a word to say about it."

Katie Lee is flabbergasted, her head sparks like loose-live battery cables touching. The room begins to whirl, and for a split second she believes she's going to pass out. Taking a couple of deep breaths, she tries to compose herself, knowing she has to keep things together if she's going to save her daughter from this madman.

"Where are you, Lyman?"

"Just outside your door step, Katie. You were so stupid to let them steal our child. Do you know how great she could've been? She was designed for immortality, for fame and fortune, but those schleps ruined her."

"You're insane!"

"Am I?"

Katie hears blackness come across the line. "Lyman, Lyman, are you there?" He hung up.

"Bastard!" Katie throws the phone across the room, but her lack of strength barely gets it past the end of the bed. Sobs overcome her, and her body shakes in tear-filled spasms.

Wanda sits down beside her and wraps Katie in her arms. "There, there, sweetheart, calm down, you don't want to hurt yourself. Tell me what Lyman said."

"Oh, my, Wanda, he said Lee's a clone. He said he combined his and my DNA to make her and left Burtrum's out, and now he's here in Santa Fe to claim his daughter."

Wanda stares into Katie's eyes. They fill with pools of spilling tears. "What?"

"Yes, that's why he called. He's going to kidnap her and try to reprogram her so that she meets his expectations that he set for her all those years ago. He's going to destroy my little girl."

Katie Lee wipes her face, whipping the covers off her legs. "Come, Wanda, help me up, and get me dressed. My daughter needs me and there's nothing that is going to stand in my way."

"Just wait a minute, Katie. You're a little wound up." Wanda tries to pull the blanket back up, but Katie pushes them away.

"Now, Wanda!" The caretaker is familiar with that tone in Katie's voice, and knows better than to question it. As loving and compassionate as Katie Lee is, you don't want to piss her off. "And get Calvin on the phone and my accountant. I'm going to pay this man off and get Burtrum back safely."

"Okay, okay, let me get a bath going for you, while you talk to Calvin." Wanda bumps her way to the end of the bed, and moaning, bends over and picks the phone up. "If you hadn't broken your cell, I wouldn't be breaking my back. Here." Reaching out her hand.

"Quit your whining, I have enough on my mind without you filling it with dribble."

Wanda picks up Katie's address book as she passes by the chest of drawers, and tosses the brown leather covered volume next to Katie. "There, dial it yourself."

"Getting a little lazy these days?" She chides.

"Nope, just thought I'd save me a few steps since I know you're going to have me running around all day," Wanda's tone is filled with playful care. "I'll be right out."

She disappears down the small hall and into the bathroom where she shuts the door behind her, locking it. Hurrying over to the bathtub she turns on the faucets. Pulling her personal cell phone out of her robe pocket, Wanda presses the number two speed dial button and listens as the phone on the other side rings. A gruff voice answers.

"What do you want, I'm busy."

"You'd better not be too busy for me. What in the hell do you think you're doing, telling Katie the truth, you almost killed the woman?"

"So, what, that'd be a burden lifted off you."

"Katie is not a burden."

"Oh yes, I forgot, my little sister is in-love with her. A go-no-where forty-year-old crush. How pathetic is that? The old hag can't even have sex."

"Knock it off Lyman. You've gone too far this time, and if you harm a hair on Burtrum Lee Conner, I'll kill you."

"You don't have the guts, Sis."

"Yeah, well you wait and see." Wanda pushes the end button without saying another word to her crazed brother. She and Lyman have kept it a secret that they are siblings. All those years ago, Lyman had gotten her the job as Katie Lee's caregiver, so that she could keep an eye on her for him.

At first everything was all right, but as the years grew, so did Wanda's fondness for Katie Lee, and she often regretted having to spy on her. But now, Lyman has gone too far, and Wanda knows that she'll go to all lengths to protect her friend.

Turning off the faucets, Wanda returns, noticing Katie Lee just hanging up. "Well?"

"He's agreed to meet us at Shidoni."

"Shidoni, where in the hell is that?"

"He says it's about ten or fifteen minutes from here. I guess it's some kind of foundry where they make all these sculptures. I don't know, that's what he said. Anyway, we can take a cab there."

"That's going to cost some bucks." Wanda has always been a penny pincher.

"Stop, now get me into the bath, we need to be up there at noon, and we have a lot of things to do before that. Stephens is wiring money to the bank across the street and we'll be able to pick it up at eleven. Until then, we'll just have to pray that Lyman doesn't find them first."

❂ ❂ ❂

"It took you long enough. What were you doing in there?" Calvin grabs Lee's arm and sits her down in a chair. "There's been a change of plans, and I need to tie you up for a little while. Your mom's just come through with the cash and I don't want you getting any ideas and taking off before I have the briefcase in my hands." He tightens the ties around her ankles, and wrists, giving just enough leeway for her to walk.

"What are you talking about, I'm not going to bolt on you. Don't you understand that I want to meet my real mother more than anything."

"I'm sorry Lee, I wish I could trust you, but I can't take the chance." He stands her up. "Come on, we've got to get out of here, I have a strange feeling all of a sudden." Picking up his back pack, Calvin shuffles Lee to the back door, stepping onto the porch. "Now, just wait here until I go get the car, and don't try anything funny, got it. Trust me, you won't get far."

Calvin loosely bounds Lee to the rail, and stuffing a bandana in her mouth, jogs away.

She can hear him panting even though he's only turned the corner.

A click on the window catches Lee's attention, and she turns to see Megan standing behind a bush, her finger to her lips.

Lee moans as Megan tip-toes up to her, and pulls the wad out of her mouth. "Megan, listen, he's taking me up to Shidoni to meet with Katie Lee. You've got to get hold of my parent's and Clair, okay. My grandma is number one on the speed dial. Call them and then contact the police."

"Why Shidoni?"

"I don't know, I think he saw a brochure on my coffee table and decided to be spontaneous. But please, you need to leave now, I think he's coming back." They peer toward the driveway.

"Okay, I'll wait until you leave and then I'll go in, okay."

"Yes, but hurry, now hide, I can hear his car."

Megan replaces the handkerchief into Lee's mouth, and scurries back behind the bushes at the side of the house. Peeking around the corner, she watches as Calvin loads Lee into the back seat, unseen.

Her heart aches as the feeling of sadness washes over her. Did she do the right thing by letting him take her again? Should she have set Lee free?

❋ ❋ ❋

Megan waits for a little while longer as the car pulls out of the driveway. Then, stealth like, she races into the house, closing the door behind her. Reaching for the phone, she presses the number one button and listens as a tin-can ring floats through her numbing brain.

Time seems to last forever before someone answers. Unfortunately, it's Jed.

"Lee?" His voice filled with concern.

"No, no, Mr. Conner, it's Megan. I'm calling from Lee's house. I just saw her and she wants me to tell you he's taking her to Shidoni. The meeting is at noon."

"Where'd you see her?"

"Here, at her house. That guy still has her, and is taking her to Shidoni to make a deal with Katie Lee, her biological mother. Do you understand?" Megan knows her tone is sharp, but for crying out loud, how many times does she have to explain it.

Jed doesn't appreciate Megan's attitude, but decides not to mention it, because, she too, is in danger and doesn't know it.

"Megan, listen to me. You need to get out of that house and meet us up at Clair's as soon as possible. It's not safe for you to be there."

"I don't understand. I really don't have anything to do with this mess. I just saw Lee, and all I'm trying to do is help her because I think she's a nice woman. I don't want to see her get hurt. Which doesn't seem to be of your concern from what I'm sensing. What you need to do is get up to

Shidoni and hel. . ."

"Hello, Megan." Jed hears an empty line, then.

"Why, Mr. Conner, hello, what a pleasant surprise to finally be able to talk to the man who stole my daughter."

"What? Who is this?"

"My name is Dr. Lyman Stone, and it wasn't just Katie Lee's child you abducted, but mine, and believe me you, when this is all said and done, I'm going to make all of you Conner's pay."

Dread fills Jed as he listens to this stranger's voice, dark and lifeless. He hopes Lyman doesn't have a clue who Megan really is. When Jed sent his PI out to find information on Megan Masterson, he had no idea what would be uncovered, information he never suspected.

"Where's Megan?"

"Oh, don't worry about her, she's just fine. She's agreed to show me where that buffoon is taking Burtrum. Then, after that, who knows. She's really of no use to me. So, Mr. Conner, I guess I'll see you in court, and no need for you to bring your checkbook, because you won't be able to buy your way out of this one." The line disconnects and Jed stands frozen, shaken white, when he hears Clair's voice.

"Jed, what is it?"

Jane comes over to him, touching his cheek with her hand. "Jed, is it Lee, did they find her?"

He walks away and sits down at the table. "No, well, yes, but no they don't have her yet."

"Jed, you're not making any sense. Here drink some of this coffee, and maybe you can
    think straight."

"Listen you two, sit down. I need to tell you something about Megan."

The anguish rippling through Jed's face sends dread down Jane's spine, and makes Clair feel sick to her stomach, both sitting simultaneously.

"What is it Jed?" Jane asks reaching for his hand.

"I know you don't like it when I do things like this, but I sent my private eye out in search of some insight into Megan's past. Apparently Katie Lee had twins. She must've given birth at the hospital, or after we left. I swear she was dead." He lowers his head, disgusted with his lie, and begins again. "From what my source says, the baby ended up in Minneapolis, Minnesota, by the name of Megan Masterson."

"You got to be kidding me. Are you insinuating, what I think you are?" Jane's voice rises a pitch.

"Yes, Jane, Megan is Lee's twin."

"They don't look anything alike, Jed. I think you're over doing it a little bit. The stress is starting to get to you." Jane pats his hand.

"I'm telling you the truth." He slides a blue envelope on the table. "Here, look for yourself."

The room falls silent. Birds chirping in the warm morning, fly off shaded branches, shimmering the lime leaves.

"You're serious, aren't you?"

"Yes, I'm telling you the truth, and now Megan's life is in danger. That was her just now calling from Lee's house. She saw Lee, who's being taken to Shidoni as we speak. I guess a meeting is going down with Katie Lee."

"He's not lying," Clair chimes in. "I knew she had twins,

I'm the one who found the second child and brought her to the church. I never told anyone, not even Katie. I just wanted that baby to be as far away from the whole scene as possible. Who would've ever guessed she'd show up in Santa Fe." Clair stands up, almost knocking over the chair. "We'll discuss this later. Right now, we need to go help Birdy."

"My lord, this is way too much!" Jane Conner plops into a chair.

"No, Mother, just wait," Jed pleads. "While Megan was talking, the phone was ripped away from her and this man comes on the line. It was Dr. Stone. He starts babbling about how Lee is his daughter, and how we ruined her life and now he's going to destroy ours! The thing is, if he finds out who Megan really is, who knows what he'll do."

"Then, we'll have to keep it between ourselves. Katie Lee and Dr. Stone don't know about Megan, so, we'll just keep this between ourselves for the time being," Clair suggests.

"Katie Lee will recognize her child right off, isn't there that mother/daughter thing they talk about all the time."

Both women glance down, neither one of them birthing a girl. Noticing this, Jed says, "Anyway, we need to get to Shidoni before something really bad happens. So, go grab what you need and meet me by the Pathfinder, okay?"

As long as Clair has known Jane, she's never been at a loss for words. But, this time, silence perched itself on her daughter in-law's tongue.

❖ ❖ ❖

"Let me go, let me go." Megan tries to wriggle out of the large man's grasp, but it's useless. She watches as the skinny, older man, who reminds her of Mr. Burns from the Simpson's, threatens Mr. Conner over the phone.

What is he talking about? He thinks he's Lee's real father? How can that be? Things are certainly getting more and more complicated, Megan concludes, deciding her efforts to free herself are fruitless. There is no way she can squirm free.

The man who calls himself Dr. Stone, hangs up and slithers over to her. Eyes flaring in raging insanity. He raises a hand as if he's going to strike her. Megan stands tall. "Go ahead, you friggin freak. I know men like you, and how they get off by hitting a woman, so go right ahead, you piss-ant for a man." Megan has no idea where this surge of courage is coming from. All she knows is that she's sick of it all and is really pissed off.

"Young lady, if I were you, I'd keep my mouth shut until you are spoken to. Now tell me, where is Calvin bringing Burtrum."

"I don't know what you're talking about. I don't know either one of them."

"Damn you little liar." This time Lyman swings his arm to strike Megan, but it's caught in mid-air as Megan hears a female voice.

"That's enough, Lyman," the tone is angry.

Dr. Stone rips his arm from the grip of the woman. "I thought I told you to stay in the car."

"You were taking so long, I wanted to know what was going on." Carla steps out from behind Lyman. "Is this her?

Your prize possession, well not yet, at least."

"No."

"She resembles you a little."

"I told you, it's not her." He pushes Carla away from him, she stumbles onto the couch. "Go wait in the car."

"No, I'm staying here, I don't trust you with this woman." Carla goes over and stands next to Megan.

"She knows where they are."

Carla asks. "Is that true?"

"Yes," Megan replies, suddenly surrendering.

Sitting down next to her, Carla takes Megan's hand and holds it in her own. "Now listen to me, I don't mean to scare you, but I think you should know what kind of man you're dealing with here. He'll stop at nothing to get his way, and I mean nothing. So, if I were you, I wouldn't waste anymore of his time, and just tell him."

Megan shouts abruptly. "What are you people? When did you stop living in reality?"

Megan doesn't see the back of Lyman's hand as it swats her cheek, sending creasing ripples of pain shooting through her head. Feeling blood flow from her nose, she falls down as pulsating shocks of darkness flash in firecracker rhythms in front of her eyes.

She hears Carla scream, before passing out.

"Damn-it, Lyman, what are you doing?"

He towers over the two women. "She either tells me what I want to know, or I'll give her a good dose of reality," he threatens, tossing a glass of water on Megan.

Coming up coughing, Megan spits on the floor.

Carla leans over Megan. "Honey, are you all right," she

whispers in her ear. "I think it's best you tell him where they're going."

Megan doesn't think twice this time. Swallowing some blood, she coughs out, "Shidoni."

"Shidoni? What the hell is that?" Lyman hisses.

Grabbing her arm, he hoists Megan up and drags her to the door. "Come on, you're going to take us there."

❀   ❀   ❀

Detective Sanchez turns onto Santa Fe Street, almost hitting a town car wheeling away from the curb. If he wasn't in a hurry he would follow the guy and ticket him for reckless driving.

Pulling into an empty space not far from Burtrum Lee's house, he turns the ignition off. The air is calm, and a strange stillness hangs low. Slowly opening the door, Jose eases out, and unclips his holster, preparing for a quick draw if need be.

Tip-toeing sideways up the driveway, he leans against the rugged adobe structure as he inches along. He careens his neck, and peers into the uncovered window.

The place looks a mess, but there doesn't seem to be any sign of someone being there. The detective sneaks around to the back door where he finds it swinging open. Quietly, he maneuvers up the steps and into the house.

Holstering his gun, he begins searching for a clue. There seems to be nothing, just a bunch of trash. Flustered, Jose turns to leave and swipes the coffee table with his jacket. Papers fly to the floor, and as he bends over to pick them up, he notices a brochure from Shidoni. Studying it more closely, he sees a spot of blood.

Is this where he's taken her? Should he take a leap of faith, and check it out? His better judgment saying, no, Sanchez stuffs the pamphlet in his coat pocket, figuring he can make it there in less than ten minutes, hopefully before something, if anything happens.

❀ ❀ ❀

Lee looks around her, as she feels the nuzzle of Calvin's gun press against her ribs. It's a dull, cold pain. She promised him that she won't take off, and that all she wants is to meet Katie Lee without anyone getting hurt, but he doesn't trust her.

So, after untying her wrists and ankles, he's been holding the gun to her ever since. Lee doesn't know which is worse.

"You know, Calvin, this place is quite amazing, too bad you don't have the time to stroll around and look at all of the sculptures."

"I'll have plenty of time to gaze at art, after I get my million dollars. For the mean- time, be quiet, and just start walking to that picnic table over there. The angle holds a good vantage point?"

"Do you have to dig that barrel into me?"

"I'm sorry, but yes. Mine and Carla's future depends on what happens in the next thirty minutes. Then you can be on your way, to do whatever you want. Make a Movie of the Week, or write a book about all of this, I don't care. You're never going to hear from me again."

Lee halts and turns to Calvin. "You know, this might sound kind of weird, but I want to thank you. I mean, if it wasn't for you I would've never known about myself, about my true self. So, whatever happens, I will always be in debt to you for that. I just want to wish you good luck, but on the other hand I don't appreciate the manner in which you did it. Did you ever think to just knock on my door?"

"You've got to be kidding, right?" Calvin pushes her forward. "Come on."

Reaching the picnic table, they hear a voice yell out. "Calvin, stop right there."

Wheeling around, they see Lyman Stone rushing toward them. His arm wrapped around the neck of Megan as he presses a cold gun against her temple.

The two inch forward as Calvin and Lee watch in awe. "Who is that, Calvin? I don't like the looks of him."

"That's Lyman Stone. The scientists who performed the cloning experiment on you."

"Oh!" Lee feels nauseas, and leaning over, throws up into the dry river bed. Yellow bile heaves out of her, as she spits foamy white saliva out of her mouth.

"Come on, sit down, Lee." Calvin hurriedly eases her down, not taking the gun or his eyes off of Lyman.

"You'd better stop there, Lyman, or else I'll get rid of her. Then where will you be?" Calvin pretends to act like he'll shoot Lee on a dime.

"I don't believe you," Lyman says, suddenly being shaken by the blast of gun fire.

"Well, you damn well better believe this," Katie Lee screams from the tiny wooden bridge her wheelchair is rumbling over. Wanda steering the back like a river guide. "Nobody move." The crippled woman aims her rifle right at Lyman as he continues to strangle Megan with his arm.

Megan, falling into a crazed haze, thinks to herself, this truly is the Southwest with everyone totting a gun.

"Katie, this is none of your business. I've come to claim what is rightfully mine. And no one, nor nothing, is going to get in my way."

"Lyman, you're acting like an insane man. Why don't we all just talk this out and do what is best for Burtrum."

"I know what is best for Burtrum, to come back to my lab and let me transform her into the great being she was destined to be before those vagrants, the Conner's, stole her."

"We rescued her," Jane Conner yells, as Jed and Clair march along-side Katie. "And we protected her then, and we'll protect her now, do you understand?"

"Now, everyone, just wait a minute!" Lee yells across the field. Suddenly she hears a shot ring out and is horrified as Calvin melts to the ground. After a second shot is fired, Carla, starts screaming, "Calvin, Calvin," as she dashes over to her husband.

Flat, Roadrunner clouds hang like puppets in the desert blue Santa Fe sky. Megan thought she heard a, *beep-beep,* somewhere. A searing pain pricks her gut, kind of like a bee sting. Sandy sunbeams glitter off the steel structures dotting the new spring grass.

Scented Russian olive trees coat the air as Megan drops to her knees. Her head is queasy, that sting, is she allergic and having a reaction. Maybe it was a spider, a lost widow tangled in her top.

Easing her hand down to the pain, she sees on her finger tips an unusual strain of red. Have I been shot? Fog rolls over her as trembling knees buckle, and Megan falls to the soft ground. She hears her name being called out, but can't figure who's it is. She's not here anymore, something strange is going on, Megan has no feeling.

Is she dying?

Lee, watches as Megan melts onto the lawn. Scampering to her, she lifts her head into her lap. "Megan, oh, Megan." She pats the woman's cheek, white with death gray splotches.

"Lee, Lee, is that you? Look, another bad day to wear white."

Lee Conner glances down to the expanding map of blood etching across Megan's blouse.

"I'm cold, Lee." Megan closes her eyes.

"Megan," Lee shakes her. "Megan." Panicked, Lee starts screaming, "Help, help, she's been shot."

Katie Lee, witnessing the events from her lonely chair, calls out to Wanda, ordering her to carry her disabled body over to Megan and Lee. Setting her down on the knoll next to them, Katie wraps her arms around the two women. "My daughters," she whispers.

"What?" Lyman screeches, jogging up to them, and kneeling next to Katie. "What are you talking about, Katie."

"I had twins, you idiot."

"It can't be true." Lyman stands.

Hysterical, Lee chokes out. "What are you talking about?"

Jed, squatting next to his daughter, rests his arm on her shoulder. "Lee, I found out that Megan is your twin."

"This is nuts, you're all crazy." Abruptly standing, Lee backs away from her family, sirens advancing. "Right now, everyone needs to leave me alone. I can't believe things have gone this far. Megan, an innocent woman, is dead because of all of you.

"This is your doing, Lyman," Katie sneers.

"I did it for us, Katie, for Lee Labs, don't you understand."

"No!" Before anyone has a chance to stop her, Katie slips her frail hand beneath her shawl, and pulling out a Derringer, aims it at Lyman. "You bastard. You killed my husband, and almost me. You tamper with mine and Burtrum's child, and now you murdered one of my daughter's."

Hearing the police arrive, Katie lowers her gun. "The only reason I didn't blow your head off is because I want you to suffer. I want you to spend the rest of your life in a tiny cell, rotting away, with no hope of a future. That's what I want!"

"Everyone, drop your weapons," Detective Sanchez's voice rises as he scampers closer to the scene.

Rushing over to Megan, he squats and feels for a pulse, but is unable to find one. "Is this Megan Masterson?"

"Yes," Lee chokes out. "My twin sister."

"And you're Burtrum Lee Conner?" He rises.

"Yes, how do you know that?"

"Your friend, I mean sister, called us last night to report a kidnapping. She led me to the motel you were at, and I found your license after the evacuation, which she caused." Detective Sanchez glances down at Megan's body. "She was a brave woman, your twin."

"Detective," Clair Conner touches the policeman's arm. "I'd like to report a murder."

"Me, too!" Katie softly speaks. "And I know who did it!"

23

Santa Fe, 1960

Katie Lee, regaining consciousness, flutters her eyelids as the soft falling snow tickles them.

The cold baby boy in her arms softly cries, he *isn't* dead! Iced tears drizzle down her frost bitten cheeks as Katie Lee, believing she's going to die, closes her arm around the infant's face, smothering the last breaths from the newborn.

She knows what Lyman did, and there's no way she'll ever let Dr. Stone have her child!

ABOUT THE AUTHOR

Mary Maurice wrote her first poem when she was in the ninth grade, and hasn't stopped writing since. Catching the fire at an early age, she continues to dedicate her time to the craft.

Ms. Maurice has completed several novels of fiction and poetry, and has performed readings in distinct cities around the country. She presently resides in Santa Fe, New Mexico.

CPSIA information can be obtained
at www.ICGtesting.com
Printed in the USA
FSOW02n2102220118
43407FS

9 781609 751975